A
LOVE
DEFERRED

*H.V. Bennett
and W.E. Lawson*

Copyright © 2009 by H.V. Bennett and W.E. Lawson

A Love Deferred
by H.V. Bennett and W.E. Lawson

Printed in the United States of America

ISBN 978-1-60791-043-5

All rights reserved solely by the author. The author guarantees all contents are original and do not infringe upon the legal rights of any other person or work. No part of this book may be reproduced in any form without the permission of the author. The views expressed in this book are not necessarily those of the publisher.

Unless otherwise indicated, Bible quotations are taken from The King James Version. Copyright © 1976 by Thomas Nelson Publishers, Inc.

www.xulonpress.com

To Poppy, Sita-Mama, and Fonz, whose love was <u>never</u> deferred.

H.V.B.

Table of Contents

Prologue ix	
Chapter 1 – <u>MIRROR, MIRROR</u> 13	
Chapter 2 – <u>WEAKNESS</u> 25	
Chapter 3 – <u>HOW IT ALL BEGAN</u> 35	
Chapter 4 – <u>NO BIG DEAL, IT'S JUST A CALL</u> 45	
Chapter 5 – <u>GETTING READY</u> 61	
Chapter 6 – <u>AN ENCHANTED EVENING</u> 71	
Chapter 7 – <u>BREAKING THE ICE</u> 83	
Chapter 8 – <u>THE LONG WAY HOME</u> 93	
Chapter n9 – <u>BACK TOGETHER AGAIN</u> 99	
Chapter 10 – <u>BLUE LIGHTS IN THE BASEMENT</u> 117	
Chapter 11 – <u>NO, ME!</u> 127	
Chapter 12 – <u>THE MIDDLE PASSAGE</u> 137	
Chapter 13 – <u>1984: THE YEAR OF MY FATHER</u> 167	
Chapter 14 – <u>1984: THROUGH THE NIGHT</u> 187	
Chapter 15 – <u>JOY IN THE MORNING</u> 203	
Chapter 16 – <u>A NEW LEAF</u> 213	
Chapter 17 – <u>SWEET REUNION</u> 235	

**Chapter 18 – THE BLOOM COMES OFF
                   THE ROSE** 287
Chapter 19 – BEEN FOUND 303
Chapter 20 – WHEN IT'S ALL SAID AND DONE....315
Epilogue - 339

PROLOGUE:

Her Story *(Ronni)*

What happens to a love deferred? Does it keep its aromatic beginnings or does it take on the pungent decay that happens to most living things when left unattended over time? I have asked myself that question dozens, no, hundreds of times over these many years – smitten, infatuated, love struck. I can't pick just one because they all apply to how I felt, and still feel about a certain someone whom I have carried in my heart, although maybe not always in the forefront, for as long as I can remember those first real feelings of warmth that a young girl gets when she knows that she has met her first love, someone she thinks could be her forever love.

Of course, there are some who know me who have told me that I must have a screw loose somewhere, to carry a torch, or maybe more appropriately, a bonfire, for someone who has never committed himself totally to me. And deep down, in the far reaches of my educated, sophisticated, otherwise level-headed mind, I know that for most of these years I have melded him in the aortic canal which is my heart, what they say rings true.

Now, I'm not looking for justification, empathy, or absolution in telling this story, but I thought it might help someone else, woman or man, who can relate in some way to what I have been, and am still, going through, to some degree, to come to grips with a bittersweet romance.

His Story *(Eric)*

I know what happens to a dream deferred. But what happens to a love deferred? I think it finds a warm, quiet place in your heart and lives there, passing judgment on any semblance of love that passes by. Mine sits in my heart and speaks constantly to my mind. It says things like, "Yeah, she'll pass for now, but what about later? She's not *her* you know? Will this one pass the test of time? Are you going to settle for this? You can do better. Why don't you just give up? You know it's not going to work out – again!"

Sometimes I wish it would just let me have my peace. Sometimes when it's silent for a while, and I think about letting someone new into my life, my mind takes over and asks, "Well, what about that thing in your heart? You know, that thing that keeps asking those questions? Go on, answer it! Because if you don't, you are making a big mistake."

A Love Deferred

I know what happens to a love deferred. It always comes back to *her*. That thing in the warm, quiet place in my heart. The love of my life.

****

Gloria Naylor once wrote that there are four sides to each story: his side, her side, the inside and the outside. Truer words have never been spoken or written. However, the years have taught us that there are two other sides as well: the side we remember and the side we wish could be. What happens to *A Love Deferred*? We invite you to find out what happens to Ronni and Eric.

CHAPTER ONE

MIRROR, MIRROR

Attention: Veronica Bradley, the cover sheet on the paper pile read. "Yep, that's me," I thought to myself as I sat in my comfortable office overlooking a sea of greenery and an expanse of housing complexes in this suburban cocoon that looked as if they were right out of *House & Garden*. I was scrupulously reviewing an important document that had a 72 hour turnaround for comment. I could never understand why it seemed as if they always waited until the last minute to circulate for review these mega *Reports To Congress*. The voluminous pages of charts and graphs were making my head spin, and the never ending paragraphs must have detailed everything there was to know about the subject matter and then some — bordering on redundant. I thought that if I just took out a handful of pages from the unread portions of the document and tossed it, there would probably still be enough left to inform the good ole' boys on Capitol Hill. But that shortcut wasn't my call. Maybe next time, I thought, smiling. For now, I knew what my weekend activity would most likely entail and it wouldn't be watching a gripping drama on one of the dozens of cable channels at home. More likely, cozying up to more of this "can't put it down" [yeah, right] must-read.

As much as I complained at this moment, I knew that this was part and parcel of the responsibilities I had worked so hard for over the years. My work in the health arena was my professional passion, and helping people get and stay healthy, my mission. Since the early 80's, I had worked on topics ranging from AIDS and HIV, to kids with cancer, to second chances at life through organ transplants, to stemming the tide of disease caused by a much too familiar, but deadly culprit – tobacco. Still I knew that the hard sell was always convincing the powerbrokers on The Hill and 1600 Pennsylvania to do their part and put their money (or more accurately, the taxpayers' money) where their endless promises always seem to lie and die.

I took my glasses off and rubbed my eyes as I took a break from the fine print I had been reading for seemingly days when actually it had only been a couple of hours. I got up from my desk, strolled to the credenza where I always kept a fresh pitcher of ice water and poured a small amount in a glass. As I sipped, I walked to the window and looked across to the subway station, watching people hurrying in and out – always hurrying to wherever they needed to go or whatever they had to do, but most likely today to get a jump-

A Love Deferred

start on the long, holiday weekend. Even in the suburbs they always had someplace to get to.

I had long ago taken off my shoes and enjoyed the feeling of the carpet under my feet. I turned and leaned against the wall as I looked around at the pictures and objects that pretty much represented my career and life so far. On one wall were the many awards, given over the last two decades, for exemplary service. "Just doing my job," I always said to myself when I read them. On another wall, a favorite framed mural that was presented to me on one of my travels to New York, more specifically, to Harlem, where I had the chance to talk to communities about the importance of good health and their well-being. I had rolled up my sleeves many times over the years with these folks and was a key force in helping to put in place, community health workers and programs to fight the scourge of drug addiction, high blood pressure, obesity, and premature death that plagued not just this community of color, but hundreds like it across the country.

As I slid down onto the window sill I looked around at the honorary Doctorate in Public Health bestowed upon me in 1998 from one of the better known Historically Black Colleges and Universities, a Key To Harlem presented to me by one of its most respected community activists, and a framed picture of me seated at the piano holding one of the many consumer health tools I helped to develop. That appeared in a 1980's Rising Stars issue of a very popular African-American magazine. I loved this photo because it was a great conversation starter. I would let the curious know that it represented my second and third loves – health and music. Some, who'd heard me sing, generously commented that I had a melodious voice, and I also always wanted to play the piano. You didn't have to look far to figure out what, or rather, who, was my first love, for I kept my most precious treasure close to me at heart level as I sat at my desk. I reached for one of the many photos on my desk of my son, Mark. The pictures showed him as a toddler playing a miniature keyboard, another showed him as a junior high student in his track and field uniform, and the most recent captured me hugging him at his high school graduation. I smiled as I thought about what a fine young man he had become. I had to admit to myself that my baby was all grown up and independent. In a few months, he would be off on his own to college and that brought on mixed emotions. I picked up my glasses to continue reading the huge manuscript still left to review and was startled when I heard my staff assistant, Maggie, come in.

"Ronni *(the name most people called me),* Corrine is on Line 1 for you. She reminded me that she was one of your oldest friends and that I should interrupt you no matter what you're doing, so I hope you don't mind. Do you want to take the call or should I take a message?" In a burst of excitement, I dropped the manuscript on my desk as if it were fiery hot, and as if the phone call had given me a momentary reprieve from the pressing business at hand. "No! I mean, yes! I'll take the call Maggie, thanks!" I exclaimed. "I haven't talked to her in quite a while." As Maggie turned to leave, I added, "Oh, and if there is nothing more for you to take care of out there, why don't you take the rest of the afternoon off and get an early start on your holiday weekend. I'll have something for you on this Report next week." Maggie asked, "Thanks Ronni, but are you sure there's nothing I can do to help you?" "I'm sure," I replied. "There's no reason why both of us should be stuck in here on such a beautiful afternoon. See you first thing Tuesday." Maggie waved and closed the door behind her to give me some privacy.

I pushed the button to Line 1: "Is this *the* Corinne Pointer?" I joked. "Make that Corinne Pointer-Rush, Ms. Bradley," she responded in a proper, but humorous way. We both laughed. It had been a few months since we laughed together during Mark's high school graduation weekend. I remembered how my oldest friend, of 35 years, and I used to talk at least twice a day as teens. College, careers, relationships, marriage, and children – not necessarily in that order – changed all that. And then five years ago, after having lived in Atlanta for a decade, Corinne, her husband Eddie, of 25 years, and their twins, Chris and Eddie, Jr., moved back to the D.C. area. Even if we didn't get a chance to see other as much, it was good to have her back on the home end. "You know I love that man of yours, too," I said, "but somehow, you'll always be Corinne Pointer to me." "Yeah, yeah, yeah," laughed Corinne. "How are you doing Ronni girl? You know we're both at that tender age now where we need to check and double-check to see if we're all there. What's new with you? I haven't talked to you since we all got together for my godson's graduation. How is my magnificent Mark doing anyway?"

I beamed at the mention of my son's name. "He's doing just great. He's finishing up a summer job down in North Carolina, staying with his dad and grandparents." I admit I was a proud, single mom and happy that Mark's dad, Jeff, and I were on good terms – something I had to pray about and we both worked hard to get through. Corinne was crucial to helping me deal with a lot of the issues and challenges of parenting, oftentimes talking me off the ledge, figuratively, when I wanted to jump. It definitely helped in the way Jeff and I worked together to bring up a well-adjusted and loving son. "Mark's dad says that he really thinks he must have grown another inch or two and gained another 5 pounds since he's been down there. Must be all that good country cooking," I said laughing. "I besta keep my good government job."

"Your good government job and then some," Corinne concurred. "You know I've been there, done that, especially with two in college at the same time, so I know where you're coming from. How soon will Mark be back home before he heads down to college in Louisiana?" she asked. I looked at the calendar on my desk. "He isn't coming back up here, Corinne. He and his dad actually took most of his stuff with them when they drove down to North Carolina. He has a few things here and we've all synchronized our schedules so that I will ship the remaining items to a hotel near the university where he and, his father, and I will be staying —separate rooms of course," I emphasized with a laugh, "a couple of days before he checks into the dorm. Mark and Jeff are going to fly in from North Carolina and I'll leave from here. If all goes according to plan, our flights should arrive in New Orleans around the same time, we've already reserved a car, and then we'll be set for the week to drive around and get a feel for Mark's new living and learning environment first hand, at least for a little bit. I added, "You know me, the planner. I'd like to make sure all the pieces are in place for Mark, or at least convince myself that they can be, before the umbilical cord is cut again." Through no fault of his own, Mark had demanded such a huge part of my focus for so many years. I knew it would take a while to make the new adjustment to not having him around everyday, but I had already made up in my mind, at least, that I could do it.

 Corinne seized the opportunity to transition the conversation to the main reason she called. "Sounds like one of those Ronni Bradley getting-it-all-together plans. And speaking of putting pieces in place, my dear sister, I called you about a chance to consider putting another major piece of your life in place this weekend," she said in a way that I knew she hoped would stir up my inquisitive nature to know more. I sat erect in my ergonomically correct office chair, "Ok, I'll

A Love Deferred

bite Corinne, what do you mean by that?" I probed. "Well," Corinne continued, "it's just that this is the third time in fifteen years I am using whatever net I can to pull you in to be with me and Eddie for chat and chew or should I say, throw down and get down with some of the old Prom crew at the Five/Fourth Fun Fest. *(This was the cookout held every five years during the 4th of July weekend, for the old prom night crew.)* You've only been a few times since we all graduated and started this and we all miss you. And before you say that you don't like doing the High School Reunion big deal, you know it's not that kind of thing. That gathering of the 10 of us after the prom really started something, and we've tried to keep it going over the years. I actually like this much better than the pomp and circumstance of that formal reunion business. And by the way you enjoyed yourself at the last one you attended, I know you did too. So come on girl, say you'll go. Besides, I think there's an incentive there this year that would make it a little more interesting than previous years, if you know what I mean," Corinne hinted again.

I found myself getting just a little impatient with my best friend. "Uh, excuse me, Ms. Pointer-Rush. Could you cease with the *Things I Need To Know* Jeopardy category and instead of me sitting here trying to ask the right question, just give me the 4-1-1, pleeeeeeze?!" Corinne sensed the edginess in my response and said, "Ok, ok, just trying to have some fun with you. Well, my dear, it appears that this year's gathering will probably be graced with the presence of a certain someone you met prom night decades ago and I'm sure will be hoping to see you there too."

I knew immediately who Corinne was talking about. Even with the slightly clumsy reference to the 6 foot 2, soft-silky voiced, salt- and pepper-topped gentleman whose name was purposefully not mentioned previously, I felt a chill go up my spine thinking about him for a brief moment. It didn't matter whether either one of us actually said the name out loud; we both knew the mystery date of decades ago was none other than Eric Lewis.

It seemed like it took minutes before I responded to Corrine's invitation, but it had actually only been a few seconds. "You know Corinne, I've got a load of work to do this weekend." I started to build on reasons why I couldn't go. "Even as I speak, I have a 3 inch thick Agency *Report to Congress* that they dumped on me today to review and comment by next Tuesday, and I'm not even half way through it yet. I know I sound like a broken record, but I just don't think I can..." Before I finished my sentence, Corinne jumped in. "I'm *not* taking no for an answer. Not this time Ronni. I know how you work, and I know that you've attacked those reports in the past and breezed through them with no problem. So stop selling it because I'm not buying it. This is old Corinne, remember....? Come on girl. Stop making excuses not to find some kind of closure to this thing with Eric, once and for all because any other course of action won't do you any good, and certainly won't give you any peace. If you need help with that paper pyramid you've got to devour, I'll come over on Saturday and we can take that document and rip it apart, read what you need to, and write the facts – just the facts, like the old days of handling those huge school projects. We were a great team then and we can be an even greater one now, since we both have some experience under out belts, or should I say, our girdles." I laughed, which, at least let Corinne know that she had my ear. I could feel that she was about to make the final pitch and let the chips fall where they may. "Look, I know a certain conversation with a certain someone is *more* than a little overdue, don't you think?" I said hesitantly, "I know what you're saying is right Corinne, but...."

"No buts, Ronni, let's do this. You can finish what you have to do with the work assignment by Sunday. The cookout isn't until Monday. So, what do you say, do we have a date? If it will help, Eddie and I will come by and pick you up. That way, you won't come in alone, and we'll be there for support. But mostly, we want you to come out and enjoy yourself with the old —and I do mean old, folks. Girl, you will laugh when you see some of these people. Time hasn't been kind to all of them, but they are all still as fun and crazy as ever, but I digress. Will you come?" As always when Corinne presented her reasons why to do something, it usually didn't leave me much room to debate or argue the why nots. I thought to myself that this is what happens when your best friend is a lawyer, and an extremely persuasive one at that. "Ronni, oh Ronni," Corinne pleaded again. Reluctantly, as was the case when I gave in to a few of Corinne's schemes over the years, I said, "Okay already. Uncle! You've convinced me. I'll come with you guys. But I'm telling you now that if I feel it's better for me to leave, I'm outta there. Deal?" I could imagine Corinne smiling to herself and pumping her fist in a victorious gesture. She knew how stubborn I could be, so she was willing to settle for the temporary victory she had won over her dear friend. "Deal," Corinne agreed. "I'll call you at home Saturday afternoon to see how you're doing with the Report. I meant what I said about helping."

"I know and I appreciate it," I said, "but I think I'll be alright. Talk to you soon." We said our goodbyes and hung up the phone. I sat staring at the phone, and did a mental playback of the conversation to understand what in the world I had just agreed to do. Then my eyes were drawn to the clock on the wall, thinking how quickly the events of my life had changed in just a few minutes time. I picked up the picture of Mark in his the track and field uniform, and went to the window again. As I focused on the sports uniform, I remembered that track was one of Eric's main interests in high school. At least that's what he had told me years ago. And although I never saw him compete against my alma mater, I imagined he must have loved the sport as much as my son. Certainly, their similarity in height, and those long legs and powerful thighs, made them both a sight to behold.

I turned to the window and looked out, oblivious now to anything on the other side of the glass, concentrating only on the partial reflection of my face in the glass. My mind wandered for a moment. Then, thinking back and borrowing from a very familiar line from an old childhood story, I said: "Mirror, mirror, on the wall, was it me or Eric who dropped the ball?" That window pane reflection wasn't giving up any answers, but maybe, just maybe, I thought, Eric Lewis might do so this weekend.

CHAPTER TWO

WEAKNESS

"I'm finally home," I thought to myself as I looked out of the passenger side window of the cab pulling up to my house. I always liked coming home, but especially today, after a grueling week in the office. I spent four rather harried days and nights on call, living at the company's in town suite, in order to put a major deal to bed. And then, as if that wasn't enough, I was victim to a freak accident by an impatient motorist driving out of the office garage, no doubt anxious to get the Independence Day weekend underway. My car had to be towed to the mechanic's shop, but at least I am in one piece. For that, I am truly thankful. The dealer said they would deliver a loaner car first thing in the morning. I asked that they drop it off early and leave the keys in a secured location at the house, because I had several errands to run before I gathered myself up and headed back East for the holidays as well. But, for now, I planned to settle in for the night.

A Love Deferred

I liked the quiet and the surroundings this house offered. It was one of the more solid investments I made when I left my last company and cashed out my stock options. I now lived here with Kit, the Wonder Dog, and my son, Trey, when he was home from college. My wife and I divorced amicably and she now lived in Southern California where she could easily access her celebrity clients and travel on photo shoots. What that really means is that I spend a lot of time alone. After handing the driver some bills I unfolded myself from the car. No matter what size vehicle I was riding in, if I was in the backseat, I felt cramped. I grabbed my bag and briefcase, thanked the driver, and started climbing the steps.

As I walked up, I checked out my little garden and saw that the lemons on the tree were ripe and needed to be picked. As I looked around the side of the house, I saw that the persimmons were growing well, too. I needed to get the gardeners to pick them because deer would start tramping over the newly planted ground cover to get to the persimmons. I got the keys from my pocket and opened the front door ready to sprint through the kitchen to enter the alarm code before it went off. I thought about the several times in the past year, that the alarm company called the police to my house while I was away because a window came loose during high winds and kept setting off the alarm. On one business trip to Singapore my office called to alert me. From thousands of miles away, I called a friend, who lived less than 20 minutes from here, and asked him to check the house

A Love Deferred

out and disable the alarm. He promised he would but didn't make it to the house until three days later. By that time, my neighbors and the police were pretty upset. I was fined $150 for "creating a public nuisance." Thanks, buddy. You always got my back, right? Yeah, right.

After turning off the alarm and dragging my bags inside, I took a walk around the house to check things out. Everything looked in order. Mrs. Timms, the lady who cleaned several houses on the block, as well as mine, made sure that everything was dusted and well kept. She came once a week whether I was in town or not. For the most part the house was always relatively clean. I felt embarrassed leaving a mess for her to clean up, so I always made the bed and washed dishes before she got here. I also insisted on doing my own laundry. That is one of the lessons I learned early in life from my mother. She taught me, and my siblings, how to wash with an old ringer washer. We even learned how to add bluing to the whites to make them brighter and how to use Argo starch on shirt collars, ironing, and the art of folding clothes neatly. Those lessons never left me. Years ago, when my wife, baby Trey, and I lived in an apartment, I used to drive several miles to a nice laundry mat, where I amazed the women there with my ability to get my clothes so much whiter than theirs and how, when I left, the clothes were always folded so neatly in the cart. Even with my neatness and no laundry, there was still plenty for Mrs. Timms to do. One of the things she did for me was pick up my mail and place it near the phone. That way I could read it while I retrieved my messages. I took my bags upstairs and poured my dirty clothes in the middle of the laundry room floor. I sorted all the dark clothes out, put them in the washer, set the water level and temperature, added some detergent and softener, and pushed start.

I went back downstairs to retrieve my messages. I pressed the button on the phone to see that there were 6 new messages and started flipping through the usual bills and advertisements. There was a message from Trey, saying he was just checking in and that he was going to be done with finals in three weeks. He wanted to know if I was going to be in town so we could hang out together. I smiled as I heard his voice. It didn't matter how old Trey was, he still sounded like the mischievous little boy I love with all my heart. I made a note on the pad by the phone to call him back as soon as I listened to the rest of the messages. The next two messages were from realtors saying they had buyers interested in purchasing my house. These calls always intrigued me because the house wasn't for sale. I guess that's just the way things are done in Northern California. The realtors call you prospecting for sales. This house was attractive because it was in the Oakland Hills with a view of the Bay and Golden Gate Bridges. On New Years Eve and July 4th when all the communities surrounding Oakland and San Francisco shot off fireworks, my neighbors and I could see at least eight communities from our balconies or porches. Thankfully, our homes were also protected from the fires that destroyed much of the community in the 80's, because the surrounding mountains provide a natural firewall. I erased these solicitations because there were no real circumstances where I could see myself selling.

The next message was from my best friend Eddie Rush. Eddie still lived in our hometown, Washington, DC. He was making his weekly call to confirm that I was still coming to the Five/Fourth holiday bash, being hosted this year by him and his wife, Corinne. They lived quite comfortably in suburban Maryland. Eddie tried to appeal to my competitive nature by challenging me to the Bid-Whist tournament, and if that wasn't enough, he had hoped to tantalize me by partially describing the menu of finger-licking barbecue chicken, melt-in-your-mouth ribs, and the slap-your-momma homemade peach cobbler that was Corinne's specialty. Although this event started as a small gathering of a few high school friends, over the years it had grown into a major family happening. As children have grown up, they have started coming to the gathering with their spouses and children in tow. Eddie ended his message, dangling only part of the last temptation to draw me to the East Coast by saying, "Call me turkey. I need to holla at you for a minute because the best reason for you to come this year can't be left in a recorded message. Hit me back. Later Bro." I chuckled after hearing that message because here was a 50 year old man still trying to sound hip and everybody knows only I can do that. Can you dig it?

I checked the last two messages and called Trey. As usual, I got the answering machine that he and his roommate shared. I left a message saying that I looked forward to seeing him and reminded him to bring his golf clubs. Next, I called, Eddie.

It was about 8:30 p.m. in D.C. so it was still a respectable time to call. On the third ring, I heard the voice of a young woman saying "Hello." It was Chris — Eddie and Corrine's daughter, and my Goddaughter. "Hi Baby Sister. How are you doing?" I asked. Chris replied cheerfully, "Hi Uncle Eric. I am just a *B.W.W.*" I said, "Excuse me, a BWW....? What's that? Laughing, the eighteen year old said, "A *B*lack *W*oman *W*alking. Can you believe my parents won't buy me a car? I mean, I'm about to be a big time college student and that should account for something," she paused and added, "Right Uncle Eric?" She quickly added, "Of course, an uncle can buy his favorite niece/Goddaughter cars, too." I answered "And elephants can fly in cartoons." At that we both burst out laughing. "Now put your dad on the phone you silly girl." I could still hear the lightheartedness in her voice as she called for her dad. Eddie picked up the phone and said "What's up dawg." I answered "It's your world; I'm just living in it." Eddie said, "Now you see that. That little exchange we just had shows how you are old school and I am new school." Before he could explain to me how hip he had remained over the years and how square I had become I said, "Okay, okay. You called me. So now I'm calling you.

What's up?" He answered by asking, "You're still coming this weekend, right? You're not going to back out at the last minute are you?" I answered, "Ed, I've got my ticket. I've got my hotel and rental car reservations. My family is expecting me to stay at least long enough to spend some quality time with them, and I can't back out, so I'm coming." "Well good," my friend said, "because I spoke with Corrine and, if all goes as we hope it will, Ronni is finally going to grace us with her presence this year. It's sad that we have only been able to get sister girl here for this once; but hey, better late than never, right?"

With the mention of Ronni's name and the thought of seeing her again after so many years, my knees suddenly felt weak and that warm feeling I always got when I thought about her came over me. I found I needed to sit down. Eddie was saying something about Ronni working on a deadline this weekend and something else about her son, Mark but I missed most of the details. "Eric are you listening to me?" I said that I was as I seated myself on a stool. "So when are you arriving?" I responded by reading my itinerary and saying once again thanks for inviting me to stay at their house but I needed to be more centrally located so I could visit my family. "Okay man," he said. "But seriously though, it's going to be good having you here. This will be the big send off for the twins." Shaking my head, I said, "I can't believe they are heading to college. You must be getting old." "Me"?" he protested, "I'm a whole month and a half younger than you, and you act as though you are my father. Now on a serious tip, when you come here, have fun! Don't think about all you have to do and who you have to see. Think about Eric Lewis for once." He added, "Promise?" I answered, "I promise. See you Sunday." "See you then." He said. With that, we both hung up.

When I looked through the window, I saw the pastel colored sky as the sun started falling below the Bay Bridge. As I turned to look away, I caught a reflection of myself and repeated to myself the words "I promise." Those two words took me back to another conversation and another promise I made to my good friend more than 30 years earlier. That promise introduced me to Ronni Bradley, the woman I would spend, from that moment on, loving more than any other woman I would ever meet afterwards, and who, whether I was ready or not, I would see in less than 72 hours. I had to smile when I thought about how Ronni and I met. It seemed like only yesterday. Still reeling a little from the phone conversation with Eddie, I thought more about that phone conversation we had three decades earlier. A conversation as it turned out, that would change our lives forever. It started out so simply, but as I think about it today, things between Ronni and I were never really simple. Life threw all kinds of twists and turns in our way that kept us from becoming the couple that we should have been all along. Life for us was no Crystal Stair to paraphrase Langston Hughes. Maybe it's the stuff that movies are made of, or maybe it's not. However, the story of how our relationship began is a story for the ages. It started with a phone call and a promise. Man, time really does fly, whether you are having fun or not.

CHAPTER THREE

HOW IT ALL BEGAN

"Ronni, I don't know how you can be so calm at a time like this, and with the prom so close," my younger sister Cecilia said. I was actually anything but calm, but I was determined not to let the situation get the best of me. What situation you might ask? I had no prom date, well, I did at first, but he was now history, at least as of 29 hours, 46 minutes, and 15 seconds ago, but who was counting. To my baby sister, that spelled social death, especially in high school alphabets. "CeeCee, what's not to be calm about?" I asked. "He was just a date." But she shot right back, "Yeah, but for P-R-O-M, which is only the biggest date night of your life, at least so far. I've seen you do some bold things before, but this has got to be the boldest." When CeeCee put it like that, I had to admit that a few goose bumps of nervousness suddenly appeared on my arms, but I had already programmed my mind not to let anything reverse my decision concerning my *would-have-been* date, David Stevens.

A Love Deferred

Looking back on it, the breakup between David and I was inevitable, but the timing was lousy. Maybe I should have hung in there a bit longer, at least until the prom was over, I thought to myself. But deep down inside, I knew that if I had to put up with any more of his drama, I never would have been really able to enjoy myself on prom night, especially in front of all of my friends, who knew my "fit to be tied" looks. My eyes usually gave everything away. Big and brown, I had been complimented on them numerous times. But they could also be bullying, menacing or mean when I was annoyed or frustrated, and David had made me reach that point.

I would have been okay to miss the prom, and staying at home watching black and white classic movies I always loved, but my best girlfriend, Corinne, insisted that I still had to go to this last bash with her and Eddie, her boyfriend. Corinne and I had been thick as thieves all through high school and this was the beginning of saying goodbye to those years together. So Corrine had a plan that would have me, and Eddie's best friend, Eric, double dating with the two of them on prom night. While it might have made great sense to Corinne, convincing me to go with the plan took some doing. "But I don't know the first thing about him and he certainly doesn't know me," I protested. "And I don't want to seem like a desperate sister who needs to be fixed up!" I declared, as if that was the end of that topic of conversation. "If I didn't want to go with the other guys from school who asked me, what makes you think I'd want to go with this one, who is a total stranger?" I challenged Corinne. "He's a stranger to you, but not to me. You know I would not put you out there like that. You are my dearest and best friend. And I promise you, he is not a *serial anything*. Trust me on this one," Corinne said.

My girl, Corinne, had a way of making things seem right, and by the time she finished with the reasons why this match should happen, I ran out of comebacks for why it shouldn't. And so, calling a truce, I apprehensively said yes, but only if Eric and I had a chance to talk at least a little bit before the prom to make sure we would be able to survive each other for that one night. Corinne told Eddie that if I didn't go, she had made up in her mind that she wouldn't go either. A stag prom was not in Eddie's plans. And now that Corinne had already started the ball rolling, Eddie knew what he had to do, and exactly how to do it.

Prom Night: Two Weeks and Counting

The phone always rang loudly at the Lewis household, and it seemed as if all the Lewis siblings took it as a starting signal to sprint for it. Even though I was one of the fastest guys on the track team at school, on the home track it was more about strategy than speed and I was no match for my sister Jenny.

A Love Deferred

"Eric it's for you" Jenny said as she handed me the phone. "It's that cute boy Eddie," she giggled as she ran away blushing. "Hey man, what are you doing to my baby sister? She's got the hots for you," I joked before saying hello. Eddie and I had a long history of joking about my baby sister but it just occurred to me that she was not so much a baby anymore. In the blur that was the last few weeks before high school graduation, hadn't I seen her sitting in the living room with some boy? I made a mental note to check into this further after talking to my good friend.

Eddie started "Well you know if you had my looks, all the girls would be after you too." We both laughed at that and then Eddie turned to a more serious subject. "Hey man, I need a big favor from you." It had always been my experience that big and favor in the same sentence meant trouble, money, or both. All I knew was I didn't need any trouble and I didn't have that much money so my answer to most people would have been pretty simple. But Eddie wasn't most people. Eddie stood shoulder to shoulder with me in a fight with the Quincy Street Boys. We both got a little bloody but stood together while some of our other friends ran. From that day forward Eddie and I never had a problem with the Quincy Street Boys.

What you had to like about Eddie was that he wasn't the biggest one of us, but he made up for his lack of size with his heart. We had been through some serious times and situations together so when he asked for a favor, I always placed

A Love Deferred

it in my special circumstances file and disregarded any past experiences and observations. "What kind of favor?" I asked never hinting at my initial concerns. He answered by saying, "Well, you see...um." My mind quickly said, "Uh, Oh. When a brother can't answer you straight, its trouble, or money, or both. But again I stayed quiet. Better to let him get his tongue untied and just get the words out there. He continued, "It's about the Prom."

I gave a quick sigh of relief because I was all set for the prom. My date was confirmed, Denise Jenkins, the cheerleader. My tux was confirmed and paid for since February. I had my brother's '72 Chevy Camaro all set. The tickets were in my dresser so any problem with the prom was his.

"What about the prom?" I asked, suddenly wondering if it had been cancelled. "Well, Corrine said she wasn't going – to ours *or* hers," he said forlornly. Now Corrine and Eddie were as close a couple as any I had known in high school. Even though she went to another school in our district, she lived not far from Ed and he even hinted that he may have more than just casual feelings for her. I also knew that Eddie had invited her to our prom and she invited him to hers so still why was there a problem. "Why won't she go?" I asked not knowing why I was being led into this line of questioning. (Years later I learned that Corrine was in the room with Eddie prompting him on what to say) but as they say, I digress. "She won't go because her best friend, Ronni Bradley, doesn't have a date for her prom," he answered.

"What are you talking about?" I replied. "Didn't you tell me her best friend was dating that guy I embarrassed on the track in the 200 hundred yards finals?" I laughed. "Isn't he taking her to the prom?" Logical question I thought but that was always the wrong approach, being logical that is. Eddie responded, "They broke up. Ronni is pretty stuck on not going and now it's having a domino effect because Corrine won't go to mine or hers unless Ronni goes to their high school's dance."

My only response was "uh huh" still not seeing what this had to do with me. Eddie continued, "Now you know I've got money invested in two tuxedo rentals and tickets to two proms. All of that money goes to waste if Corrine's friend doesn't get a date." Then it hit me just what the big favor was. My answer was an emphatic "No way man. I see where this is headed and I can't help you." Eddie said "You don't understand brother. This is a real opportunity for you." Not seeing it I asked, "What do you mean, opportunity?" Right then and there Eddie knew he had me, but I didn't know it until it was way too late. That's when he went into his prepared speech. "You see," he said, "Ronni isn't looking for a date. She says she's okay with sitting this one out. But what a waste." "What do you mean a waste?" I asked. "*Brother*" he said, "she is a knockout. She is tall, very pretty, and sexy in an understated way and she has this voice." Thinking I understood the other physical characteristics he described I asked, "What voice?" He said, "When she talks she makes everything sound, I don't know, sensual. The best part is she's not trying to sound that way. That's just how she talks."

I stood there, on my end of the line, slightly intrigued but still skeptical. "Well if she's got all that going for her, why isn't some other guy, or guys, for that matter asking her to the prom? I mean, I don't even go to her school," I said. Eddie quickly answered, "She has been asked by other guys but she is very picky. She doesn't want to go with just anybody." "Well why do you think she'll go with me?" "Because Corrine knows you and she likes you. She has always wanted to introduce you to Ronni but she was dating that David guy. Now that David's out of the picture and given the unusual circumstances, she thought it might be a chance for you two to meet. Listen man, it's only for one night. The tickets are paid for. All you have to do is show up. That's all. No commitments."

I had to admit that I was in a no lose situation, but still I had to be completely sure I wasn't being set up. So I asked the one question that would set my mind at ease. "Ed, be straight with me." I said. "Would you take her to the prom if you weren't taking Corrine?" He paused for a second and said, "Brother, if you don't take her, I was thinking about inviting her and taking two dates to the prom." I thought I heard some laughter in the background and I asked, "Is someone else there with you, and he lied "No. It's just the television. So what's it going to be? I don't want to seem desperate but I am sort of." I answered him by saying "Well,

A Love Deferred

Okay, I'm in. So now what? I mean I can't just show up on her doorstep the night of the prom right?" I asked. Ed replied, "I've got it all worked out." "I see," I said. "You must have been giving this a lot of thought." Eddie laughed and said "Yes I have my bleed, because there is more at stake than just the prom here." "Oh," I said. "And what else can be on the line here?" "After the prom man," he answered. "Don't you know that girls are more likely to give up their sweetness on prom night? That is, if you set the mood and play you cards right." After that, I heard a loud "OUCH!" from Eddie. Caught off guard by the sound I asked, "Man what's wrong with you?" Eddie replied, "I slammed my finger in the drawer or something," "Uh huh," I said not really seeing. Then I continued, "Well, I doubt there's any chance of that happening. I'll probably be lucky if I get a nice handshake," I joked, "especially with someone I have yet to meet."

"I'm glad you brought that up," Eddie said. "Corrine and I think it would be a nice touch if you called Ronni and actually invited her to the prom." "I thought you said that I didn't have to do anything? That she was going to expect me to be her date?" I protested. "No, No, No my brother," Ed answered. "Ronni knows about you, but she doesn't know you. She is trusting Corrine's word that you are a good guy, but she won't go on hearsay alone. Also, if she thinks you are doing this only out of pity or because you feel sorry for her, she won't go. You have to call her and get to know her. Bring up the prom in your conversation when you've both warmed up to each other a little. Even though this is kind of prearranged, if you feel it, make her feel you're not a total rent-a-date. Pouring on a little sincerity can go a long way," he finished. "Now how do I just pour on the sincerity out of the blue?" I asked. "I don't even know her." A little frustrated, Ed answered, "Surely you can think of something. After all aren't you a jock and an Honor Society poster child going to that Brainiac College in Chicago? Use what you know man and go with your instincts. I know you can figure this out," he said. I tried to stay on Eddie's wavelength. "All of that is true, but those things are only relevant to academics. This situation is related to someone's feelings." "Yeah," Ed said earnestly, "which makes me even surer you are the right person to ask Ronni, because I know you will respect her feelings." And then emphasizing every word, Ed said, "You are one of the truly good guys that I know. And Ronni deserves to be with a good guy that night." I recognized and respected where Ed was going, but still tried to lighten the moment just a bit again by saying, "Alright, alright, please stop before the violins start playing." Ed then recited seven numbers and said, "Ronni's phone number. Seeing as though their prom is two weeks away, I think you should call her today. Remember her name is Ronni Bradley." Before he hung up he said "You know I would never steer you wrong, right?" I nodded dumbly at the phone as if he could see me and said, "Yeah brother." Figuring he had said and done all he could at this point, Ed wrapped up our conversation, confidently saying, "Trust me. You are going to thank me that I called you and not somebody else." I joked, "How do I know I wasn't the fifth person you called and the only one gullible enough to say yes to this arrangement of yours." Ed laughed, "You don't know, but it's too late to back out now. Call me back after you speak with her. I want to know how everything goes." I said that I would. He repeated Ronni's number and before we hung up he said "Promise you'll call today." I said "I promise." With that we hung up. But before I made any phone calls, I went looking for my sister Jenny to ask about that boy.

CHAPTER FOUR

NO BIG DEAL, IT'S JUST A CALL

✏️

"Look for clear skies and a warm California evening," said the smooth jazz DJ on the radio. It's a funny thing. For as long as I'd lived in sunny California, I haven't quite gotten use to the summer heat, mudslides, brushfires, or earthquakes. But it is still California and anyone who lives here will tell you that we are blessed with some of the most beautiful terrain in the country and perhaps the world. That's what I was thinking about when I went outside to give my plants a much needed watering. Afterwards I sat on my front steps still thinking about how much I looked forward to seeing Trey at school break and my phone call with Eddie. The first call brought pleasure and the second, apprehension. But I still couldn't help but focus on the prospect of seeing Ronni again after so many years.

I looked up into the hills and saw a small family of deer rooting about in the vegetation high above. Watching them and thinking, I was surprised and happy when I heard the scrabble of dog toes on concrete and Kit's bark as he ran up the steps to greet me. My neighbor, Jeff allowed me to leave Kit with him whenever I was going to be away for an extended period. He always told me it's because Kit and his dog Buster, got along so well. I also think it's because Kit is a little dog and when he takes the two dogs for walks in the park, it allows him to strike up conversations with more variety of women. Whatever the reason, I was thankful to Jeff for watching Kit. As Kit sat next to me, I continued to piece together the story of how Ronni and I met. That part of our story was pretty clear. It's the part leading to our, what, break-up? That's unclear. How many times have I replayed our first conversation in my mind? I have probably embellished it. Made it more than what it really was. But here's how I remember it.

Be Prepared

The first law of Boy Scouting is "A scout is trustworthy." If nothing else, I was very trustworthy. So when I told Eddie that I was going to call Ronni soon, I meant it. However, we lived in a small house with one phone to share with two teenage girls and two teenage boys. There was also the problem of finding the right moment when things were quiet enough to have the kind of conversation I needed to have with Ronni and also leave her with a good impression of me.

If I was reading this situation correctly, I still had to sell her on the idea of going to the prom with me. Just as I had questions about her, she probably had the same questions about me. Getting on the bus and asking her face to face was out of the question. Going to her house on a bus??? What kind of impression would that make? I finally settled on going to my brother, Ben's apartment and making the call from there.

Ben was always supportive of me and I could ask him for some tips about what I should say to Ronni, the girl with the "voice." I walked to Ben's place which was only eight blocks from our house. So far I had two older brothers who were married, or engaged, who lived within ten blocks of the house we grew up in. I made a note to myself "The first chance you get, move away from Washington, D.C." This wasn't an indictment on D.C., my friends, or my family. It's just that I always felt that there is too much world out there to discover outside of D.C., Maryland and Virginia. I needed to fly to new places, taste new foods, experience new things and maybe become a new person. I continued to walk during my musings and before I knew it, I had arrived at Ben's place. I shouldn't call it "Ben's Place" because his fiancée' Mary was always there. I should just call it Ben and Mary's place. But for now Ben's place is fine.

I rang the doorbell and, no surprise, Mary answered. "Hello" her voice came through the box. "Hi" I said pleasantly. "It's Ben's cool brother Eric. Can I come in?" She laughed and said, "Ben doesn't have a cool brother named

Eric, but I will let you in anyway." I always walked the four flights to their apartment because it seemed to be the right thing to do. I can't explain it better than that. When I got to their door Mary answered after my knock. She said, "What's this cool brother thing? You are the furthest person from cool that I know." I tried to sound indignant when I answered "How can you say that? Who do you know that's cooler than me?" Mary actually looked liked she was thinking about the answer and then she answered, "Everybody." We both laughed and hugged, our usual greeting.

Mary was really cool. She grew up in New York City and she was a radical in the mold of Angela Davis. She was medium height and build, brown skinned, and wore her hair in a short tight Afro. But she came across as someone you didn't want to get crosswise with so I always tried to stay on her good side. However, one thing we always ended up doing was debating. I don't know how it always worked out that way but we always saw things differently. Sometimes our debates got stormy but we always ended up hugging and saying "I'll get you next time." Before I left for college later that summer, Mary and I had a final talk. She told me that she intentionally took the opposite side in some of our debates so I could learn that there will always be more sides to a topic than just my side and that I should always be open to at least listening to other people's opinions. I can't tell you how much that lesson meant to me, or the hundred dollars she slipped into my pocket when we hugged.

Mary asked, "So what brings you here this Saturday afternoon? It's too nice to want to be inside," she added. "I have to be in because I am studying for finals but you should be out enjoying yourself." I agreed with her but added, "I really came to see if I could make a phone call." Mary asked "what's wrong, the phone's not working at your house?" Then she said, quite perceptively, "Oh. It's one of those calls." I quickly said "this is different." I hurriedly explained the situation. Mary smiled a knowing smile and nodded after hearing my explanation. She waved to the phone and said "Just leave a quarter after you are done." I griped "a quarter! You used to only ask for a dime." She said, "I get the feeling this call is going to be longer than two minutes." I asked her seriously, "Do you have any words of wisdom of what I should say to Ronni?" Mary smiled and put her arm around my shoulder, like she always did when she was about to share some knowledge, and said, "Just be a gentleman. You know, be yourself. Be the Eric that isn't always trying to compete or show off and you'll be just fine." She added, "I'll go in the bedroom to give you some privacy." I stood for a moment thinking about Mary and how much I liked her. I wish I told her more often how I felt about her. I wish I knew then that she would not be with us in less than four years due to cancer. I wish I had the words to say, even now.

****

Making the Call

I walked back inside with Kit following close behind. I smiled, thinking that it's times like these when you realize that technology is a wonderful thing. I opened one of my computer photo archives to a picture of a younger, Afro-wearing me in a dark blue suit and Ronni standing nearby in the background. In the next picture, she was smiling back at me. I was surprised that even today seeing this picture still had an effect on me. I could still remember her voice, as clearly as when I first spoke to her and how she could... BUZZ! The alarm on the washer went off breaking my reverie. I walked to the laundry room, took the darks out of the washer and threw them in the dryer. I set the heat and timer and started the darks drying while I got a load of whites going in the washer. I undressed and put on some jeans and loafers before going back to the office. Once there, I settled back into my chair and looked at another picture of this attractive, young couple – Ronni and me — standing outside her parent's home in Northeast, D.C. I couldn't help but think about our first conversation. It's funny now to think about how difficult it was for me to dial those seven numbers, and how quickly I settled down when we actually spoke for the first time.

****

Okay. Everything is set. I am here. The place is quiet. I have privacy. Now all I have to do is dial the number. But all of a sudden, I'm starting to get nervous. I actually felt a chill come over me. I couldn't recall ever feeling quite this way before but, I sort of felt that this was an enormous step I was about to take and it all just hit me at that moment. I stopped and thought for a moment that maybe I had better put together an outline of what I would say when I finally spoke to Ronni. I picked up one of Mary's notepads and scribbled down some things to say just to get the conversation started. It was probably lame that I did this, but it was the best I could think to do.

I wrote down things like, "Hi, my name is Eric Lewis, may I speak to Ronni?" And "Hi Ronni. We haven't met but I would like to see if what Ed and Corrine said about you is true." I even wrote that she should laugh at that. But what if she didn't laugh? This is getting to be more complicated than I planned, I thought to myself. As I was sitting there confused about how to proceed, Mary came out of the bedroom, to get one of her textbooks and said, "Boy that was a quick phone call. Maybe you only owe a dime after all." I told her, "I haven't called yet. I can't get the words right." She looked at me and shook her head. She said simply "All those brains but no smarts. Just pick up the phone and talk to her like a normal person you knucklehead." After hearing her say that, I knew she was right. I shouldn't complicate things more than they already were. Mary got her cup of tea and after she left I picked up the phone and dialed." As I dialed I started thinking about all the phone calls I made before. What was so difficult about this one? I felt like one of those phone solicitors using the phone book to cold call anyone who would listen long enough for me to get my story about all the wonderful things I could do. Simple! Not on your life.

****

I left work, mega *Report* in hand, and couldn't believe how crowded the subway trains were on my way to Allen and Allen Hair Salon. I was already running nearly 40 minutes late. Anita and her husband Andre ran a thriving hair styling business out of their home. Many of the clients had been with them since back in the day when their shop was in the hood. For a special occasion, or any occasion, the men and women who frequented their establishment, then and now, knew we had to make the trek wherever these hair doctors extraordinaire set up shop, to get our manes laid in true style and glamour. I was preparing to take my licks when I walked in the door. I was used to it by now and was actually relieved it was their daughter, Tina, who answered the door instead of one of them. "Ok, get ready," I told myself as I walked down the stairs to the basement salon. As expected, my man Andre lit in first. "Oh, oh Anita, look! Ronni is here early!" Anita let out a loud laugh and I had to join her, because 40

A Love Deferred

minutes late *was* early for me. "Y'all know I got to travel all the way from Hooterville [the name I affectionately called the suburban area where I worked.]. "One shuttle bus, two subway trains, and a taxicab ride later, I'm here. Gimme a break and work your magic on this head. I may have something *special* planned this weekend", I said.

Even though the salon was pretty busy, Anita got to me quickly. As she whisked me from her main chair, to the washing bowl chair, we talked about our children, and school, and teachers, and movies, and church, and singing, and some of our latest pet peeves and relationships of course. It's just something about a hair salon setting that makes people become instant experts on affairs on just about anything – money, family, affairs of the heart. Oh yes, especially the latter. I was so involved in our marathon conversation; I didn't even hear my cell phone ringing. Anita's daughter motioned to me, "Miss Ronni, your phone is ringing. Do you want me to get it for you before it stops?" I sat up, my towel draped around my neck, and now pulling it around my head, said, "Yes, please baby, thank you." She pulled the phone out of the cell phone holder on my purse, pushed down the button and immediately handed it to me. Thanks baby." Anita knew this meant she could temporarily move on to the head of someone else, at least for a short time, while I took my phone break. I was pleasantly surprised to find out who was on the other end...

A Love Deferred

****

The phone rang four or five times and then "Hello" answered a friendly, slightly older female voice on the other end of the line. "Good evening," I paused for a second, deducing that it was Ronni's mother. "Is this Mrs. Bradley?" I asked. "Yes," she said slightly guarded. "Who is this? At that point, I realized I may have potentially sounded like a phone solicitor and tried to remedy that right away. "Mrs. Bradley, I'm sorry to disturb you. My name is Eric Lewis, a friend of Corinne Pointer, and I was calling to speak to Ronni." In a slightly less guarded tone, Mrs. Bradley asked if Ronni was expecting my call and I answered as calmly as I could, saying, "I think so Mrs. Bradley. I believe Corinne told her I would be calling." "Okay," Mrs. Bradley's tone softened, "let me get her on the phone for you." I said "thank you very much Mrs. Bradley. It was nice talking to you." Mrs. Bradley asked me to hold on while she got Ronni and put the phone down. When she left, thoughts went through my head, wondering if I had poured the "Mrs. Bradley" thing on too strong. I think I may have started to sound like Eddie – not *my* Eddie, but the overly polite, but slightly annoying best friend to Wally Cleaver on that old show, "Leave it to Beaver." Definitely not the best way to start this off, so I made a mental note not to take the rest of my conversation with Ronni down this path.

A Love Deferred

I heard Mrs. Bradley's voice in the background calling "Ronni, telephone." I next heard the sound of a person ascending or descending some stairs and faintly saying "Who is it, Mom? I was about to wash my hair." Her mother replied good-naturedly, "Who am I, your personal secretary?" she laughed. Not wanting to tell anything more, she said, "Just pick up the phone and you will see who it is for yourself." A few seconds later the moment I thought I had prepared myself for happened. "Hello." Her voice caught me off-guard but I quickly composed myself and said "Hi Ronni, this is Eric Lewis, Eddie's friend. I hope this is a good time to talk, because if it's not..." Ronni cut me off with a soft laugh and said "Now is a good time to talk. Just let me go someplace where we can talk more privately." After a few seconds I could hear a door closing and Ronni saying, "So you are *the* Eric Lewis that Corrine and Eddie have talked so much about." I answered, "If what they said was good, I am," trying to lighten the moment a bit more. "If you don't mind me asking, what did they say about me?" When she answered, I thought more about her voice —*the voice* — as Eddie called it. I couldn't put my finger on it then but later I could best describe her voice as exotic. It was a combination of Phyllis Hyman singing and Eartha Kitt, purring like Cat Woman. [Years later I would joke with Eddie that Ronni could have been a millionaire if she started one of those infamous phone lines. But by that time I had heard her sing in her church choir I knew it would have been profane to have

55

her voice – "the voice"— anywhere on one of those lines.] "Corrine said that you are a really nice guy and that we would get along well," She answered politely. "She didn't say anything else?" I asked. "She didn't mention my wonderful sense of humor and how I was sometimes mistaken for *John Shaft* on the streets?" (*"Shaft"*, starring Richard Rountree was the big movie earlier that school year. Believe me; no one would have mistaken me for him). She laughed and said "No, she failed to mention either of those things. I'll have to ask her to be more thorough the next time she describes a brother to me. By the way what did Eddie have to say about me?" Truthfully I answered, "Eddie described you as a person I have to see to believe. When he told me that, the only person I could think of that fit that description was Lola Folana. So in comparison to Lola Folana, how would you describe yourself? She laughed again and said, "I'll only say that maybe he thinks I have her dance movements – ha! As for anything else, I'd really rather have you make your own observations, based on personal study."

Ronni and I talked and agreed on a lot of things. Ronni added that this conversation was refreshing compared to recent ones she had with some other members of the opposite sex. I asked, "What do you mean by that? I know you must talk to guys all the time." She got a little more serious adding, "Yes, I do talk to guys, but what I find is a lot of the conversations ends up being superficial. It becomes a lot of jive talking on his part and not much substance. If a guy wants to make it a one way conversation by talking mostly about himself, I just figure when that happens, he doesn't need me on the other end. He'd do better recording all that he has to say and then playing it back to his heart's content, because at that point, he is the only one who is really interested in hearing it." We both laughed. That seemed to lighten the moment. "Look, I don't want to sound like a jaded sister, because I'm not. I really would like to meet a nice guy, a guy of substance, who takes the time to engage *in* conversation with me, *not at* me, or even *about me*. Those guys seem harder and harder to find. You know sometimes when you don't respond to some of these so-called "brothers" the way they think you should, they curse at you and try to humiliate you." Before Ronni could go on I said, "I am sorry you have to put up with those things. You mentioned what you thought was the worst part but I have to let you know that there could be rougher times ahead for you. Some brothers just aren't going to change. You see, we invented jive talk so it's only going to evolve. As you get older and more attractive, the jive and the brothers who talk it will get older but, unfortunately, not necessarily more mature. As you walk down the streets you can only expect more of the comments and rebuffs when you don't respond. That's part of the harsh, real deal for some brothers, but not all of us. There are still some brothers who have been raised the right way." Ronni said that she could see I had put a lot of thought into this." I let her know that I had and all this had added to my conviction to treat all sisters with the same respect that I would want for my mother, grandmother and sisters." I thought this was as good a time as any to change the subject somewhat. "Ronni, when I spoke with Corrine and Eddie they mentioned you weren't going to your prom. Is that still true?" Ronni said "Yes, I suppose it's true."

"Is it because you don't have a dress, or a ticket?" She laughed and said "No to both questions. I have a dress and I have a ticket. Two tickets as a matter of fact." "So it sounds to me like you have a dress and some tickets that are going to go to waste. That is, of course, if you don't change your mind and go alone," I said. Ronni replied, "Going alone is not an option for me. But you are right. If I don't use the tickets, they will go to waste." "May I make a proposition?" I said. "Why don't you let me buy those prom tickets from you? Then all I would need to do is find someone to go with me." As if thinking about that problem I mused, "Let me see...Let me see....Who could I get at this late date that has a dress and doesn't have a date for the prom?" Then as if it just dawned on me I said "Wait a minute, you have a dress, and you just said you aren't doing anything next Friday." Next, carefully and sincerely I asked, "Ronni, would you do me the honor of being my date for the prom?"

I'm sure Ronni thought my approach was a little corny, but her response let me know she decided to play along anyway. "Hmmm," Ronni said trying to sound a little serious. But even over the phone, I could tell she was struggling, trying to hold back a laugh. "Let me think about it and get back to you, Eric. Hold on." I heard her lay the phone down and let out a girlish giggle. For a moment, I wondered if I had made more than a fool of myself. But then, almost as quickly as she put the phone down, she picked it up again. "You're in luck, Mr. Lewis. It just so happens my calendar is free next Friday. So, looks like we're going to the prom together." With those words, I told her that I would make arrangements and get back to her soon. As we said our goodbyes and hung up, I sat there wishing I had a car and the courage to call Ronni back to invite her to the movies or just talk some more. But I didn't have a car or movie money. So, I thought it best to leave her with the image of a prince and not a pauper. After saying goodbye to Mary, I walked the eight blocks home and started planning for the prom.

CHAPTER FIVE

GETTING READY

"**H**ey mom, it's me," the voice on the other end of the phone said cheerfully. My whole countenance changed. "Hey country bumpkin," I said laughing. It was my son, Mark on the phone. I sat up and then stood up with a big smile on my face and immediately Anita and Andre — I guess anyone who knew me for that fact — knew it was my heart on the other end of the line. They all started yelling, telling me to say hi to Mark for them. "Everybody at the hair doctor's says hello Mark. So what's up with you babe?" Mark answered, "Not a whole lot Mom. Dad and I just finished fixing dinner for Grandma and Granddaddy and then he and I are gonna ride to Charlotte to catch a couple of movies." I remembered how the movie-thon had been Mark's and his dad's special outing since he was a young child. They could go from flick to flick and never get bored. I tried to hang with them a couple of times, but after awhile, I ended up wanting to see just the opposite of the things they generally wanted to see, so I opted out of other movie-thons. I was glad they still enjoyed doing something like that though. Now, when they went bowling, that was a different thing. It was definitely on then!

My spirit of competition never waned when it came to things like that. It didn't matter what the challenge most times, or whether I'd done it recently or not at all, I always acted like I could. That's what Mark got from me I guess because he could talk a good game like his momma. That part of the chip was definitely off my block. "So mom, what are you doing this weekend? Got any special plans?" Mark always worried about me sitting around. He didn't want me to be alone, but what I would tell him, from time to time, was that I actually enjoyed some of those moments. Sure I could call up a buddy and do something, but it was funny how I was just as content to stay home and just be quiet. I think it went back to my childhood. Even though there were six kids in the house and my mom and dad, and constant activity and chatter, I could find a quiet place in the room I shared with my two sisters and hang there and be fine. My mom and sometimes my dad, and even my sisters and brothers, occasionally made it their business to make sure my solitude was anything but that. I usually had to convince Mark that his mom was okay.

Special plans he asked. Hmmmm, do I tell him that I'm going to get together with the man who could have been his dad or even his step dad? Not!!! Especially on the phone.

A Love Deferred

"I'm actually going to hang with your Aunt Corinne and Uncle Eddie and the twins this weekend at a cookout honey," I said. I was glad that I could tell him something that wasn't made up. "Good mom. That should be fun and I know that it will be good eating," Mark said and I could tell by his voice that he was relieved that I wouldn't be sitting at home the entire weekend. "Yeah," I continued, "I'm here now trying to get my do done by the hair docs just for that occasion. Although once that barbecue smell and the humidity hit this hairdo it will all be over," I laughed. "But, a woman's got to do what a woman's got to do!" I heard Mark laugh at that. "Mom, you got it goin' on no matter what you do to yourself. You'll always be beautiful to me." "See baby, that's why you are going to make some woman – your wife – real, real happy one day. But not until after you finish college, get a good job, and meet a woman who loves the Lord, right?" I asked, repeating the vow that I had Mark memorize from a child on and repeat every now and then just to make sure he had it down. Mark responded, "Yes, mom, you're right. Look Mom, make sure you say hi to everyone for me this weekend and tell them to all have a great time. I'll call you again on Sunday alright?" "Alright baby, I love you," I said, water starting to drip through the towel. I knew it was time to sign off. "I love you too Mom. Talk to you soon." With that Mark hung up the phone. My, how I love that boy I thought.

I turned to Anita with one of those forlorn looks. She just motioned to me to sit in her chair. Then I realized it was back to the task at hand. Monday would come soon enough. As if I thought everyone in the shop knew what was on my mind, I said, "Ok, Anita girl, get me ready!"

****

I got up from my computer and walked downstairs to the kitchen. I was still smiling about the first conversation I had with Ronni. It was so natural. So right. I don't know how we allowed ourselves to lose what we had. But I wasn't going to beat myself up over it again. Not now anyway. I went to the refrigerator and took out a turkey sandwich left over from last week. It would be a little tough but better than nothing. I also grabbed a can of Pepsi and went back upstairs. I went back to my computer still not quite ready to get to work on my emails. I opened another picture file of Ronni and me standing in front of her house. All smiles. I looked at her looking at me in the picture and I think I knew even then that I cared for her more than I wanted to believe. I picked up the remote for my stereo system and turned on the CD player. I pushed the random button and as clear as a bell I could hear the all too familiar song stylings of Eddie, and Marvin, The Supremes and other "Classic" songsters. I love old music, I mean classic music. Funny how at my age, I oftentimes forget what I did a week ago, but when I hear a classic Temptations song, I can vividly recall where I was when the song was played, who I was with, what I was doing, and what was going on in the world. These songs reminded me of the day of Ronni's Prom and what I did to *get ready*. I spun my chair around, looked out the window toward the bay and traveled back, at least in my mind, to 1972.

****

Somewhere in the background seems like all I kept hearing was that beat and what now seemed like a direct order from my Tempts charging me to "get ready." It seemed very appropriate because that's exactly what I was doing. It was now Friday, the morning of the prom and the time between the conversations I had with Ronni by phone was now a blur. I remember calling Eddie after getting home and giving him a few details of the call but mostly reporting that he could relax and start planning to attend the Prom. I still attended a week of classes but most of our real class-work was through. Most of the seniors spent a lot of time passing yearbooks around, getting autographs and exchanging numbers. I was surprised to see the number of girls who signed my yearbook and actually wrote messages that included their home numbers. I made a note to myself to call one or two of them later this summer just to see what happens. Eddie and I spoke later that morning and we decided that I would drive my brother's car to pick up Ronni that evening. Then

I would drive Ronni to his house and we would all drive together in his father's car to the hotel where the prom was being held. With those logistics taken care of, I left school early so I could go home and get ready for the prom. I got on the bus, showed the driver my student pass, and dropped in my dime fare.

We rode north on one of the busiest streets in D.C., Georgia Avenue, and passed landmarks like the Howard Theater, where the James Brown's revue was still announced on the marquee, Ed Murphy's Supper Club, Howard University and D.C. Teacher's College. We passed the Guild Shop where I got my high school letter jacket and later my fraternity sweater. We also passed the Omega Psi Phi national headquarters before arriving at the corner of Georgia and Columbia Road. I stepped off the bus and crossed the street to the Bluebird Tonsorial Parlor. I always thought that was too fancy a name for a barbershop but that's the name it had for over forty years, or so I was told. I walked into the shop and there was Mr. Walker and his brother Fred. Fred was busy cutting hair while Mr. Walker sat in his chair reading a newspaper. In the corner there were two guys playing checkers and Rickey Adams was sweeping up the shop. As usual the Walker brothers wore caps on their heads. That was another thing I found odd but cool about the shop. They defied convention. There was also a heated debate about whether Marion Barry would make a good mayor for D.C. after the job he did at Pride, Incorporated. One side believed that Walter Washington was doing a fine job and Marion Barry was just a joke and had no place in politics. The other side was of the opinion that Walter Washington was an establishment puppet and was only a figurehead. I enjoyed listening to these debates and was surprised when Mr. Walker said "What do you think young blood?" and was actually referring to me.

While he motioned for me to be seated I stammered "Well, I have met both of them and they both have strong points." I was going to add more but Mr. Walker said "You see Fred. That boy has a good head on his shoulders." Fred added, "Yeah he's what you call it." And fumbling for the word he said "Articulate." "Yeah, that's right." Mr. Walker said. "He's articulate." Taking pride as if he taught me everything I knew. "You know I been cutting the boy's head since he was a baby. Some of my smarts must have rubbed off on him." With that that the shop erupted in laughter and off started the barbs and banter. A half hour later, my hair cut was done. Although he didn't approve of the Afro style, Mr. Walker knew how to shape it and make it look good. He put on an ample amount of Afro Sheen and handed me a mirror, the last step before brushing off any loose hair and taking off the apron. I looked in the mirror and checked myself out. Although I looked good, I knew I would never look as good as some guys but not as bad as others. So the hair cut was acceptable for what is was worth. When I nodded. He took off and shook the apron that covered me, which was Ricky's cue to start sweeping. I reached in my pocket to pay for the cut when Mr. Walker said "No charge today Youngblood."

Before I could say anything he said, "Early graduation gift." He handed me an envelope with a card inside and said, "This is from Fred and me. We heard you are going to a big college in Chicago. Take this and make us proud." With that I shook both barbers' hands and said "thank you." I took the envelope and waved as I left. Later when I got home, I found that the envelope contained a card that read simply, "Congratulations Graduate from Fred and George Walker." It also contained five brand new $20 bills. I put the card and money away with my small savings and made a note to myself to say a special prayer of thanks that night. My next stop was the dry cleaners. I couldn't afford a second tuxedo rental so I decided to wear my navy blue suit. I figured I could dress it up with a white shirt and a nice tie and make myself look presentable. I mean how much did I have to invest for one night with this girl? I would be presentable and pleasant but realistically, after tonight it would be all over so a suit would do just fine.

When I got home, I checked the refrigerator to make sure the corsage was there as my sister promised. It was so I went upstairs and laid out my suit and a freshly starched and ironed white shirt. I picked out a tie and laid it next to the shirt and suit then I polished my shoes. With my clothes ready and about an hour and a half to go before having to pick up Ronni I took a nice hot bath. I was careful not to mess up my hair while I was in the tub but I wanted be extra clean. I toweled dry and put on baby oil instead of lotion. I sprayed some Afro Sheen on my 'fro and picked it out to its full length. Finally, I splashed on some Hai Karate aftershave and was good to go. I did it in that order because by the time I arrived at Ronni's house, the after shave would have toned down considerably. I still had thirty minutes before it was time to leave so I sat and played a few records on the stereo before getting dressed. This was one of the few times I had the luxury of having the bedroom to myself for such a long period of time because my brothers were still at work and school.

    I played the Stylistics, the O'Jays, Delphonics and Whispers. I started getting dressed while listening to the Miracles, Stevie Wonder and the Jackson 5. When I finished dressing, I turned the stereo off and walked downstairs for inspection by my grandmother. She said "Baby, come closer so I can get a good look at you." This was her old trick so she could give me a big kiss on my cheek and say "you are my love lamb." I stood there and accepted it like I had for as long as I could remember and also smiling because it was so warm and predictable. Grandma added, "Now who couldn't love that sweet face." She shouted to my Grandfather, "Walter come in here and see your grandson before he leaves." Granddad called back "He's going to walk right by me on the porch. I will see him then." With that I got the usual speech about being a gentleman, and watch what you drink. "You know they slip drugs in punch nowadays so just be careful." I promised I would and before she could grab me I grabbed my tiny Grandmother and gave her a big hug and said "I love you Grandma. See you later." With that I walked out the front door and talked to my Granddad who said "Went a little heavy on that aftershave huh?" We both laughed and he said "You need any money?" I answered "No sir, I'm all set." He asked "You remember what to do if there is any trouble, right?" I answered "Yes sir. Call home and get to a safe place." He said "Above all make sure you keep this young lady safe." I promised I would and with that, I twirled my brother's keys, got in the car and took off.

****

CHAPTER SIX

AN ENCHANTED EVENING

I was still looking out the window when my phone rang. I looked at the caller ID on the handset at my desk and laughed as I picked up the phone. It was my sister Jenny. All grown up now, a successful attorney, wife and mother. "Hey baby sister" I said happily into the phone. "Don't you baby sister me Eric Lewis." She snapped back. "And I love you too" I replied not surprised by the verbal attack. "Don't try your little I love you trick. Save that for those valley girls out there." She fumed. I said in my best Rodney King impersonation "Can't we all get along" words I knew would get her laughing. Sure enough she started laughing and she said "You know you're not right." "First of all let me start by saying Happy Birthday and many happy returns." "Uh huh," Jenny said. "You're only four days late. I guess my gift is in the mail" she continued. "As a matter of fact I am bringing it with me when I come this weekend. I'm saving the postage" I said while making a note to get Jenny a birthday gift. She said "I know you just wrote a note to remind yourself to buy me a gift. So just to make sure you get something I like, I want a jade necklace. And not some cheap Chinatown jade either" she added. "And you know that I know the difference." I stammered, "Now how are you going to call me and place an order for a Birthday gift? Whatever happened to a gift being something sent from the heart and the receiver just accepting it?" I said jokingly and also pleased that I now knew what to get her. "Puleeze Eric."

Jenny said "You know as well as I do that I am doing you a favor by telling you what to get me. What happened did you forget me again? Go on. Tell the truth." She admonished. "No badgering the witness." I said. "Overruled" she answered smoothly. "Answer the question." "I plead the fif" I said trying to sound like Dave Chapelle. With that we both laughed. "Hey the kids are sleeping but they would really get a kick out of seeing you. I don't get it but they seem to like you" she joked. "Maybe it's because I never got out of the sixth grade" I laughed. We both had a good laugh and before hanging up I gave her the details of my itinerary and promised I would see her this weekend. I took a bite of the sandwich and almost gagged. I decided to get on my bike, ride down the hill and pick up some fresh tacos at the Burrito Village in Berkeley. The problem is going down the hill was one thing, but getting back up was something else. My stomach won out though so I put on some decent shoes, helmet and pads and took off. As I was gliding along, my mind on auto-pilot. I saw a young man getting into a suped up Camaro Z28 metallic blue just like my brother's. While looking at him I was thinking about me and how I got in the car the night of the prom.

****

I took my jacket off, folded it and laid it on the back seat. Then I got in the car and started the engine knowing that my granddad was watching me like a hawk. My Grandfather, now retired, was a professional truck driver for 40 years. One of the highlights of his year was his company's Annual dinner where they recognized long service employees and retirees. His pride at getting dressed up and wearing his company pin on his lapel was great to see but his 40 years of perfect driving experience gave him license to tell all of us how to drive. So I was very careful to show I was checking traffic before pulling into traffic, I had my hands on the steering at 12 and 3 o'clock and I was within the speed limit. However, when I reached the corner I relaxed and went to my normal one-handed driving. I cranked the music up in the new Camaro and began cruising toward Northeast D.C.

I only lived about 15 miles from Ronni but there are no straight routes from my house to hers. Having never been to her house, I followed the bus route I would have taken under normal circumstances. I always felt a little uncomfortable driving in parts of the city, other than around where I lived, because it felt as though I was crossing invisible boundaries and entering into new and dark territories. I reached Ronni's street a short time later and was turned around briefly when I found it was one way, and not the way I was driving. No problem, I thought. Just go to the first street and turn right on; another right and then I'd be there. But I still got mixed up when I had to cross a diagonal street and missed the entrance to Ronni's street which turned out to be three short blocks long. When I finally circled back and turned on to her street, I easily found the house. As it turned out there were folks hanging out on the block — advance scouts I said to myself. There was a space open directly in front of the house, almost too good to be true. I hadn't really planned for any kind of inspection, basically, say hello to Ronni and her parents and then take off. Good plan I thought but that's not how it would work out.

I parallel parked the car using only two cuts. My granddad would have been proud. I gathered up the corsage and stepped out of the car. That's when I noticed several neighbors on their porches giving me the once over. Maybe it was just my imagination, but I started feeling a little pressure then. I walked slowly to the door of Ronni's house checking the house number to be sure I wasn't going to the wrong door and slowly so I didn't trip or something else embarrassing. I opened the screen door and tapped on the front door, not too hard, but firm... "Just a minute, I'm coming," the voice on the other side of the door shouted. "Okay, Lewis, you're on,"

A Love Deferred

I thought to myself. The door opened, and I made the proper introductions to the older man standing opposite me, who, not surprisingly was Ronni's dad. We shook hands and he welcomed me in the door. We chatted some more as he led me into the house. As I walked, I noticed it was only slightly cooler inside than it was outside and felt a little trickle of sweat start down my back. I'm sure it was more my nerves than it was the heat, but I wasn't going to let on.

Mr. Bradley introduced me to Mrs. Bradley and I felt a calm come over me, having spoken with her previously. I almost felt as if I had bonded with her and, hoping that I earned brownie points the day I spoke with her, she must have helped pave the way with Mr. Bradley before my arrival. I thought it odd at first that none of Ronni's other five sisters and brothers, except her baby sister, were home, but Mrs. Bradley said they all decided to clear out so Ronni and I wouldn't feel so much on display. Wow, I liked them already. I looked around the tidy living room trying not to be obvious also seeing if I could spot Ronni. I saw photographs of young girls and boys, family pictures and pictures that were probably aunts, uncles, or grandparents. I continued to take in all the remnants of life there including photographs and of all things, little bells from around the world. I thought about my own living room where there were no photographs, pictures, snapshots — you get my meaning. No signs of past life, just present existence. In fact, as I think about it, I don't' recall any photos of me as a baby, or anytime during my young life that documents any of my achievements so far. No pictures of my first steps, my first word, winning the Spelling Bee, my first race, hell not even my last race. I made a note and a promise to myself that when I get to a point in my life where I can afford a camera, to document every moment I can.

****

I was determined to take full advantage of the prom night pageantry, so I waited upstairs until my dad called me down. My sister Cee Cee, who heard the knock at the front door and tried to rush me, wasn't feeling my plan. "Come on Ronni, he's not going to wait forever," she said impatiently." "Hush Cee Cee," I said. "I'm trying to hear some of the conversation between Eric and Daddy." As I listened, I could only hear bits and pieces. My father had a presence about him that could be a little unsettling. [Eric would later tell me that he analyzed his discomfort as two Alpha males vying for the attention of one female. Of course this wasn't the same as in the wild but, when my father needed to make a point, Eric felt obliged or frightened to just say, "Yes sir"]. "My dad was a former policeman and, even at 5 feet 6, he had a very imposing voice and presence. And if that didn't work, he also had a gun hidden someplace in the house – a fleeting thought that, for a moment, made me smile, thinking if this Eric guy didn't treat me right, he'd better watch out for dad. The very fact that Eric made it in the house let me know that he passed the first phase of what I would always refer to as my father's *Three Phase Test* he conducted, probably subconsciously, on any male suitors entering his castle. *Phase One* passed, I thought. My father *Sees No Evil.*"

"Can you see him?" I asked Cecilia. "No, not without him seeing me. The angle of the banister on the stairs was just too awkward to allow anyone to be sneaky – something that we actually knew from years of unsuccessfully trying to sneak a peak at gifts being placed under the tree in the wee hours of Christmas mornings. Too bad, I thought. I needed a spy to let me know if how he described himself to me in one of our phone conversations was actually true – over six feet, lean, but not skinny, and a little salt and pepper in his afro. That last part intrigued me because we were both only 18 years old.

I could hear daddy say, "You know that's my baby girl you are taking out tonight." I heard Eric answer, "Yes sir, I do." My father continued, "I only know you through what my daughter and my wife say about you. All I want is at the end of this evening Ronni will still have kind things to say about you. Do you understand?" I imagined Eric responded respectfully and correctly, and probably looked to my mom for some sort of expression that would show that she believed he would follow to the letter, the charge given him by my father. *Phase Two* passed: My Father *Hears No Evil.*

And so, here we both were, seconds away from meeting for the very first time. "Ronni," my dad called to me, "are you ready? Eric is here." "Coming daddy," I answered, trying to sound as calm as possible, even though I could feel the butterflies fluttering in my stomach. With my dad's speech over, I walked to the top of the stairs, preparing to go down, when I heard Eric say," Mr. and Mrs. Bradley, I just want to let you both know that it is my intention, to make this a night Ronni will enjoy and remember." When I heard that, I thought, *Phase Three* passed: Eric *Speaks No Evil*. I don't think he could have given me a better cue to enter. Besides, I thought I'd better get down there and save him from too much of my dad's inquisition, before both of us were too nervous to start. As confident as I was trying to portray myself, I was actually pretty quiet and shy around most folks until I got to know them better, a luxury I didn't have leading up to tonight's events.

Seems everyone in my family wanted to get into the act that night. My sister CeeCee rushed down ahead of me, cleared her throat and announced very dramatically, "Ladies and gentlemen, I now present to you my big sister Ronni, who is surely the Bradley Prom Queen for the Night!" I had to laugh at that. I was glad CeeCee, with her crazy self, was here to share in this moment. With that, conversations ended and all you could hear were the sounds of my heels on the wooden stairs. I slowly made my way down the stairs, and as I turned to enter the living room, I could see the smiles of pride on my parents' faces. I gave them both warm, long hugs. And then, I turned to the tall, young man standing in the living room. When our eyes locked, I became a woman of few words, at least in my mind, when all I could think was "Wow." Aside from the fact that he wasn't wearing a tuxedo, [something I dismissed because this was a last minute thing] he was striking in the tailored navy blue suit he wore. I definitely liked what I saw. His first words relaxed me.

****

The moment I realized I had been anticipating so intently was now here. I rose to my feet and noticed that my heart was beating way too fast. It was the same feeling I had before the start of any race or game I ever participated in. That same adrenalin was rushing through me and it made me a little light headed at first. Then I saw her. She was descending the stairs slowly, probably so she wouldn't slip or trip on her long gown. Years later as I thought back on that moment, Ronni was just as I imagined. No, let me make that clearer. I didn't let myself imagine what she would look so I wouldn't allow myself to be disappointed. But I never imagined this. I had gone to my own school's prom only two weeks ago and I had already forgotten it. The pictures, who cares. This is what prom night should be like for everyone.

I waited patiently as she hugged her mom and dad and turned towards me. Her beautiful face was slightly enhanced with makeup, lip gloss and eye liner, just enough to make her brown eyes really stand out. Her lips were full and inviting.

A Love Deferred

Her hair was a perfectly coiffed, medium length Afro. She was stunning, and all I could say was "Good evening Ms. Bradley, I am Eric Lewis. Let me be one of the first to say how beautiful you look this evening." Ronni smiled and answered, "And you, Mr. Lewis, don't look half bad yourself." We both let out a light laugh and it helped calm us. I reached back and picked up the box that contained her corsage and didn't think my hands were steady enough to pin it. Her mom must have picked up on it, and offered to do it. Saved again by Mrs. Bradley. I continued to try to take the sight of Ronni in without staring. She was wearing this intoxicating fragrance. For years after that night, the slightest hint of that fragrance took me back to that night and that moment, no matter who was wearing it. Ronni walked gracefully as we posed for a couple of the obligatory prom night pictures her sister insisted on taking.

As our eyes met, she smiled at me. I think I smiled back but I am not sure. I was starting to feel self conscious. I started to question all my decisions leading up to that night. Why hadn't I worn a Tux? I could have kicked myself. Ronni made a special point to give her parents another hug and a kiss and from the looks all around it was clear, this was her night. We made our way to the door and found a few of the neighbors outside watching our every move. We said our good nights to her family, and headed towards the car. I opened the passenger side to let her in, again taking full inventory of this Dream Girl. I had to make sure I thanked my buddy

A Love Deferred

Eddie. He called this one right for sure. 'Got everything?" I asked Ronni. She looked in her small purse, looked at me and answered, "Yes." With that, we were headed off to meet Corinne and Eddie.

When we arrived at Eddie's house we found much the same scene as at Ronni's — family members taking pictures, kids hanging around, and neighborhood well wishers. When Ronni stepped out of the car there were whistles and cat calls from some of the boys but nothing to get excited about. "I told you, it's only going to get worse." I whispered to Ronni as I escorted her to Eddie's driveway. Ronni and Corrine gave each other hugs and a once over then they began chatting. Ed's mother came over and gave me a quick hug and insisted that she get a picture of Ed and me together. Ed's father and brother were completing the last minute clean up of the car and when they were done walked over and spoke to all of us. "Now, I know this is a big night for all of you," his father said, "but I want you to be safe tonight as well. Don't let fun make you forget to keep your mind on the road and being aware of the situations you put yourselves in." He ended his speech by saying "If you get into any trouble call us right away." We all shook our heads and said that we understood and would call if any trouble arose. After a few more pictures and waves goodbye, we bundled ourselves into the car and drove off towards the Grand Hyatt Hotel in downtown D.C.

The ride to the hotel was uneventful. There was light conversation and nice music on the radio. Ronnie and I sat in the back seat of the car and although we were hitting it off quite well, still sat a respectful distance from each other. I found myself stealing glances at her when we weren't talking and I caught her doing the same.

CHAPTER SEVEN

BREAKING THE ICE

When we arrived at the hotel, there was a frenzy of activity outside. Couples arriving at the same time met and greeted each other at the entrance taking pictures and having fun. Once inside, Corrine and Ronni saw and hugged friends and complimented and received compliments on their hair and gowns. I have to say, totally unbiased of course, Ronni and Corrine, were stunning. Ed and I were basically holding our own and since we didn't know anyone, other than Corrine and Ronni, we couldn't really contribute much to the conversations. Of course, we were introduced to everyone but almost immediately, I forgot their names. I couldn't shake the feeling that I was on alien ground and I was looking for some way to stabilize myself in that environment. The only answer I could come up with was staying close to our little group and hoping to make the best of the situation.

A Love Deferred

****

Once inside the prom, we all sat at a table with a couple of other friends. Eric and I occasionally joked about the sports rivalry between our two schools, but nothing, indeed nothing, too personal. If our eyes connected for too long, a nervous impulse we both seemed to suffer from, had one, or both of us slowly shift our focus elsewhere. Our conversation paled in comparison to the lively banter happening with the other couples at the table, but then again that wasn't so strange, considering the others knew each other longer than a couple of weeks and probably met each other well before tonight.

****

The conversation was cordial and at times funny but I still felt subdued. The music was provided by a DJ and he was very good at sensing the mood of the crowd and mixing the music just right. I love to dance, but Ronni probably thought I had two left feet because it took me a little while to get in gear to keep her on the dance floor. There was mostly fast dancing. I know we did at least one disco line but I stayed away from the slow songs.

****

Eric, ever the perfect gentleman made sure refreshments and snacks were there for me, but there was only so many punch and pigs-in-a-blanket I could stomach to fill the void before I choked on them. There were intermittent dances, which helped move the evening along slowly, but it took at least an hour before Eric and I felt a real social connection.

****

At one point, all four of the female dates made an exodus to the ladies room. That gave me a chance to talk to Ed alone for the first time since the dancing started. "Nice prom, huh?" He said. I said "Very nice. You were right about Ronni you know. She is very nice." I replied. "Yeah she looks great. How are things going between you two?" I answered "I think they are going pretty well. We just don't know each other well enough." "Well you've got all summer, starting with the rest of tonight," Eddie hinted as he smiled at our dates returning to the table.

I thought about Eddie's comments as I joined him in watching Ronni and Corrine walking back to our table. It was pleasant to think about spending more time with Ronni. I briefly fantasized about talking on the phone for hours with her. Going to concerts, movies or just walking and holding hands with her. Then I was back at the Prom and the reality set in that it was almost over.

A Love Deferred

The DJ announced that the Prom would be ending soon and that he wanted all couples on the dance floor for the remaining songs. What happened next could almost be described as magical, if you believed in such things. The first violins strains from the Dells classic "Stay in My Corner" came through the speakers and en masse the floor filled with couples. Ed, Corrine and the other couples were long gone and it was just Ronni and I left at the table. The dance floor was over flowing and people were jostling for position, so I held my hand out to Ronni and asked "May I have this dance?" She didn't answer; she just rose and took my arm. We found a place on the dance floor and then the magic began.

****

What Eric and I didn't or couldn't share in awkward moments earlier, came through much better in our time on the last few records, a medley of love songs. There must have been something magical about the lights going a little dimmer, the music slowing, the chatter in the otherwise noisy room dulling about 200 decibels, and the flashing of the party ball above our heads, reflecting rainbow colors — yellow, red, and blue — across our faces that had us to finally look into each others eyes and strike up a really nice conversation. The nervous impulses had totally disappeared. Hallelujah!

A Love Deferred

****

I took Ronni in my arms and held her close to me. At that moment, we weren't aware of anyone else but us. We moved well together for two people just meeting. With her height, it was easy for her to rest her head on my shoulder as we danced. We were so close that I could finally talk to her without raising my voice. I could still smell her perfume and I was spellbound. We glided as much as danced and I could feel her soft, warm body move even closer to me as we danced slowly to the music. I whispered, "So are you having a good time?" She nodded and in a rich, mellow tone, answered, "Yes, I am." We talked some more as we danced but mostly we savored the moments until the song ended. When the song was over, we didn't immediately leave our embrace. I looked into her eyes and they might have said "It's okay if you want to kiss me"...or maybe not. So I took the safe road and said "Thank you" and we walked back to our table, gathered our things and left as the lights were turned up signaling the end of the dance.

****

Following the prom, Eric, Corinne, Eddie and I joined a few others at the home of another future graduate where we continued the party with board games, more music and dancing, and even later fixing a full breakfast. We talked endlessly about our high school years and what was ahead of us. While I was staying put in the area to attend college, Corinne and a few others, including Eric, were headed in other directions north, south and Midwest to pursue their higher education. So this night's gathering would always hold a special place for all of us. The looks on Eric's and my face throughout the night, and now, very early morning hours, let others in the room know what we had probably filed in the back of our minds, but now was evident in our motions, and that is that we had clicked and really enjoyed each other's company – a relief to Corinne and Edward, who would have never heard the end of it had we not.

It was turning light when Eric pulled up in front of my house. As he opened the door to let me out of the passenger side, I shivered slightly. "Cold?" he asked. "Maybe just a little," I said. Eric took his suit jacket off and draped it around my shoulders. "Thank you," I said. "My pleasure," Eric beamed. As we reached the front door, we were again faced with an awkward moment, wondering whether this one magical night would warrant a second or even a third date.

****

When we reached Ronni's front door, the mood was pleasant but melancholy. We both knew that this night, this moment was fast approaching its end and there was nothing either one of us could do to prolong it. Ronni was the first to speak.

****

"I had a really nice time Eric. I want to thank you. I know that you could have been a million places tonight instead of with me. You're a really good guy and I enjoyed our time together," I said, wanting to thank him, but not wanting to overdo it and make him uncomfortable. "The pleasure was all mine Ronni." He hesitated for a brief second, and then as if to make sure I really understood the sincerity in his remark, he emphasized *"Really."* Still the gentleman, he hugged me and I gave him his coat as he said good night and started to walk down the front porch steps. But then he turned and, for the life of me, I could not make out the expression on his face.

****

"If I walk away from this wonderful evening," I said, "without saying, telling, doing what I really feel, I will regret it. "I looked directly in Ronni's beautiful eyes and could tell she was a bit taken aback.

****

"Oh, God!" I immediately thought, "Regrets?! I knew this was too good to be true. Brace yourself sister."

****

"This is one of those once in a lifetime moments," I told Ronni, as I climbed the few steps back to her. "I know having only officially met you tonight, this might seem more than a little presumptuous of me, but I do regret that other than the few phone calls we've had, I haven't known you long enough, at least in calendar time, to end this special night with what I know would be a wonderful end-of-prom kiss."

****

My response was equally surprising when I said, "I don't know what it is about you and me Eric, but what we were able to share tonight made me feel as if I'd known you for years, and I don't say that lightly. So, *old friend,*" I said spontaneously, "would you like to make up for lost time?" What Eric didn't say with words, he said in the tender actions that followed. It was as if we were the only two people in the climax of a play and as the stage went dark, a solitary spotlight shining down on us lit our frames. Eric took my left hand with his right and slowly, gently, pulled me towards him. Slave to the magnetic trance of the moment, I followed his lead, gazing absorbedly into his eyes.

In the seconds before our lips touched, I heard jingling; that I thought surely must have been some ringing in my head as the blood rushed upwards. The sound was actually the ring of keys that Eric held firmly in his left hand before, but now releasing them to the front porch rocker, wanting nothing but the warmth of his palms to touch my bare shoulder and back that the halter dress exposed. He slid his hands under the suit jacket that he slipped back over my shoulders, on to my back, which I thought must surely be overheated because of that blood rushing thing happening again. And then, as if in chorus, we both released some here-to-fore hidden passion that must have been kept under emotional lock and key, in that one long goodnight kiss on the front porch that rang in the daylight, and appeared to be the beginning of something. Just what, I wasn't sure.

****

I don't remember the exact words Ronni said but I do remember her folding into my arms, looking into my eyes, and one of the sweetest, most tender kisses I have ever experienced. Ever. It was the kind of kiss that had the promise of so much more. We finally broke from our embrace and said our goodnights. Ronni turned, unlocked the door and went inside. The last I saw was her smile and the kiss she blew me.

Weeks after I left her porch that morning, I went back to accepting what was in front of me. I went back to the girl I had previously dated in senior year, knowing what the end of that relationship was destined to be, but still not rushing it to its conclusion. I called, and even went out with a couple more who signed my yearbook. But I didn't call Ronni. Maybe I wasn't ready for what she might have to offer. What a foolish decision on my part that turned out to be. I didn't know that I wouldn't see Ronni again for another three years.

CHAPTER EIGHT

THE LONG WAY HOME

The airport shuttle driver dropped me at the terminal at Oakland's airport two hours before my flight departure time. For a city the size of Oakland, I always thought that the terminal was too small for the volume of flights it handled. That leads to longer lines and wait times. It also means higher ticket prices. The alternative is of course to cross the bridge and fly out of San Francisco. So I am always left with deciding on convenience or price. Today I chose convenience. As I rolled my bag inside the building, I found that I was actually excited about going home after being away so long. I ticked off in my mind the places I had traveled to since my last trip to D.C. three years ago. "Let's see there was, Beijing, Shanghai, Singapore, Manila, Taiwan, Kuala Lampur, Hong Kong, Venice, Paris, London, Calgary, Montreal, and Bangkok. And that doesn't count all of my domestic travel. I've even been to Bora Bora since my last trip to D.C. I smiled as I thought about the stash of foreign cash I tucked into my bag for my niece's collection and the Jade necklace for my sister. Yes this was going to be a fine trip after all.

I made my way to the ticket counter and found that I could stand in the long line waiting for service from an agent or the much shorter line at the self service counter. I opted for the latter. I went through the prompts and options, handed over my checked luggage and made my way to the security area. This part of the trip is the Black Man's nightmare. If other Black men are like me, we don't like situations where other people can single you out on a whim and more often than not, I either get buzzed going through the metal detector where I get the "Male body check on line 1"or I get the TSA person asking "May I check you bag sir?" as if I really had any choice. Don't get me wrong, I understand the reasons for the stepped up security. I just don't understand why it's never caught anybody and why it seems to focus on me.

When I got to the front of the line, I placed my lap top in a separate bin, placed my camera bag on the line, poured the contents of my pockets into a container, took off my shoes, belt and watch, and placed them all on the conveyor belt. For some reason, I am always nervous stepping through the metal detector. BUZZ! The alarm went off. "Why, why, why?" I thought. Two TSA people rushed over to me. "Are you sure you have no metal objects on you? Please check your pockets and walk through again." Of course after checking my pockets and going through again, under their careful scrutiny I might add, no alarms. And I hadn't changed a dog gone thing. "Sometimes they just go off for Black people." I mumbled. "Did you say something?" the inspector asked. I just got my things and headed to the gate, not bothering to look back and surlier than before.

Okay, it's now 45 minutes before take-off so I picked up some reading materials, and a crossword magazine then found a seat at the gate. Judging by the number of people in the area, this flight was going to be long and crowded. I figured the best thing for me to do was try to get some sleep if I could. If I was reading this weekend right, there was going to be a lot of partying and late night talking. Besides Eddie, Corrine, and the twins, there would be three other couples and at least some of there children and of course, Ronni. Even with all the people around me in the gate area, I still felt alone when I thought about her and what I let slip away so many years ago. What had I been thinking? Oh yeah, that's right, I was thinking that I was the big "Playah" from D.C. and I could have a woman on North Campus, South Campus, at church, in Chicago in the suburbs, or wherever. Before long Ronni was just a face in the midst of a lot of pretty faces. What I forgot to do was look into their hearts to see who truly loved me. If I had only done that, it would have led me back to Ronni.

I was shaken from my reverie with the gate agent's announcement that Flight 107 to Washington's Reagan National was now ready for boarding. "We will be boarding by row numbers so please approach the gate only after your row is called." She went on to say, "Please have your boarding pass out. I knew I would be allowed to board since I was a Platinum Miles member so I just stepped up to the podium handed her my ticket and went on board. "Have a good flight Mr. Lewis," she said as I entered the jet-way. "Thanks," I said as I joined the few people ahead of me. I liked to get on board, get situated and watch the other people boarding. I called it my just in case security. I like getting a read on other passengers, just in case I might have to take security into my own hands. I also liked to see if I could guess before hand who would be sitting next to me on the flight. No matter how much I tried to will it, it never turned out to be the person I picked. Today was no exception. Today I got a yacker. This guy started talking from the moment he sat down. I pulled out the *New York Times* crossword magazine and started working on it, hoping he'd get the hint. Thankfully, he did. Before long, with no one to talk to, my seat mate was dead to the world and snoring lightly.

The flight was progressing smoothly until about an hour into it when we hit some particularly violent turbulence. The kind where the fasten seat belts sign came on and the flight attendants were instructed to take their seats. After five minutes of bumping around at seemingly supersonic speed, I let my mind relax. I released my death-grip on my seat's arm rest and let my mind go back to the summer of 1975. Soon

the turbulence was far away and I was a young man walking
the hot streets of D.C.

CHAPTER NINE

BACK TOGETHER AGAIN?

I was home for the summer and decided to visit my oldest brother's home after work one June afternoon. I really just liked spending time with my nieces and nephew. I always thought they were the most wonderful and well adjusted children and I enjoyed talking to them about cartoons and playing games. I also wanted to ensure that I was their favorite uncle, so I showed up for everything including birthday parties, and other fun events. I celebrated the good times and shared in the bad times. However, my real treat was spending time with my niece Raja. Raja had difficulty comprehending things. But no matter what, she would touch my nose with her special fingers to let me know that she recognized me and I would kiss her forehead to let her know I recognized her. We would sit and read until she fell asleep which didn't take long because the constant seizures she suffered, took their toll on her little body. After she fell asleep, I handed her off to my sister in-law and decided it was time to go home for dinner.

When I stepped outside, I heard the sound of a piano coming from my friend Jessie's house. Jessie and I practically grew up together and I always knew she was a singer but the sounds coming from her house were extraordinarily good, and somewhat, out of place for this neighborhood. I wasn't the only one to think that judging by the "Looky Lou's" sitting on porches and listening to the gospel sounds coming from my friend's house. I hadn't seen Jessie, who would be entering her senior year at Chapel Hill, or her sister Terry, who would be a junior at Mount Holyoke, in quite a while, so I thought I would just pop in and say hello. I crossed the street and knocked on the screen door. I was pretty sure no one heard me because there was no interruption in the singing. I stood there for a moment as I heard the harmonious voices sing "He didn't have to do it."

Their soulfulness touched me as I am sure it did our other neighbors in earshot. For a little while, their singing cleansed the arguing, fighting, drug dealing or trouble of any kind on that little street. There was just the music. I listened a little more as they sang "I'm glad so glad, that he did." *(Even today as I think about that song, I think about how Jesus hung, bled and died for all of us, even me. And I'm glad that he did).* Maybe, I needed to hear that song at that moment because I felt lifted by it. As I stood there thinking about the song and deciding whether to knock again or wait until they finished singing, Jessie's mom came to the door. "I thought I heard someone knocking." Then she stopped and saw it was me and said "Lord, come in here and give me a hug. When did you get home and why haven't you been by to see me sooner?"

I greeted Mrs. Booker, told her that I had been home for a week, but because I started working almost immediately, I hadn't had a chance to come see her sooner. "No excuses young man," she said. "Well it's good to see you. Let me get a good look at you." She stepped back and put the glasses that hung around her neck onto her nose and said, "Where is that skinny little boy that used to hang out on my porch all those years? You have really grown up and I know Jessie and Terry will love to see you. Come on in," she urged. I said, "It sounds like they are rehearsing so I won't intrude. I'll just come back some other time." "Boy you better come in here and speak to my girls. You don't have to stay but say hello while you are here." I said that I would and walked into the den where I was surprised to see not only Jessie and Terry but Corrine and another young woman named Joy. Jessie and Terry screamed and came over to give me hugs our usual greeting. I went over and hugged Corrine who had gone on to Temple and sort of separated from Eddie.

Eddie and I still kept in contact during the school year and we planned to hang out this summer. So I was pretty well caught up on their situation. Still smiling, she introduced me to Joy, a classmate and friend from school. I shook her hand

and was just about to introduce myself when *she* entered the room. And then I saw her. Apparently while I was talking to Mrs. Booker earlier, Ronni excused herself from the rest of the group to use the bathroom. She took my breath away. Tall, like I remembered, and her skin was flawless. She had cut her hair shorter and it made her look even more regal. She had truly become a woman in the three years since I had last seen her. Beautiful face, and shapely body, long slender legs and those lips — I was in a trance when I went over and gave her a warm hug. I was broken from my trance by Jessie's voice saying, "It is a small world. I didn't know you knew Corrine and Ronni. How did you guys meet?" With that Ronni spoke, a slight gleam in her eye, or at least I thought it was, saying "I think I'll leave that to Mr. Lewis to tell" I started by saying "Well, it was one enchanted evening a little more than three years ago…"

****

I listened intently as Eric started to share some of the less intimate details of how we met, and though I know this isn't precise, I thought about a line from one of my favorite classic movies, Casablanca, "Of all the joints, in all the places, he shows up here." Was I supposed to run into his arms? I think not! Although I had to admit that those arms had really filled out nicely. Hmmmm…he must be working out somewhere up there in Chicago. And then I remembered how those arms

A Love Deferred

felt wrapped around me that cool, spring morning following the prom, and... "No. Stop it Ronni!" I caught myself. "Girl, get a grip!"

The truth is I wasn't sure how I was supposed to react to seeing Eric now, here, today. Should I be angry? Should I be happy to see him? Should I act like it had only been 36 hours instead of 36 months since we last met, and so everything between us was okay? Standing here listening to him, I felt exposed. Corinne was the glue that brought everyone in this room together. I was her childhood friend; Eric was her high school sweetheart's best friend; Terry and Joy were her college friends; and, Jessie was Terry's sister. With the exception of Eric, Corinne had brought everyone else in this room together tonight because of our love of singing, and more specifically, singing gospel music. So we decided to form a group for the summer. My girl Corinne, played a mean piano, it just didn't rub off on me.

So, other than Corinne, I really didn't know these young ladies very well yet. But then again, I guess I really didn't know Mr. Lewis that well either. Is what I thought I learned about him, knew about him, believed about him three years ago all based on a reality I concocted and wanted to believe, that was strictly emotion-driven? Had my radar been so off after breaking up with David that I was a sitting target, falling for the first intelligent speaking, and seemingly sensitive guy with a plan? None of these thoughts comforted me right now, and in the midst of this reunion among old friends,

I zoned out and my mind took me to a small, dark room, with a single light. I couldn't make out faces, but could tell there were others in the room with me. There was laughter and mumbling I tried hard to make out at first. And just when I thought it couldn't get any worse, it did.

These people started circling around me and laughing harder still. As they passed in front of me, one said: "You know they always say women take leaps with their hearts, and men with their – well, you figure it out!" Still another leaned in and said, "Face it sister, you fell for it hook, line, and sinker!" And then, the third and final one leaned in, adding insult to injury, saying, "My sistas, another one bites the dust!" The laughter continued and then, in the light, I could make out the faces. They were Jessie, Terry, and Joy. But how could that be? Ok, Ronni, mind games over. Come on back.

By the time I came back into focus on the conversation at hand, I could tell that Jessie, Terry, and Joy were pretty much hanging on Eric's every word and movement, laughing and high-fiving and for a moment, I thought it was all at my expense. I wanted to escape, run out, disappear like the Wicked Witch from the Wizard of OZ, do something; but my feet wouldn't budge, not one step. "Ok, I thought to myself, you can handle this. You are, after all, Thomas and Catherine Bradley's daughter, are you not? So woman-up Ronni Bradley!" My hearing finally kicked in to full gear and I realized they were all reliving old times that didn't pertain to me at all. When I looked at Corinne, I could tell that she had been looking at me longer, probably studying my facial expressions and uncharacteristic silence, especially when a discussion about me was part of the topic of conversation.

She came over to me, and without drawing attention asked if I was alright. "Sure, girl. He just kinda caught me off guard. Did you know he knew Jessie and Terry?" I asked. "No," she said, "and I guess it wouldn't have connected unless they had brought up his name in conversation before now, because this is the first time I've ever been to their house. Look, I can't even imagine what you're thinking about now, but just know that I have your back, alright." I appreciated Corinne's friendship, at this moment more than ever. She was probably the best person, the *only* person, who could have appreciated and had even the slightest clue of the melodrama unfolding in this room tonight. The other side of the room seemed to be having such a good time that Corinne knew our rehearsal was pretty much over. She started to walk over to the others and said, "Hey, let's call it a night. I think we covered some great material and have the beginnings of a really good and assorted repertoire. We can plan to get together again next week. What looks good for everybody?" As they all tried to figure out dates and times, Eric made his way over to me. I didn't know what to expect or how I would react. I just started asking the Lord to help me.

****

I told the shortened version of how Ronni and I met. It must have been interesting because these ladies kept sighing and, as if they would miss a word if they did, hardly blinked. I guess people still love a good love story, or at least in our case a "like" story. I couldn't help but notice how Ronni looked at me as I spoke. Her gaze made me very conscious of the fact that I probably looked very different to her from the time we last saw each other. Where she had aged much more gracefully, I probably had not. I had filled out some and I watched my waist size go from 29 to 32 in three short years. I worked out a lot so I wasn't getting fat but I was getting bigger. I had grown an inch in height and now had a goatee. Where she was casually dressed in a tee shirt, jeans, and sandals that only made her look better to me, I was in work clothes that were quite uncomfortable. Cognizant of her looking at me, I became even more uncomfortable. Now, with the story told and everyone sort of accepting me as an old friend, I took a really good look at Ronni and found she was doing the same to me. Man she looked good. A million questions went through my mind as I looked at her, "What had she been doing over the past three years? Was she dating? Should I ask her out? Would she even go out with me? Is any relationship between us destined to fail? I looked into her brown eyes and wondered all these things.

I took a circuitous but purposeful path to Ronni. While I was making my way over to her I was trying to think of what to say. Sorry I haven't called during the past three years wouldn't cut it. Now was the time to be real. The phoney Eric, the Eric with the smooth lines, the funny Eric, the cool Eric, the cute Eric, had no place here. He would be smelled out as the stinking rat he was and squashed, never to be heard from again. No. If ever there was a time for the real Eric to appear it was now. So when I finally stepped in front of her, I stretched out my hand to take hers and said, "Hi Ronni. You know you did it to me again." "What's *it*?" she asked cautiously. "You took my breath away," I stated simply. "Listen, I know it's been a long time since we last spoke, but can we sit down and talk away from here and everyone, over lunch or dinner sometime?" I added, "My treat of course." I didn't realize our conversation could be heard until Joy said, "Well, if she won't go, I will." With those words, the tension was broken somewhat and Ronni said,"Okay. Look, I've got to catch my ride with Corinne, so why don't you call me and we'll set something up." She took a few steps to leave and then turned back to me saying, "I shouldn't assume anything here, so do you still have my number?" I answered sheepishly that I didn't and went on to explain how I lost it along with my phone book some time ago. I didn't want to go into the story of an enraged ex-girlfriend trashing my dorm room and tearing the book up in the process. Terry produced a pen and piece of paper and Ronni wrote her number and address down in large print. We all walked outside together saying goodnight to Mrs. Booker, Jessie and Terry. I walked Corrine, Ronni and Joy to Corrine's father's car and opened the doors for them. Before Ronni got in I asked when would be a good time to call. She leaned in closer to me and whispered, "Three years ago." She caught herself and said, "I'm sorry. I didn't mean that. Tomorrow night is good." With that, she sat in the front passenger seat and I closed the door. After waving goodbye to everyone they drove off and I slowly walked home.

****

The plane ride smoothed out considerably and I just settled back to relax the rest of the way to D.C. I asked a passing flight attendant for some water and watched a little of the in-flight movie but my mind kept going back to the summer of '75 and Ronni. It was uncomfortable thinking about that period now, so many years later, but I had to have the events clear in my head so kept on reliving that summer. The good and the bad.

****

Twenty four hours had passed since rehearsal and I didn't want to lose a moment. I believed I was given a second chance with Ronni and I didn't want to blow it. Of all days to have to work late. When I got home it was a little before nine. I stopped to chat with my grandparents, washed up and changed into more comfortable clothes. My grandmother complained about my afro, saying it made me look like a Wolf-man, and pleaded for me to get it cut. My grandfather was more interested in what was going on with Wagon Train than my hair so I asked "So what situation are they in this week?" Before he could explain my grandmother joined us and said "It's always the same." She added, "It's Indians, thieves, soldiers, or cut-throats. It's always the same." Granddad agreed she's pretty much right. We watched in silence for a while and they were fighting Indians this week. I excused myself about 30 minutes later and called Ronni. I found that I was a little nervous but excited at the same time.

****

Somehow I knew the call coming in was Eric. The phone rang three times before I picked it up. "Hello. It's me Ronni." It was Eric. After hearing his voice I said "I didn't know whether you would call. I really didn't mean what I said at Terry's house." Eric said "Yes you did and you were right. I should have called that summer, and that fall, and that winter, and...." I stopped him. "I get your point. So tell me why you didn't? Was it something I did or said?" He quickly answered, "No it wasn't you at all. I hope you haven't been thinking that all these years?" "Not really," I said. "But I guess seeing you again, inquiring minds want to know. I mean one minute we were sharing a wonderful night together with promise, and the next no-call, no-show, no-Eric. What was I supposed to think?" He was unable to answer right away. When he spoke he said "I allowed myself to get distracted by other situations. I should have called you; should have come by. I'm sorry I didn't." Eric went on to say, "I know that we've probably both changed a lot over the years and we probably have a lot to talk about. Can I interest you in having dinner with me soon so we can talk?" I thought about Eric's invitation and said, "I'll go out with you if you promise to really talk." I'm sure my comeback made him wonder where he would begin. He responded, "As long as you are willing to tell me what's been up with you the past few years as well." I agreed and we set a date to get together that weekend for dinner and a movie.

****

The Friday night cross-town traffic challenged me twice. First I went from Northwest DC to Northeast DC to pick up Ronni..... Then I went from Northeast DC to upper Northwest to get to the 7:00 o'clock show, only to find a line around the corner of the theater to see the hot new movie, "*Jaws.*" After finding a parking space and standing in line to buy tickets, we missed the ticket sales for the 7:00 and 8:00 o'clock shows but we were able to get tickets for the 9:00 p.m. show. While waiting, we bought some slices of pizza and sodas and we really talked. Without giving too much detail, I talked about my break-up with the girl I took to my prom and then the rapid pace of activities leading up to going away to school. I talked about going away to find out that you have to take control of your life and not the other way around. I talked about adjusting to the new environment of campus and dorm life, fraternity life, sports and of course girls. I talked about some of the things I learned about women and how I was sure it was just the tip of the iceberg. I talked about a series of relationships some beginning before the other ended. I talked about sex and sensuality, the good and the bad, and how it related to spirituality. I told her how confused I had become and how sometimes I felt I had lost myself as a person. Finally, I went on to talk about how many bad decisions I had made and how I felt I would have to live with some of them the rest of my life. I ended by telling her that I was hoping this summer would give me the opportunity to find myself and become the person I always hoped to be.

****

I looked at Eric all during the conversation, occasionally providing an understanding nod, and shaking my her head at other times, but overall saying nothing until the end when I acknowledged, although a bit guardedly, that it appeared as if he had been through some things over the past three years. It was close to the time for us to get in line for the next show so I told Eric that I'd tell him my story later. But I did have a few questions for him. "I didn't want to interrupt when you were talking because it seemed that you needed to get those things out in the open." He I nodded and said "I do feel a little better Ronni. Maybe it's because you were always such a good listener." "She added "Or," maybe, I added "maybe, "you are seeking something, and talking it out is just a start?" With those words we were ushered inside the packed theater and began looking for two seats together. We found them, a little too close to the front, but alright considering. After the seemingly incessant previews, the movie started.

****

I could tell this was going to be just my kind of movie but Ronni, seemed nervous. I asked her if she was alright and she said, "This really isn't my typical movie so don't be surprised by my reactions." I said, "After seeing the *Exorcist*, nothing else can scare me." She answered "Never saw it and never will." The next thing I knew the theater became quiet, all the lights were dim and on-screen there was a woman swimming in the ocean while her boyfriend lay drunk in the sand. The next thing I heard was a collective scream when the shark grabbed the swimmer and I felt as if the shark had grabbed me too as Ronni's nails dug into my arm and she hid her face in my shirt sleeve that was being twisted so tight that my blood flow was slowed. Popcorn flew from the row behind me when the woman behind us screamed. I could tell this was going to be my kind of movie and two hours later, I was right. Ronni left the theater a little shaken, but composed herself shortly thereafter. We made our way back to my car talking about scenes in the movie and checking bruises left on my right arm after her attacks of squeamishness. We got in the car and drove off.

****

I sat there in the passenger seat asking myself what it was I wanted to prove here tonight. I knew I couldn't handle the movie, but decided to try to be a big girl and watched it, mostly through two fingers on my right hand or more accurately, with eyes closed tightly. It took several minutes, driving away from the theater, before I began to feel like my old self again. From the corner of my eye, I could see Eric looking over my way occasionally, just to make sure I was alright. I cleared my throat and said, "You know all that screaming and stuff made me a bit hungry. I know it's late, but I'm not quite ready to go home. Maybe we can grab a light bite to eat from somewhere and finish our earlier conversation. You up for it?" Eric looked at me and said, "That sounds good to me." Since it was Friday night a lot of the downtown establishments stayed open until the wee hours of the morning. We found a great parking space steps away from a quaint restaurant and went in. I don't know if the waiter read our faces or not, but sat us in a cozy, private table, almost as if he knew, without needing to ask, that we

A Love Deferred

had things to talk about. After he took our order for sandwiches and drinks, we found ourselves fumbling with the place settings and looking around, commenting on the ambiance, perhaps as a way to give us both time to prepare for the real reason we were there. I could tell we were both relieved when the waiter served us quickly, which meant we now, had time to talk uninterrupted. I took a few bites off my sandwich, sipped my ice tea, and fixed my eyes on Eric. "Okay, Ronni, you're on," I told myself. And as if Eric heard my thoughts, he looked directly in my eyes and I said "There really was no one after you."

Eric said, "Are you telling me that you didn't date at all after prom?" I corrected him saying, "No, I'm not saying that. What I am saying is that I can tell you that there has not been any serious relationship for a while. I poured myself into getting my education after prom. The college I chose to attend here in the city held my registration for a year, which enabled me to work for the Feds full-time and save more money to help my parents out. My mom and dad would have made a way to foot our part of the tuition, but I couldn't put that on them. And when the college said I wouldn't lose anything if I delayed freshman entrance until 1973, I couldn't pass it up." "Wow, I'm really impressed but the pressure had to be overwhelming, Eric said. But long hours spent with the craziest and fun-loving sisters on campus, we all try to keep it real. We know how to party and have a good time, but when we have to buckle down and keep our nose in the books when it comes to academics, we support each other that way too.

"Even though I commute to school, I have spent just as many nights and weekends on campus, doing what's necessary to get it done! I have met some cool guys hanging out with my girls, but our interaction has been kept to a slow burn and not a towering inferno." I don't even know if Eric understood what I was saying, but it was the best way for me to put it out there. "So are you dating anyone now?" he asked. As if to get a rise out of him, I looked at my watch and said, "Not at this time." I tried to be serious but couldn't help but smile. "I guess I deserved that too," he said. "Yeah, you did," I agreed. We continued to eat our sandwiches and talk about other topics - music, movies, family, and church. Almost closing out the restaurant, we decided it was time to head home.

As we pulled up to my house, I couldn't help but shake my head and let out a laugh. "What's funny?" Eric asked. "Tell me so I can laugh too." I continued shaking my head and looked right at him, but a little more inexpressive. "You know, this parting thing could become a bad habit with us, and it's something that I don't want to get used to Eric. So before we go any further, why don't you tell me right now, what it is you think you want to happen and then I can react." He turned the car off and took the key out. I knew I had his undivided attention. "Ronni, I want to be straight with you. I want to get to know everything there is to know about you, what makes you laugh, what you like, what ticks you off, well actually I think I got some of that already," he laughed nervously. "Is it too late for us to start again?" he asked. I didn't speak a word, but looked at him for a few seconds, then took off my watch, put it in my pocket, and said, "If the timing is right, it's never too late Eric." We gave each other a nice, but not overly passionate, good night kiss. Eric started to open his door to get out. "No, Eric, don't get out. I'll just go on in." As I got out of the car, my moves were definite. I closed the door, leaned slightly in the window, and said, "Good night." He said good night and as I turned to walk up the steps, I could feel his eyes on me. I thought, "Yeah, I bet I got you wondering now huh? You are going to have to woo this sister Eric Lewis because I am worth it!" I took out my keys, opened the door and went inside, never looking back. That night paved the way to a wonderful summer, full of days and nights of discovery.

CHAPTER TEN

BLUE LIGHTS IN THE BASEMENT

The announcement came over the 777's speaker system that we would be landing in Washington, D.C. soon and to please turn off your portable electronic devices, put up your tray tables and everything you needed to do to prepare for landing. I put away my magazines and looked out at the evening sky over D.C. I smiled as I thought about the fun weekend ahead. But while I was thinking about that fun weekend, I was also thinking about that last summer with Ronni. I thought about how hot it was outside and how hot it got sometimes in her basement. I wasn't thinking about the outside temperature when I thought about the heat in Ronnie's basement. I was thinking about the heat that two healthy young people generate when they are attracted to each other. No amount of air conditioning can cool that heat down but, as we found out, there we rather things that could.

A Love Deferred

****

If you had company and wanted privacy in the Bradley household, your best bet was to be the first to claim the basement. It was a cozy, comfortable room with a small table and chairs, television, stereo set, sofa, and lounge chair. We had an awesome music collection, dating back to the pre-Motown years. My mom and dad used to throw the hottest house parties when we were growing up and I think we must have kept every 45 record and 33 rpm album they ever played downstairs. You could also find some great 8 track and regular cassettes. During the summer, it was one of the coolest places to be in the house, so it always puzzled me why my family wasn't down there more. And then I realized why - it was summer, and like any red blooded young person, my siblings were out enjoying the summer nights. My mom generally found her respite in her bedroom upstairs, always busying herself with something to do in somebody's room; although she generally liked to read her Bible or listen to gospel music or a good sermon playing on one of her favorite stations.

If my Dad wasn't resting in his chair in the living room watching television, you could bet he was enjoying one of his favorite sports - baseball, and his Baltimore Orioles, or the Washington Senators on the radio. When the coolness of the summer night hit, he loved to go out on our front porch with his transistor radio, smoke his cigarettes [which we

A Love Deferred

always tried to make him quit] and take comfort in the fact that as long as he could hear a game every now and then, all was right with the world. I can remember, on occasion, sitting with my Dad and trying my best to listen or watch, or at least try to do one or the other, to baseball games. It wasn't so much that I enjoyed the sport, because I thought it very boring, and I never understood how my dad could stay awake through nine, and sometimes even more, innings of the infrequent action, punctuated by brief flurries all described by some announcer's droning voice. The silence between the action was just like a sleeping pill for me. But what I loved about baseball had nothing to do with the game itself. It was watching my dad's face as he explained, or at least tried to explain to me, the ins and outs of certain plays and calls. I loved how his face lit up when one of his favorite players was coming up to bat.

With my siblings scattered about outside, and my mom and dad focused on other activities, Eric and I generally liked coming back to my house after going to the movies, a concert, a friend's house, or rehearsal with the group. Whenever Eric approached my dad, I could tell he was still a little intimidated by, or maybe just plain afraid of him. I think my dad could sense it, and while he would never let on that he shouldn't be afraid, probably felt that a little bit of fear was the best weapon to use to insure that his daughter wasn't being mistreated. "Good evening, Mr. Bradley. Nice night for baseball, huh sir" Eric would say as he extended his hand, hoping to get on my dad's good side. I'm sure he hoped his hand wasn't sweating. "Good Evening. I guess it will be nice if my team wins," my dad would respond. I would run over ready to plant a big kiss on his cheek, stroke his wavy, white hair, and jokingly say, "Oh Poppy, you have more than one team, so how do you know who you're cheering for?" He would act as if he were pushing me away, smiling all the while. I would then ask if any of my brothers or sisters were in the basement, and tell him that Eric and I were going down to watch TV or listen to some music and play a few games. Board games were a Bradley staple. I would then give him one more kiss, take Eric's hand, and start to go in. He would get my attention by calling me "Lotsa," reminding me that it shouldn't be too late a night because the next day was either work or church. He would then give Eric his famous *don't forget I'm watching you* fatherly look and we'd disappear into the house

****

Ronni and I were lounging in the comfortable sofa, watching TV. As the evening wore on, and the more we kissed, the hotter it got. I fumbled under her blouse to caress her body, watching her excited response. Sometimes if I made it to one point, I tried my hand at exploring other parts as well, but just as we'd get to the height of passion a voice would come from above. It was the booming voice of her father saying "It's too quiet down there. What are you kids up to?" He would take a couple of steps down which would cause our own flurry of activity that would redo all that I was successful undoing.

****

It was always hard going back to focusing on other things, like games, when our body chemistry was boiling, but we tried. Eric and I set up the Scrabble board. It was nothing for us to go at it, all out, trying to one-up the other. If he challenged me, I had to accept it. It was in my blood. I turned the television channel to one of my favorite network shows, and we played Scrabble for nearly thirty minutes, talking trash, just to stay occupied on something else. I could tell that Eric wasn't really into it as much anymore. He found the remote to the stereo and turned it on. Following his lead, I turned the television off. Eric found the *Quiet Storm* station, a must have in any urban city. The sizzling one and two liners coming from the disk jockey, voice raised just above a whisper, combined with the smooth rhythmic tunes, little by little commanded our full attention and made it a challenge for me, for Eric, for anyone under its spell, to stay focused on anything else. "You know what I'd like to do now?" Eric asked. It was such an open-ended question that I didn't know whether I should answer, so I just looked at him.

In one spur-of-the-moment gesture, he picked up the Scrabble board, emptied all the tiles into the cardboard box bottom, placed it on the table, took my hand and started dancing with me. Slow. The song on the radio was "Stay in My Corner," our song. There was a breeze coming in the open window, and I imagine my dad might have heard some of the strings and vocals escaping out of it onto the porch. Even though the light in the room was bright, we made this our *blue lights in the basement* moment. "You know Ronni; I don't know why your dad makes me so nervous. It's as if he's reading my mind before I'm even thinking of anything and planting some kind of psychic inhibitor that won't allow it to happen." I laughed. "He may seem like a lion to you, but to me, he's just a lovable, huggable, teddy bear." "Speaking of huggable," Eric brought me in closer. "*Honey, I love you... Stay,*" was the very familiar refrain from the song. "Will you always fit so perfectly in my arms Miss Bradley?" I whispered, "Always is a long time and only time will tell." Nothing else was said. "*I love you.....Stay....yeah yeah yeah yeah, yeah, I love you.*" The music faded.

****

We would half-heartedly go back to our kissing and touching, but after Ronni's father came back again with the "I don't hear any noise down there" speech, I would give up. That kind of pressure was too much for a brother night after

A Love Deferred

night. Can I get an Amen Brothers? He had me more nervous than a long-tail cat in a roomful of rocking chairs. Every creak on the floor above meant he might be coming back. It was during one of our one-on-one competitions that a somewhat important fact came out. The conversation went something like this, "So Eric Wendell Lewis, it looks like I have beaten you by 750 points in Scrabble. Do you wish to concede or do you want to fight to the bitter end?" "I don't think you'll ever get me to concede to anything Ronni Bradley. I answered. "But of course you knew I wouldn't. My head is bloodied but unbowed." "Eric," Ronni said suddenly. ".I've noticed you never call me by my full name. Do you even know my middle name?" At that moment it struck me that I really didn't know her middle name. How could that have happened? My immediate response was "Uh, er uh, of course I know you middle name. It's..." "Eric Wendell Lewis, do you mean to tell me, in the time we've spent together, you haven't taken the time to commit to memory an important, intimate detail like my name?" Again I answered "Of course I know your middle name. In a moment of desperation, I said, "It's uh, Sweetie, isn't it?" Immediately, I put my hands up in a defensive posture and closed my eyes waiting to ward off the punch to my shoulder that normally came. But it didn't. Instead, Ronni, humored by how pitiful I must have looked, fell down on the sofa laughing. From that day forward, the name Sweetie Bradley became our inside secret. And from that night forward, Sweetie Bradley was my special name for her and I was the only person ever allowed to call her that. I looked forward to using it often. That night before I left, she kissed me goodnight as usual, and landed another punch in my shoulder. I guess as a painful reminder of what's in a name.

As it got closer to the time for me to return to school my seduction efforts got more intense but ultimately were unsuccessful that summer. Not necessarily because Ronni was unwilling. It was more because we had no place to go where we could comfortably do what we both wanted to do. It's all about timing between the two of us and we still didn't understand that simple fact.

****

How do I tell this man who has gotten totally under my skin that I am falling in love with him? What I also knew was that I had a week to find that hidden voice before he would return to college for his senior year.

****

Ronni and I enjoyed our summer together. I still played hoops and hung out with Eddie when I could. We still sang with Terry, Joy, Corrine, and Jessie but the long, hot days and humid nights were quickly coming to an end, which meant we would be separated yet again. How would what we discovered this summer hold up to the test of time was unsure. As I started my senior year, and Ronni, her junior year, I only hoped it wouldn't be another three years before we spoke or saw each other again.

****

"Feel free to date." Those were basically the last words I said to Eric over the phone the night before he left for college, and then wanted to take them right back. We both knew that there was something special between us, but I think we were afraid (for lack of a better term) to fully give in to it. So we both pretty much tried to keep the tone of our goodbye conversation from becoming too deep or too serious. But I guess that trying to play it suave and one step removed from expressing true feelings was a formula for failure and yes, heartache. I would find out the hard way.

CHAPTER ELEVEN

NO! ME!

My senior year in 1977 proved to be a particularly busy one, juggling academics and part-time work. By Thursday, which was the end of my academic week, all I wanted to do was come home, eat dinner, get a hot bath and veg out. This particular Thursday night proved to be no exception. When I walked in the door, the aroma of fried chicken filled the living room and it drew me back towards the kitchen. "Hi mom." I went up to place a kiss on her cheek, careful not to break her rhythm, dipping the legs in the flour, and then in the deep fryer. I tried to grab one of the golden brown pieces already cooked, but my mother was on to me. With her flour covered hand, she shooed me away. "Girl, if you want to keep that hand, you'd better move it," she said laughing. "How was your day mom?" I asked. "Pretty good baby. I've been up and down those steps more than I should with a few loads of clothes so I guess my legs are feeling it right now," she said. My mother could always busy herself in our home. I think she was happiest when she was busy, but it could take a toll on her too. She tried to tend to everybody's needs, even though we worked to rid her of some of that and have her do more away from home, with my dad and her friends from church. With the three of my older brothers and sisters out on their own, I was now the oldest of the three remaining children. I loved and respected my mom dearly, but we also had challenges in our relationship that probably had more to do with a woman coming-of-age in the household of another woman than anything else. Even with the occasional schism, I admired my mom and would laugh to myself when I realized that, with the exception of being a neat freak, I was more like her than not. I pursed my lips like my mom when something vexed me. If angered, I took on a very proper persona, making my words more definite to get my point across. But, also like my mom, I inherited her laughter and competitive spirit. I put down my books, washed my hands and helped with the remaining tasks to prepare the dinner that night. Afterwards, my younger sister, Cee, and I cleaned up the kitchen - I washed, she dried and put away, while my mom retreated to a hot bath and my dad rested with his radio in the living room.

The phone rang and my mom answered it upstairs. "Ronni, telephone," she yelled. "Okay, mom." Whoever it was, they had perfect timing. I had just washed the last pot and handed it to my sister. I dried my hands and picked up the phone in the kitchen. "Got it mom, thanks." She hung it

A Love Deferred

up on her end. "Hello." There was a very familiar voice on the other end. "Hey Ronni girl, what's up?" Jessie asked. When our gospel group stopped singing that summer and we went in other directions, I hadn't kept up with Jessie and her sister that much. But it was good to hear her now. "Just trying to keep it all together girl. What's up with you?" I asked. She said that her health had been a real challenge lately and she had gone for several tests, waiting for a diagnosis or something that would help give her some answers. She added that she was just being really prayerful. I let her know that I would pray for her as well.

"Are you still singing?" she asked. I let her know that I had joined the Young Adult Choir at Joy's church, which was now mine as well. Jessie knew that Corinne was playing for the choir there, but hadn't heard about me. "That's a blessing girl," Jessie said. "I know that you're getting good Word under Pastor Thomas. "You know that's true," I added. "He is just so awesome and speaks so plainly that you can't help but learn from it. I'm not saying I have it all in order, but this is the first time in a long time that I've been challenged to pick up that Bible and read it girl." I wanted to know more about her and her family and was told that her mom and dad were great, and her sister Terry was forging ahead with her career. Terry was so energetic and outspoken that I knew if anyone would be heard, she would be. We went on for a few minutes more like this, but there was something I couldn't quite put my finger on that was different about this conversation. And that something became clear with Jessie's next words.

"Ronni, I don't know quite how to ask this, other than to just put it out there," said Jessie. "Did you know that our *dear brother* Eric is single no more?" All I thought I heard was "Eric, and, single no more." It felt like an hour passed before I responded. I could only hope what came out made sense. "When Jessie? Who? Married?" Jessie continued, "Yep. This weekend. To a girl he knew in college. I didn't call to gossip, but something in my spirit told me that you didn't know because nobody heard from you. I told Corinne this morning and asked if you had said anything about it, and she didn't think you knew either because you would have mentioned something to her." I pulled myself together. "No, I didn't know and I guess I wouldn't have if you hadn't called me tonight. I don't know what to say." "Neither do I Ronni. I always thought that you and Eric would be getting together. There was never any question in my mind, or for that matter, Terry or Joy or probably even Corinne, based on what we saw happen with the two of you last summer. I didn't understand it, and even asked Eric to explain it to me, but didn't get a clear answer. I don't want to put you in an awkward position, but you might want to consider calling him tonight or tomorrow to get some answers. That is, if you feel led," she said. I didn't know quite what I was feeling. True, we never spoke the word marriage, but in the far reaches of my mind and certainly my heart I kind of thought that's where we may have been heading. I guess the heart can be unpredictable. "Look," Jessie said, "I'm going to get off now because I know you have some things to think about. Just in case you want to call Eric, here's the number in Boston." Jessie read off ten numbers. I thanked her for her concern about me. "Hey, it's the least us sisters can do. Love you girl. If you want to talk, I'm here." With that, we said our goodbyes and hung up.

By now, CeeCee had finished cleaning the kitchen and gone upstairs with my mom. My dad was still sitting in the living room, still listening to his game. I sat on that basement step and tried to collect my thoughts. What do I do? Do I call? Do I back off? What am I feeling right now? How am I supposed to feel? What is Eric thinking about getting married and not having the decency to call me? Why am I so upset? I was the one who told him to "feel free to date other people," an open relationship, full of bull phrase that, now in retrospect, probably translated to "I'm not ready to be committed to one person yet." I got up off the step and opened the door, stepping back in to the kitchen. "Ronni, you still on the phone?" my Dad asked. "I just got off Daddy, but I need to make one more call — long distance, if that's ok." "Okay, but don't tie it up too much longer." "Yes sir."

I picked up the receiver again and began to dial all but the last digit of Eric's number. For a minute I thought I'd just hang it up and let it be. But the part of me that needed some kind of explanation or maybe closure, got up enough nerve to push the last number. Back on the step, with door closed, the phone rang on the other end. By the third ring, someone picked up. "Hello," Eric said. Too late to hang up now I thought. "Hi, Eric, it's Ronni." Of course I know he knew it was me without announcing myself, but a touch of nerves generally clouds the obvious. "Oh, Hi Ronni. How are you?" [All I could think was: Do you *really* want to know brother?] "I'm fine. At least I was until I found out this evening that you're getting married. What gives Eric? Talk to me." He cleared his throat. "It's true Ronni, I am getting married." He paused. "This Saturday at her family's church in Boston." I wasn't interested in that kind of detail, so I knew to get what I wanted, I would have to ask specific questions. "To whom Eric?" He told me that it was Linda Simms, a young lady whom he had been seeing off and on during his junior year, before the summer we got together. Apparently, they never really had closure, and when he came back his senior year, a series of unplanned events brought them back together. He talked about how he was always torn, trying to get clarity on the two women in his life who had his heart. I couldn't resist, when I asked a bit sarcastically" And who might that other woman be?" "You," he said. "Look I know this isn't an easy discussion for us to have, and certainly not easy words for you to hear Ronni. I wanted to call you, to write you, to tell you before it got to this point, but just couldn't find the right time." Well, I got news for you brother, I thought to myself. This ain't it either. I knew that I couldn't and wouldn't listen to this much longer. "Eric, just tell me up front, do you love her?"

****

I didn't know what to say. Of all times and of all people to call me, it had to be Ronni Bradley. It seemed that it was never the right time for us. We were never together long enough and being apart only served to keep us apart. Ronni's question gave me a jolt. I was so busy thinking about getting married that I never gave a thought about why I was getting married. Was I in love or in love with the concept? Was I trying to prove something or was this something that was meant to be? I could tell her about Linda and how on a cold evening during my junior year I offered her my jacket with a promise from her that she would bring it back to me the next day. I could have told her that after delivering my jacket Linda and I talked for more than two hours about how we had been on campus for almost four years but never got to know each other. I could have told her about how we got closer emotionally one Sunday morning at church when I was holding her hand during prayer and she broke down and cried because of problems she was having with her family and all I could think to do was to hold her and tell her everything was going to be alright. I could have told her that from that moment on until now, she became my world and I became hers. I didn't tell her how we broke up in the spring of our junior year because of jealousy and mistrust. I couldn't say that the summer that Ronni and I discovered each other was the summer following the breakup. I could have told her that Linda and I reconciled at the beginning of our senior year. But I didn't say any of those things. None of them seemed adequate to explain to this person who was also, at one time, my love. So what was I to say? One thing about Ronni, she always, always knew how to hit you right between the eyes with her silver bullet questions. So I answered by telling her a little about Linda, but ultimately I was getting married this weekend and none of it really mattered. There was no place for "Sorry, I meant to call but I just didn't have the time (or courage) to call." No, none of that would do. So I just had to pull up my jock strap and own this one. I tried making some weak explanation, looking for some small approval from Ronni, but how unrealistic could I have been? I could tell by her voice that my feeble attempt at explaining had placed a wedge somewhere between her heart and her head and I couldn't have felt any lower.

****

"It was my mistake to think what *we had* last summer mattered. I've got my answers now, or as close to any as I'll ever get. There's really nothing else for us to talk about. Have a good life Eric." I could hear him call my name, "Ronni, wait!" "Goodbye Eric." I said, and hung up.

A Love Deferred

****

Way to go Eric," I thought. If I could rewind about to 5 minutes earlier, maybe how the conversation ended would have been different. But the only person I was now kidding was myself. I never really did answer Ronni's question about whether I loved Linda. Now I guess that's not important.

****

I sat there like a bird that had been wounded – wanting to fly away, but not able to. Sure, I was angry at Eric, but more at myself for taking my thoughts there. I would be okay, tomorrow, or the next day or the next, but right now, I just needed to wallow in some self pity for a bit. It was my reality check. I got up from the step, hung up the phone again and just stood for a minute in the kitchen. I heard the announcer on the radio calling the baseball game. I heard my father speaking back to the radio as if the coaches could hear his reaction to an unexecuted play. The game broke for a commercial and my dad got quiet. I turned off the light in the kitchen and started walking towards him, trying to act like nothing was wrong. My Dad could see through my pretense a mile away. I sat on the floor next to him and asked who was winning. "My team is ahead, but not by much. It's the bottom of the 7th, so they may pull it off if they don't keep making mistakes," he said.

He knew I really didn't care about the game, but also knew I was trying to get my focus off my problem at hand. I laid my head on his lap and closed my eyes. Instinctively, he put his hand on my head, stroking my hair softly, offering the fatherly touch that his daughter needed just then. I tried to fight back the tears, but it was no use. He didn't ask what was wrong, but said, "*Har*monica, you'll be alright." Monica was my middle name. Because he knew I loved music so much, Daddy called me *Har*monic*a* during very special moments. This was surely one of them. He continued, "You just need to know that you can't dance on every number. Whatever it is, God will get you through it and you will move on. Remember, your Momma and I love you and are right here for you." I don't even remember who won the baseball game that night. All I remember is closing my eyes and being comforted in the knowledge that everything was going to be alright because my Daddy said so, and this was one man's love and word that I knew was a sure thing.

****

CHAPTER TWELVE

THE MIDDLE PASSAGE

The plane landed safely at the airport in D.C. and after retrieving my bags I stepped into the steamy afternoon heat that I had all but forgotten over the past several years. Ah yes, this is why I don't come to D.C in the summer I told myself. I waited in the relative shade of the terminal overhang until a shuttle bus pulled up and transported me to the Rental Car location situated near, but not on, the airport property. I tried to fool myself with Jedi mind tricks by saying "you are not hot, you are not hot." But the more I tried to fool myself the hotter I got. I figured the only solution would be to get in the car, and turn the AC to sub-freezing at full blast.

At least the AC worked and it was a good thing too. The traffic on the 14th Street Bridge leading into the city was a nightmare. However, instead of ditching the route I knew best and getting off at the first exit I could, I kept going into the city, on my Map Quest route and arrived at my Georgetown Hotel, one-hour and twenty minutes from the time I picked up my rental car. I found after my 45th birthday, I was becoming more impatient. I couldn't stand to wait too long and because of that, I missed out on so many opportunities that required nurturing, it made me sad to think about it.

Hot and sticky after checking in, I went to my room, unpacked my bag and hung up my clothes. With that done, I peeled off the outfit I was wearing, took a warm shower, and stretched out on the bed. Nothing was starting until later that evening so it was alright if I took a short nap. In reality, alright or not, I couldn't have taken another step. As I slept a jumble of images entered my dreams; my son, Ronni, my job, my ex-wives and my friends. I slept deeply and my mind went back to my first wedding and the question Ronni asked "Do you love her?" Now over a quarter century later, I still can't answer that question.

****

Our wedding day was filled with tradition and heritage. It was held in a church just outside of Boston. Linda's uncle was the pastor and performed the ceremony. There were at least two hundred anxious onlookers, family members and guests, waiting for the service to begin. I was running a little late but my oldest brother Lonnie, also my best man, waited patiently as I got dressed. He saw me struggling to line up the bow-tie on my wing collared shirt. He stood in front of me and calmly placed it for me. "Nervous?" he asked. "A little," I answered, "no, make that a lot." He said, "Well you ought to be. This is a big step you are making. Now what I'm about to ask may seem strange at this late date but I'm going to ask it anyway." I looked at him and said, "Nothing ever stopped you before Big Brother, so what's your question?"

He asked simply, "Do you know what you are doing?" I started to answer and he cut me off with his hand. "Just listen for a moment. Karen and I have been married almost twenty years. We married right out of high school and I still love her. But there is not a day that goes by that I don't regret having married so young." I looked at him really listening to what he was saying. My brother was always someone worth listening to and if he thought this conversation was important to have now, it probably was. "I don't regret our children, because they have been true blessings. I don't regret living in the same house with the same woman all those years. But I do regret not having the opportunity to explore what I could have done, what I could have been or where I could have gone. What I'm saying is this Eric. I don't want to see you doing the same thing and maybe feeling the way I do. So I am going to make you an offer." Lonnie looked me square in the eyes. "There is brand new Buick in the driveway outside. Here are the keys. I want you to pack your bags, get in it and drive away. I will go to the church and explain things. You just get away." I couldn't believe what I was hearing. Here is my oldest brother trying to get me to leave my fiancé at the altar. The worst part is I was really considering it. The problem though is that there were already too may nay-sayers taking odds on how long this marriage would last. I had to do this. Besides, we were only 15 minutes from the appointed hour.

"Thanks Big Brother. I know what you are saying and I know why, but it's too late. I have to go through with this. If I don't what does that say about me?" He looked at me with a tear in his eye and said, "I had to try, but no matter what, I am always here for you." We hugged and left for the church.

****

My twenties and the latter part of the 70's had its share of ups and downs. Certainly after Eric married, I had to realize that there were other paths for me to travel and a whole lot of other things in my life to do, that my college years at a small women's college in Georgetown opened up for me. When I thought my career track was heading towards becoming a hot, young producer/director, I was fortunate to intern at Lorimar Studios in Burbank, California, when *Roots* and *Dallas* were the hottest things on the tube, coming out of the studio. The highlights of my time spent there were not only meeting Kunta Kinte a.k.a. Levar Burton, but interviewing a very young, John Travolta, a.k.a. Vinny Barbarino, for my college newspaper. Even then, he had unbelievable charisma and personality. When I thought I wanted to delve into the

A Love Deferred

political arena, I interned for a local Congressman on Capitol Hill. The halls of Congress were alluring and I, along with my fellow interns, thought we were preparing ourselves to continue to blaze the trail that stalwart occupants like Ronald Dellums, Shirley Chisholm, and Barbara Jordan had paved. Even when the internship officially ended, I would stay connected to many of the people I befriended while there. I would, on occasion, attend one or two of the political receptions, of which there were many, to stay up on issues and to continue to meet some of the up and coming movers and shakers.

Eventually, the halls of Congress introduced me to Gregory Whitman, a Hill staffer, moderately older than I, who would altruistically expose me to a lot more not only intellectually and politically, but later, sensually, as well. In my early 20's, I was still someone who had not shared in an intimate experience with the opposite sex – or to state it more directly, I was still a virgin. This was certainly not a condemnation on me, because I always felt that this very personal exploration would take place with the man who would be my husband, and I have to admit that I also believed, based on our reunion that summer of 1975, that man, without question, would be Eric. A lot of things had changed since then, and here I was with Gregory, not a replacement Eric, but someone who, I had to admit, may have possessed a few of his characteristics.

Gregory and I enjoyed the theater, concerts, and intimate meals at more than a few of the bistros in walking distance from his Hill office and his home. We always seemed to exhaust topics and then go back again. I could tell he would play Devil's Advocate at times just to get me riled; and even when I finally caught on, I still, unbeknownst to him, played along. We challenged each other and it not only became an intellectual stimulant, but a subtle, but maybe not so subtle, form of foreplay. And then one unusually warm spring night in April, after dining on a pre-birthday meal he had prepared for me at his home, and after demolishing him in a cutthroat game of backgammon, which fed my overly competitive temperament, Gregory took me into his arms and for my first sexual experience, he very gently introduced me to a world of passion I never knew existed. It wasn't preplanned, at least not on my part. Afterwards, as I lay next to him, a million thoughts and feelings went through my mind, and I was uncharacteristically quiet for the remainder of the evening and days later. I held polite, but brief telephone conversations with Gregory, and graciously declined any social get-togethers for quite some time. Even when we did see each other, I believe Gregory knew that our relationship had been damaged, maybe more so, because of the moral and spiritual weights that I now carried, than anything else. Our relationship lasted another few months before it finally ended. I suppose the sayings that you always remember your first *time is true.*

A Love Deferred

****

Every time I thought about Ronni, I had to think about Eddie Rush, one of my oldest friends. It was because of him that Ronni and I met, and I don't know whether I should thank him for the pleasurable time she and I shared or hate him because of all the emotional upheavals Ronni and I had over the years. I thought about the day in 1979 that Eddie called from his Graduate School dorm room and told me that he and Corrine had decided to get married. "Yeah man," he said. "We both tried dating other people but we always came back to each other." Stunned but pleased I said, "Well let me be the first to congratulate you. When's the big day?" "Next Saturday" he blurted. Almost as if he were anticipating my next question, he said. "No, she's not pregnant or anything. We would have told you sooner, but we originally thought about just eloping and showing up at your doorstep hitched. But we thought about our parents, and decided that wouldn't be the right thing to do to them. So, we are having a small ceremony in Baltimore. You have to come and be my best man. Tell me you and Linda can make it." Thinking about my dwindling bank account and my nearly maxed out credit cards I said, "Of course we'll be there. We wouldn't miss this for the world." We continued talking about the upcoming wedding and the logistics around Linda and me getting to Baltimore. Luckily there were no tuxedoes to worry about. This should be a truly simple affair. Only, anything to do with

Eddie was never really simple. And, of course if Corrine was going to be there, Ronni most certainly would be there too. So I had to prepare myself emotionally for seeing her. Maybe this trip will be good for Linda and me. Things hadn't been that good between us for quite some time. Maybe a nice road trip would help our relationship. Maybe.

We arrived in Baltimore on Friday evening after deciding to drive to save money. The trip was uneventful. We shared pleasant conversation and we made it in a little over 12 hours. We drove directly to the church where the wedding rehearsal was about to start. Eddie and I shook hands and he and Linda embraced. Of my friends, Eddie was the only one that Linda was able to connect with. I greeted his parents and introduced them to Linda before moving on to greet Corrine. I gave her a hug and kiss and was chatting with her when, out of the corner of my eye, I saw Ronni. I walked to the front of the church where the rest of the wedding party was gathering. I was introduced to everyone by Eddie and greeted Ronni with a hug and a kiss on the cheek. I couldn't help but notice how beautiful she was. She was wearing her hair in a short curly cut and had just the right amount of make-up to accent her eyes perfectly. I could also feel the heat of Linda's eyes on my back as I looked at Ronni: *Strike One.* I wasn't the only one looking though. It seemed that gravity just pulled everyone and everything into Ronni's sphere of influence. But, gracious as ever she made sure that everyone knew this was Corrine's night. Would I be repeating myself by saying she looked great? Eddie came to my side saying, "Brother, don't get fooled by her looks of happiness." I was about to inquire further but the minister called the rehearsal to order and we got down to business.

****

Since Eric and I were Best Man and Maid of Honor respectively, we were destined to be paired during the rehearsal. It was a little awkward for us to be this close and not be able to talk like we used to, but a lot had happened since the prom, our last formal gathering, taking furtive glances at each other and thinking how lucky we were to be there together. That wasn't the case tonight. We were so uncharacteristically uncomfortable that everyone noticed it and those that didn't know our history couldn't understand why. We stumbled through part of the rehearsal. Corinne, ever the perceiver, asked for a quick break for everyone to stretch and get something to drink. She made her way over to my side then Eric's. Then she took hold of Eric's and my hands, and, very discreetly walked us outside. "Look you two," she said. "The tension between you is so thick a blind man could see it. Can you please set your issues aside for the next 48 hours and at least pretend to tolerate each other for me, for Eddie? Remember, we're the ones you should feel overjoyed for. I looked at Eric, cleared my throat, and said, "I don't have a problem with that, do you?" Eric looked me in the eyes, then looked in his wife's direction and turned back saying, "I don't have to pretend to like you Ronni. Let's go show our good friends some love and do this right." Eric held his hand out and as I was about to shake it when a visible spark of static electricity stopped us from completing the gesture. The spark was so sharp that Corrine jumped back. She whispered to us both, "I knew there were sparks between you two but nothing like this." We walked back to rejoin the rest of the wedding party to continue rehearsing.

****

As we walked back to the front of the church, Ronni made a detour to greet a tall, rather nice looking man who must have entered the sanctuary while we were on break. I looked at him and thought he looked vaguely familiar but couldn't place his face readily. A twinge of jealously suddenly went through me as they kissed hello. But I pushed that back inside and focused on the celebration-at-hand. The rehearsal continued with no further incidents. As we were preparing to go to the rehearsal dinner I walked Linda over to introduce her to Ronni. Ronni was talking quietly with her friend as we approached. I cleared my throat and said, "I hope I'm not interrupting anything important." Her friend said, "Not at all," as he got up from the pew and extended his hand. "Hi, I'm Aaron Peterson and you, I know, are Eric Lewis. I feel like we've met, having heard about some of the antics Eddie tells about the two of you." When he mentioned his name, Aaron Peterson, I immediately recognized him as the once popular area high school and college basketball player who had a promising NBA future cut short by a career-ending injury. "Nobody has to introduce you," I replied. "I remember watching you play college and pro ball. What are you doing now? That's when Linda cleared her throat and I remembered the main reason why we journeyed this way: *Strike Two*. "I'm sorry baby," I said. "Where is my head? Please forgive me." I pointed to Ronni and Aaron, then Linda. "Ronni Bradley, Aaron Peterson, this is my wife, Linda Lewis." Ronni stood up. She and Linda were very gracious in their greeting, as was Aaron. Linda and Ronni made small talk while Aaron and I kept talking about basketball and his present career. Out of the corner of my eye, I saw Corinne come over to Linda and Ronni and direct them outside, as we all prepared to leave for dinner. Aaron and I lagged a little behind the group but not by much. I have to admit I was a bit surprised when we got outside and found the women laughing like old friends. I didn't know whether I liked that or not but it certainly helped the rest of the evening go more smoothly.

****

The next day was sunny and clear. Aaron and a couple of other groomsmen joined me late into last night, taking

A Love Deferred

Eddie out on his last night as a free man. We went to a local lounge and had a long, night of story telling, laughing, and a bit of drinking, but not much because, unlike our college years, Eddie and I had backed off much of the brew and were now such lighter drinkers than we sometimes cared to admit to our original crew. I met Eddie in his hotel room early to make sure that he was going to be alright. As I knocked on Eddie's door I was surprised to see him up and spry. "Brother, I didn't know how bright-eyed and bushy-tailed you were going to be after last night," I confided with my friend. He said, "Last night was fun but nothing like some of the nights at my Frat House in College. By the way, thanks for pulling that together for me." "Not at all. The pleasure was all mine," I said. "Well you're up and ready to head to the church." I observed. "Anything else we need before heading out?" I asked. "Nope." Eddie replied. "I've been up for hours," he said. "I couldn't wait for this day to come. Let's go." I joined in his enthusiasm and said, "Let's go then." I couldn't help but think back on my wedding day. Was I this excited about getting married? The thought, the question bothered me but this was Eddie and Corrine's day and I was going to do my best to make this a day they both would remember.

While we drove to the church, I thought about my wedding day and the excitement I had. But looking at my situation now, I only wished I had listened more fervently to my brother when he told me to get away. It didn't take me long to realize the wisdom in what he was saying. I knew after three months of marriage we had made a terrible mistake. But now after being married so long it was a gaping chasm between us, that neither one of us dared to cross. There is no blame to pass to one person or another. We were way too different on so many fundamental levels, and there was no hope of recovery. We functioned as a couple superficially, but never beyond that. Money was always an issue. We had enough to cover the basics but very little extra for savings or fun things. As I think about it, we never had fun. We never really had laughter. We had sex but no love. We had family and friends who acted as a buffer for us but there is only so much they can do. We did hurtful things to each other and realized that we needed help to determine if there was anything left of our relationship to salvage. We went to church and sought counsel, but even that didn't appear to work. I don't know. Maybe we both thought it too late to apply the spiritual salve being offered, to the deep wounds that we endured. Whatever the reason, our marriage was broken and it was beyond repair. We were operating on borrowed and fragile time, and anytime it would be over.

****

Eddie and Corrine's wedding was beautiful. When we entered the chapel through the side door with Pastor Thomas, we could see the crowd of anxious well wishers. In the back, I caught a glimpse of Corrine, dressed in a beautiful white gown with a simple veil and holding a bouquet of yellow roses. Underneath the veil though, you could see her smiling from ear to ear. I made sure Eddie didn't see her, or it would have been all I could do to keep him by my side. I looked around and saw Linda with a somewhat pleasant look on her face. I waved to her. Aaron Peterson was sitting close by, but his attention was drawn to the rear when the wedding march began. Jessie, Terry and Joy provided the music. As maid of honor, Ronni followed two other bridesmaids. It may have been Corinne's day, but Ronni was stunning. Nothing she could do would change that. The crowd emitted more than enough positive feelings to the couple to insure that they knew how much they were loved. More importantly, everyone knew that Eddie and Corrine had found their soul mates in each other. The wedding party, all now assembled in the front of the church, turned and faced the couple, now standing side by side. Ronni and I stole glances at each other. We performed our duties — producing rings, raising veils, and whatever else Pastor Thomas directed us to do, just as we rehearsed. "And what God has joined together, let no man put asunder," the pastor said with authority. "You may now kiss your bride." Eddie took Corrine in his arms and said, "Hello Mrs. Rush." Amidst tumultuous applause, Eddie sealed the deal with a kiss that made even this former player proud. "Ladies and Gentlemen, I now present to you Mr. and Mrs. Edward Rush," Pastor Thomas announced, ending the official ceremony. As the wedding recessional was played, I could see Ronni's tears of joy as we walked down the aisle and into the foyer together. But instead of me consoling her as I would have in the past, it was Aaron who was now holding her and telling her how beautiful she was. As I watched them, Linda came up behind me and said "Kind of makes you wonder what you missed doesn't it?" Before I could reply she turned and walked away. *Strike Three.* I could only imagine what awaited me in the penalty phase.

We showered the newlyweds with rice. They bundled into their car as they headed for their Island honeymoon. A reception would be held when they returned. I saw Ronni standing alone and thought it was a good time to say my goodbyes before I left to find Linda and head back to Chicago. I started walking toward her and was nearly halfway there when Aaron appeared to come out of nowhere. I stopped in my tracks. Aaron said something to Ronni and embraced her. As they headed in the opposite direction, Ronni noticed me, we shared a wave, and she disappeared.

****

Aaron was in such a festive mood during Eddie and Corrine's wedding, that I believed he and I were back on track. For weeks leading up the nuptials, our relationship had been going down a rocky road. In the beginning, it was all violins, hearts and flowers. We enjoyed being together. Even after a hectic workday, I often enjoyed preparing home cooked meals at his or my place. While we were both career motivated, Aaron had a five-year goal to become one of his firm's youngest partners. When we first started dating, he was already three and a half years into his plan. At first, no matter how challenging his workload, he could always find some comic relief to help him keep perspective on other things that were important in his life – his mom and dad, his church, and me. But one by one the list of priorities outside the firm began to lose favor with him. His elderly parents were so concerned with his disappearing act that they confided in me, I suppose to see what influence I might have. The Sunday worship service we always attended together became more and more of a solo act for me. Even Pastor Thomas was pleased to see Aaron at the wedding. More than a few times in the past, pastor had hinted at wedding bells for him and me. But he also became increasingly concerned about his absence. I tried to give him what I thought were credible excuses, but after awhile, even I couldn't feign sincerity.

Aaron's post-wedding celebratory mood was short-lived. He had taken on an international caseload that, if handled correctly, would put him a step closer to his goal. He would tell me that the sweet smell of success was so powerful that it was making his head spin. But what was spinning and out of control was Aaron. He demanded, no, commanded people around him to do the simplest of tasks that he could have handled himself. I thought it only pertained to his personal life, until a quick call to his office one day, provided one of his paralegals a chance to air some of her grievances. It seems Aaron's behavior was becoming unbearable there as well, at least to those he considered his underlings. This type of caste system never used to appeal to Aaron, at least not the Aaron I thought I knew. Even with all the obvious signs, I still tried to hang in and make our relationship work, thinking this madness would soon be over. Soon didn't come soon enough.

It was November 30th, and Aaron impulsively accepted a last minute invitation for the two of us to join one of the senior partners and his wife for a play and dinner. It seems there was a last minute cancellation from the intended invitees. While the invite was a feather in Aaron's cap, it could not have come at a worse time for me. December 1st was World AIDS Day, and I was part of a detail finalizing plans for a humanitarian visit by the First Lady to the research and treatment facility where I worked in suburban Maryland. Included in the planning was a short visit with patients being treated on the hospital's HIV/AIDS unit, and a brief press conference afterwards. We were all juggling plans that included handling every aspect addressing security and the media, not to mention the safety and privacy of patients on the unit. This consumed my every working minute and that of other staff persons handling the event. I told Aaron that the possibility of my presence as his date, and especially on-time this night, was extremely tentative. Aaron was so

A Love Deferred

focused on what he needed from me that I don't think he heard one word I said. Reluctantly, I told him that I would do my best to make an appearance at the theater but could not guarantee a time. "Just do the best you can Ronni," he said. This is for us." He said he would meet me in the lobby before the play started. "Aaron you are not hearing me. I'm not sure I…," I started to say, but was cut off by Aaron saying, "Love you babe, gotta run!" It was the biggest rise I had out of him in some time. Oh well, I'd do the best I could. The only thing I had going for me was the fact that the suit I wore could easily transition to an after five event. How much after five was the $64,000 question. It was already 4 p.m., and as much as I hated to admit, the devil was very much in the details of this White House visit. "As I hung up the phone, I thought, "Oh well, I can't put out any fires just standing here. Better get back to work."

As I stepped out of the subway station, I glanced at my watch. It was 7:45. The two-act play was already well into the first act. I hurriedly walked the long block to the theater. Too tired to wonder how Aaron would react, I was just glad to have arrived on this side of town. When I didn't see Aaron in the lobby, I walked up to the ticket booth. I could barely get my name out before the middle aged gentleman on the other side of the glass said, "Yes Miss Bradley, we have a ticket here just for you." He tore the perforated ticket, handed it to me and pointed in the direction I should walk. "Enjoy the show," he said. "You really haven't missed that much." I thanked him and hurried to the door. I showed the usher the ticket and followed her to my seat. Once seated, the low theater lighting made it impossible for me to determine whether Aaron's expression was one of relief that I was finally there, or annoyance because I was late. During the intermission I was formally introduced to Mr. Huntington and his wife. As we all talked and drank, Aaron's coolness towards me seemed to dissipate enough for us to have a very pleasant conversation. The lights in the lobby flickered, indicating the end of intermission. We all dutifully returned to our seats. It was a good play, well-acted, and, under normal circumstances, would have been quite enjoyable. I was challenged to keep my focus on the stage and off of what I left behind at the office. It was the perfectionist in me that wouldn't let me let go of that feeling that there must be some small detail we neglected that could make tomorrow's visit a fiasco. Why couldn't I just listen to that little voice inside telling me that everything was fine?

After the play, we dined at one of Washington's exclusive restaurants, in walking distance from the theater. It was so late, I would have been fine with a bowl of soup or a light salad, but Aaron insisted I order an entrée. Perhaps he thought to do anything less would have offended our host, who generously declared that the meal was on him. I couldn't muster up enough energy or appetite and knew I would never finish the crab stuffed salmon, mixed vegetables, and salad I ordered. Aaron and Mr. Huntington talked endlessly, from one topic to the next. Under normal circumstances, I would have been able to hold my own with them, but even conversation proved a grueling task. At one point, I could feel myself staring blankly at my water glass. I knew it was those few sips of wine that zapped my last bit of social grace and sent me into a stage of sleep apnea. "Ronni dear, are you alright?" I could hear Mrs. Huntington ask, but I found it difficult to speak. Then I felt Aaron nudge me, asking, "Ronni, Ronni, what's wrong with you?" In that instant, I awoke, lowering my head and placing my hand on my forehead, never more embarrassed. "Please forgive me," I said humbly. "It's been a very long day for me and I guess my reserve energy is all tapped out." The Huntingtons apologized for keeping me out so late, understanding what awaited me at work the next day. Mr. Huntington summoned the waiter and I excused myself for one last trip to the ladies' room before leaving. I placed a cold hand towel on my weary eyes to give me a little boost, but it wasn't much help. When I returned to the table, everyone was standing. We all gathered our playbills and other personal items and walked towards the front door. The Huntingtons had a car waiting for them at the entrance. Apparently, earlier, Mr. Huntington had given the driver a guesstimate on what time to pick them up. He offered to drop us off, but Aaron declined, saying that the unseasonably warm night air and the two block walk to the garage near the firm would do us both some good. Aaron and I said our good nights and headed out.

Aaron was strangely quiet during our walk. I was so exhausted, I welcomed the silence, figuring I wouldn't be much of a conversationalist now anyway. We reached the garage in no time at all. When Aaron handed the parking attendant a ticket, he disappeared down the ramp. It took the attendant less than five minutes to retrieve the black Mercedes, but in that time, I felt a vibe from Aaron that worried me. The expression on his face was just as puzzling. "Aaron, you ok? You look more than tired," I said. "I'm fine Ronni," he said dryly. Just then the attendant drove up in front of us. The firm had a parking arrangement for some of its staff, and Aaron didn't have to pay, but he did give the attendant a tip. "Get in Ronni, I'll take you home," he said as he sat behind the wheel. Clearly something was wrong. In all the time we had been dating, Aaron never once left it to me to open *any* door. As I fastened my seat belt, I thought that this was not the night to make a mountain out of a molehill. This was not the night for anything other than sleep to occur. But I also knew that right now, no matter what he said, Aaron was not fine. Four traffic lights into our drive, the silence was deafening. I couldn't hold back any longer. "Aaron, I can feel something is wrong. Talk to me, please," I said. Finally at the fifth traffic light, which was a long one, Aaron spoke. "Ronni, all I needed from you tonight was to be there for me - with me. You don't get a second chance to make a good first impression and you blew it", he said in a tone that, I admit, rubbed me the wrong way. My older sister once told me that an unwritten rule in Relationship 101 was to avoid confrontation when you are tired, because you inevitably say something that you can't take back. But my face felt flushed and I knew it was already too late for me to retreat.

"I blew it?!" I was defensive now. You are not putting this all on me I thought. I continued, "I know this was an important night for you Aaron and I did my best to comply because I love you and want what's best for you. But you put me in an inflexible situation when you accepted Mr. Huntington's invitation without first checking my availability. Did you ever once consider that? If I could have taken some energy booster shot to keep me going, after my hectic day at work, I would have. I figured showing up, even in the state I was in, was better than a no-show. And now you sit here and crucify me." A car behind us honked, signifying that the light had changed. Aaron abruptly took off down the road while the three competing temperatures – Aaron's, mine, and the car's – continued to rise. I was surprised that he actually saw and stopped at the next red light a few blocks away. "It's about sacrifice Ronni!" he blurted out. "I'm doing this for us, and I expect more from you to help me. Is that asking too much? Any other woman..." I cut him off.

"I'm not any other woman Aaron. You should know that much by now. I've stood by and let you hurl damning accusations at me, your staff, and even your parents, God bless them. When will you realize we're all working with you, not against you?" Aaron looked at me clueless. "I'm tired Aaron.

A Love Deferred

Not just tonight, but just plain old tired of everything. I need to get off your bandwagon and exit gracefully while I — we, still have some dignity left. Please pull over? I'll get a cab home from here." He crossed two lanes and pulled the car over to an abrupt stop. Thank God there was no other traffic nearby.

Aaron shot back, "Ronni, you're talking nonsense! You *are* important in my life. You all are. Don't be foolish and walk out on a good thing because your emotions have you all bent out of shape." I looked at him with an expression of resignation. "Somehow, I would expect a comment like that from the Aaron I see before me now." I continued, "I don't think you could possibly know the first thing about my emotions unless I wrote them in a legal brief and served it to you in a subpoena." In that split second, I felt a rush of wind and shouted, "No Aaron, don't!" *SLAP!* Too late. All I remember was the force of his back hand landing on my right cheek. I cried out in pain. Aaron covered his face in shame. As I applied my palm to my injured cheek, I wept softly.

"Ronni, I didn't mean it. You know I didn't, don't you? It's just this partnership thing has me so worked up. You're right. I'm not myself. But I'm more myself with you than anyone else, and I'm so sorry for hurting you. I'll never do it again." The tears he fought back made him choke on the last words I remember him speaking to me. "I — I love you Ronni Bradley. I can't survive without you baby." All I saw before me now was a man with whom I knew I had no future. "That may be true Aaron, but I know that if I stay with you, I won't survive your love. Goodbye." I gathered my things, opened the door, and got out of the car.

I hailed a cab at the corner. I don't even recall seeing Aaron's car go by. When the driver looked at me to ask my destination, I wondered if my face gave me away. It wasn't swollen, but extremely tender. I would apply a cold compress to it when I got home. As I looked out the window, one question kept going through my mind: "Why, how, did what just happen, happen *to me*?" I have a cousin whose husband, when he had a few too many, would often use her as his personal punching bag. Whenever she told me, I was outraged, telling her to throw the monster out. But she never did. She said she wanted the kids to have their father around, and, she said, she still loved him. Thinking about it now made me cringe, vividly remembering how his last expression of *that* kind of love landed her in the hospital for a couple of days. She finally got the message the her safety, and that of her two children, were far more important. In the end, she packed up the kids and left. Today, she is a survivor. As the cab pulled up in front of my apartment building, I wondered whether Aaron's behavior tonight was a fluke, or a taste of things to come if we had stayed together. I had no answers. But I did know that I wasn't willing to put myself in harm's way to find out. I paid the driver and got out of the car, using the entrance light overhead to help locate the keys in my purse and open the door. In the serenity and the sanctuary of my home, I exhaled. As the cab pulled off, I vowed *never* to let any man hit me — *ever again*.

The Reckoning

One day in January 1983 I came home to find all my belongings packed and in the middle of our living room. Linda and her brother were there with a letter in hand stating that she had filed for a "dissolution" of marriage citing irreconcilable differences. At that moment I felt desperate and immediately tried to seek ways to work things out, but she calmly said, "If we couldn't work things out in six years, what difference would another six months, six days, or hell, six minutes make? "I'm sorry Eric, I've made up my mind. I think it's best you leave." With those words spoken I left. No argument, no animosity, no tears. It was over.

I stayed with a friend for a few days until I could get my feet under me and regain my bearings. I found an apartment in Chicago, with a Lake Shore Drive address no less, and moved in by the end of the week. I stayed there as much as I could cleansing myself, thinking about my life and what I should do next. I was trying to shed myself of the internal emotions I was feeling about this break-up and all the things I knew I should have done, but ultimately, had no energy to do during the past six years. I set about the task of restarting my life. I made sure my job situation was secure. I found a new

A Love Deferred

Church home, since Linda made it clear she was not leaving our old church. I could have stayed, but that would probably make things uncomfortable for a lot of people. I redoubled my class efforts as I worked on getting my Master's degree. I changed my area of study and started all over again. A lot of things were new in my life and slowly the haze began to rise. I began to regain a rhythm and the regularity was comforting in a way.

One Friday evening, I was home watching television and eating take out Chinese food when my buzzer rang. I wasn't expecting any guests and in fact, had never had any guests since moving here. When I answered, "Who is it?" into the intercom I was surprised to hear my best friend's voice reply, "It's me, Eddie." I immediately buzzed him in and waited by the elevator for him to arrive. A minute later when the elevator door opened and my friend stepped out, bags in hand, I knew my weekend plans had changed. We hugged and immediately started making plans for a real dinner. That night and the next two days we spent our time talking about what happened between me and Linda but just as important what was going on in his life with his studies and Corrine. He briefly mentioned Ronni and that he had seen her in a restaurant with a date, not Aaron, some months ago. He said "You should give her a call." I answered "You said yourself that she is dating somebody. Besides, what am I going to say? Hi Ronni. It's me Eric. Well I don't know if you heard but I'm available again so what do you say? Do you want to try yet again? I don't think so Eddie. And don't think that I haven't thought about calling. Now how about you and Corrine?" Eddie cleared his throat and said "Things are going great. In fact, we just found out she is pregnant with twins." I jumped up ecstatic for my friend. I said, "We really have something to celebrate now." So that's what we did that weekend.

Eddie coming to see me was the best thing that could have happened to me that weekend. It was his visit that made me realize I had been in a freefall and needed to right myself, right now. He made me realize that I did have friends and family that supported me. But most of all we just had fun and he let me know that was alright too.

At the end of the weekend, Eddie went back to his life in Baltimore, and I went back to mine here in Chicago, with a promise that we would talk more and I would think about making that call. Eddie and I did talk more, but I didn't call Ronni. I wasn't ready to keep that part of the promise.

****

Three months into my new life, I was healing well. I was still in pain over my divorce, but I wasn't debilitated by it. The sting, I found out would stay with me forever and I would just have to live with that. One night in April 1983, Lonnie called to check in on me. As we were ending our call he asked "When are you coming home?" I told him I was going to take some time soon and drive down. He said

"Good because I ran into someone who said she knows you. "Who was she?" I asked mildly curious. "Her name is Ronni Bradley. Everything stopped around me. I could feel my heartbeat speed up as it always did when I thought about her but I composed myself and asked "How did you happen to run into her?" (I wanted to ask is she still fine as ever? But that would have been too much if he had said yes). "She, Terry and Jessie sing in a choir that visited our church. When service was over Terry and Jessie came over to speak to Karen and me and they introduced Ronni. They told her I was your older brother and she asked about you. By the way, she is very attractive." I asked Lonnie "What did you tell her?" I told her you were now single and still living in Chicago.... By the way, Terry and Jessie didn't know either. I hope I didn't overstep by telling them." I told my big brother, "Of course not. It's no secret and it was going to have to be told sometime. So was that the end of the conversation?" "Not quite" he answered. "As everyone was leaving Ronni made her way back to me and asked how you were really doing emotionally. I told her I thought you were doing alright and you are getting back on your feet. She looked genuinely concerned." I thanked my brother for sharing that information. I wanted to immediately call the number I knew I could generally reach Ronni at, but I hesitated trying to put all of this information in perspective. Maybe she's just feeling sorry for me, or worse, maybe she just wants to say I told you so. In the end it really didn't matter because I really

A Love Deferred

wanted, no needed to talk to Ronni Bradley. But emotionally, now was not the right time for us. I was a wreck and I knew it. Just as important she would know it too. If I go back to Ronni, I have to go back whole and as undamaged as possible. She shouldn't have to deal with any baggage I may have, so I won't bring any. It's going to take a while for me to fix myself I realized. So if I'm going to be any good to anybody, I'd better start today.

****

I woke up in my hotel room not totally refreshed but somewhat rested. I went about the tasks of getting ready to leave with my dreams/memories still fresh in my mind. I also thought about how far I'd come and what I have learned about life and myself along the way. One of the things I learned is that if you want something bad enough, you have to go out and get it. I'm afraid that's where I am now with Ronni. It's now or never for us. At least that's how I see it. I don't know if she feels the same anymore but I intend to find out this weekend. After looking at myself one last time in the mirror, I got my room key from the dresser, turned off the light and walked out the door.

CHAPTER THIRTEEN

1984 – THE YEAR OF MY FATHER

It was still light outside, although it was already 7pm Sunday evening. I returned home from church several hours ago and almost immediately delved right back into reviewing the Report. I had held my legs in one position on my bed for so long that I needed to stretch, and quickly. But when I looked across the expanse of my king-sized bedspread, I realized that I had created a paper patchwork design that didn't leave me much room to stretch out my 5 foot, 10 inch frame, most of which consisted of my long legs. I put the cluster of paper I held in my hand in a neat pile on my body pillow, slowly draped my legs over the side of the bed, so as not to disrupt what I had already reviewed, stood up, lifted my arms high in the air, grasped my hands behind my head and let out a loud shout. It felt good. I then looked over at the clock radio on my night stand and suddenly realized that, for the past three hours, I had been reading and

A Love Deferred

reviewing this Congressional Report nonstop. As tired as I was, I patted myself on the back, when I realized that I was now more than two-thirds through this mass of dead trees.

The radio station continued to play some of the most soothing tunes. As was my practice when I had to concentrate, I tuned to one of those music stations that I would listen to with my father. Stations that played nothing but the classics. Hearing one of those songs now took me back to 1984, "The Year of My Father." A year that I will never forget. Listening today, I imagined hearing a couple of lines from one of my dad's favorite crooners, Frank Sinatra, singing something just for me. In the song he was asking:

"When you were twenty-nine, was it a very good year? Was it a very good year, for hopes and dreams?"

Hopes and dreams indeed. 1984 started off as a year that held much promise. Not just for me personally, but for the entire country as well. It was a presidential election year. It was also an Olympic year and the U.S. had strong hopes to bring home the gold. And then there was the ballyhoo about what the year held based on George Orwell's book, *1984*.

On a more personal note, it was a milestone year for me too. I was transitioning out of my twenties and turning the big 3-0 in the spring. Contrary to what some people told me they experienced when going from 29 to 30, I had no uneasiness, anxiety or trepidation about the transition. I lost no sleep wondering if I would be losing part of myself, crossing the imaginary threshold that would no longer identify me as a young adult. There were a few new things in my life, however. I had recently started a new career in health communications at a national research hospital. I had also started dating Barry Williams, a manager at a major healthcare insurer in the area. We met under the oddest circumstances. My father, who had been living with cancer for many years, was now in the last stages of the disease. Barry, ten years my senior, struck up a friendship when I visited his branch office, seeking clarity on a few discrepancies I needed cleared up regarding my dad's care and coverage. I was actually poised to "do battle" the day that I went to his office. I felt I had been given the run around over the phone, which did not sit right with me, especially when it came to my dad's care. But when I met and talked to Barry, a lot of the answers started falling into place. Barry was relatively easy to talk to. By the way he conducted business, I could tell I wasn't the first to champion this particular cause for a loved one. But what he said intrigued him was my approach. He would comment, after we dated awhile, that I had him eating out of my hand from the day of our introduction. Of course, I was flattered.

My dad, my Poppy, one of the strongest and most loving Black men I knew, who took care of all of us, now needed a lot of taking care of himself. It was not easy for any of us to hear the doctor's prognosis in early 1984. Six months was what the Oncologists said. But he and the other so called experts had tried to predict a couple of times before and it seemed like they scratched their heads when my father defied their timetable. The Bible says that the *effectual, fervent prayers of the righteous availeth much.* Of all those who love and surround my dad, we who understand the power of prayer surrounded him with such prayers. Not that we were trying to bargain with God or anything. We knew that in times past, these "practicing" physicians tried to make that call, but God proved to us all, time and again that He was the only one who could make the ultimate decision and He wasn't yet ready to call him home. We knew He had other things for Poppy to do first. Even as he sat, weakened in his favorite chair, listening to his radio in the living room, my father still commanded the admiration, love, and respect of anyone who was in his presence. He was frail now, the result of a decreasing appetite and our struggle to get him to keep liquids in his system, that sometimes left him borderline dehydrated. The medications that he took for his pain would not allow him to be as articulate as he used to be, but he still got his point across through body language.

 I saw my mom tend to my father's needs round-the-clock as much as she could. She continued to cook and clean for him, and to get him to talk as much as she could. She was his woman, and as I watched how she took care of her man, I admired the hell out of her. I always loved to hear my mom talk about how she met this man, who, born in 1896, was more than twenty-six years her senior. She said he was smooth and one of the sharpest dressers in his day. He was always in a hat, suit jacket and tie, back in the days when these were staple items for a man's everyday look. My mom, who was very social and a looker herself, said she caught his attention, and his interest in her never waned. This couple, once married, had six stair-step children between the late 40's and 50's. This man, who took up parenting at age 53 was very near retirement age when he fathered his last child at age 60. I saw my mom trying to anticipate his needs before his moans of pain and uneasiness directed her to do so. I saw how tired she was physically, but how strong she was spiritually to push her body to do what needed to be done, what she believed was hers exclusively to do. Of course, the children, my brothers and sisters, and even the few grandchildren who were old enough to understand what was happening, helped as much as we could.

It would not be hard for anyone to understand how important this man was in our lives. There was no way you could take his kindness for weakness. His quiet spirit had always shown us an inner strength that taught us how to take stock of situations before reacting, and then to use more brains than brawn to get things done. The family was the foundation in my dad's eyes and he worked hard to keep that foundation strong. Even as we grew up with a much older father than most children in our peer groups, we were not lacking for anything. As a matter of fact, his maturity may have pushed him to insure that he shared himself much more with his family. Who was this man we loved so dearly? He was the man who took his role as father very seriously. My father often reviewed our homework. I recall one day when he was looking over mine, he found a separate sheet of paper that highlighted some of the words to a very familiar Temptations song, "Papa Was A Rolling Stone." My father, who was not familiar with the song, believed I was writing about him. Even with my siblings backing me up, it was not until we dug the 45 record out of our collection and played it for him, that he calmed down. Out of respect for him, we never played that song in his presence again.

Who was this man we love so dearly? He was the man who, when we were young, made Sundays after church my mom's day of rest and our special time for outings, gathering all six of us up for a ride on the public bus to McDonald's, which was a big treat back then. After that we visited his sister's (our favorite aunt's) house or one of the several museums in the downtown area. He was the man who, along with my mom, packed up the real Brady Bunch and, for our first out-of-town experience, loaded us on the train and let us experience the 1964 New York World's Fair. Who was this man we love so dearly? He was the man who made education a priority in our home; someone who taught us how to aim for excellence; someone who, while never able to complete his higher education, attended college for a time in the early 1900's when it was not the usual course for African-American men. He was the real encourager for my seeking and completing my higher education. It was a sacrifice for my family to keep me in college and, when I received my Associates degree, and thought to end it there, my father would not hear of it. His support, his guidance, and his love were the overwhelming factors in my staying the course.

One of my favorite memories during my pursuit of higher education had nothing to do with education at all. I attended a small, woman's college that, while slowly coming of age, was still steeped in a lot of tradition. One of those traditions was the annual Father/Daughter dance. With the exception of graduation, this was the single, most important social event at the college and it didn't take long to peruse the dance floor to see the cross section of children of privilege, some of whom were with their dads, but many more who, stood alone and lonely; and then there were couples like me and my dad. I could not have been any more privileged than when I walked on to the dance floor with my Poppy. We stood out for a couple of reasons. First, we were one of the few African-American couples on the floor. Secondly, even though there was at least a 5 inch difference in our height (I was taller), what really made us stand out was the precision with which my father glided me gracefully across the floor doing the two-step. I could tell everyone in the room had their eyes on us. Fred Astaire and Ginger Rogers had nothing on us. I still get goose bumps reliving those special moments

A Love Deferred

in my mind, and smile when I think that these are the stories that I can't wait to share with my child/ren, and their children, when the time comes. In my dreams, the music never stops, and I am in that ballroom at school, dancing with my father again.

But now, here we were, seeing our hero fading away. We were always in touch with the doctors and other healthcare providers, either on the phone, or person-to-person meetings with my mom and dad or in whatever combinations worked best to get my dad back and forth to his appointments. He wanted to be home for as long as he could, and my mom was going to respect his wishes. We supported her in every step she took to make it happen. It was a few weeks before Thanksgiving and my father's health had definitely taken a turn for the worse. It was clear that, even with a home health nurse coming in on occasion, the emotional toll on my mom was too much for her to bear. We moved him to a nearby hospital and split into groups to make sure someone was there every hour, everyday with him. It was the only way we could insure that my mom would take some time to rest herself. My sister CeeCee and I went over together, mostly because we lived together and also because we would always sing to daddy. I would bend over and kiss him softly on his cheek and say, "Hi Poppy. It's me, Harmonica, and CeeCee, here to serenade you." He would always find the strength to smile. My father was an excellent singer. He used to sing lead for a group called the Starlight Singers in New

York in his *B.C.* (*B*efore *C*atherine) days. Years later, he sang with a male gospel group, and when he stopped singing, he would travel wherever they sang in the Metropolitan area to hear them. CeeCee and I were generally right by his side. So, here we were, standing at our dad's bedside singing a medley of gospel songs, many of the old standards. But even in his highly sedated state, Poppy could tell every time my sister or I hit a sour note and if he couldn't speak it, would grimace and let us know it wasn't right. Amazing!

Working in a medical environment, my colleagues on the job were not only very understanding of my plight, but helped me to make sure I understood all that was happening to my dad. I often wondered, with all the state-of-the-art, technological advances and top medical minds that surrounded me here on campus, why we hadn't beat cancer yet. Surely, the answer must be in one of the hundreds of thousands of test tubes and Petri dishes being pored over here or somewhere in the world. I thought the answer couldn't come soon enough for my family and me.

I also had some of the best spiritual support from Corinne and Eddie, the members of my church and Pastor Thomas, who was more like a father to me than a pastor. I recall one day when he sat me down after church and told me that if there was anything that I needed to say or to share, he was there for me. It wasn't that he hadn't offered that before, but that particular Sunday, his offer hit a nerve. For the first time in a long time, I voiced the fact that I know we don't always understand God's plan. I said that I knew my father would not be with us much longer and, while it hurt to see him suffering, it hurt just as much to think about not having him around, for me, for my mom, for my family. At that point, I did what I had only done in private when I totally broke down and cried, what seemed like, nonstop tears. Pastor Thomas put his arm around my shoulder and, as I began to release the anguish I had held onto for so long, he prayed for me and for my family. *The effectual, fervent prayers of the righteous can do much.* Even in the midst of my endless tears, I felt, as the old folks in the church used to say, part of my help coming on.

There was nothing special about the morning of November 20th. It was a cool morning, but by the time I made it to work, I started to warm up. I went through my routine and addressed my tasks as best I could, but everything I attempted to do as I would have normally, took an incredible amount of energy, and I was already way over my reserve. My supervisor offered to let me take a couple of days off, but I felt I needed to continue to move about as much as I could with my regular life for as long as I could. This was the alternate day for visiting my dad, which meant that my older sisters would go visit him that evening, and, once I went home and changed clothes, I would walk the six blocks to check on my mom at the house. This particular day, it was torture trying to complete an eight hour tour, and after

A Love Deferred

trudging through five, I went to my supervisor, eyes slightly blood shot, to let her know that I needed to go home.

The subway ride from suburban Maryland to Northeast D.C. seemed to take forever, but I finally made it to our apartment. I needed rest and headache medicine and was about to pick up the phone to call Cee Cee at work to ask her to check on mom on her way home, when it started to ring. At one point, I considered not answering it, assuming it was an unwanted solicitor. But I was immediately brought back to the sobering reality of what any phone call could mean. "Hello," I said wearily. Even before the other person on the phone spoke, I could hear the sniffles. I thought, "God, why couldn't it have been some stupid salesperson on the line." I knew it was a woman's sound, but my senses were so dulled that I couldn't make out whether it was my sister CeeCee or Marie. "Who is this? CeeCee? Marie?" All the voice could barely get out was, "Ronni, you need to come to the hospice." "What's wrong? What's happening Marie? Tell me? Daddy?" Marie started crying uncontrollably and someone nearby took the phone from her. The next voice I heard was CeeCee's. "Ronni," she paused, her voice trembling, "Daddy's gone. He died thirty minutes ago. You need to come now." I couldn't find my voice box, so just held the phone and then held it away from me for a second like whoever this was, was playing a cruel joke on me. Yes, I knew that my father was slipping away and had been for some time, but hearing it now, over the phone, felt like a sledge hammer making a direct hit on my heart.

I could hear my sister calling my name louder, "Ronni! Do you hear me?" I think I answered yes, but just barely. "Okay," Cee Cee said. "Look, Barry is on his way to get you, so be ready to come out. Just come out when he blows. Don't stay there Ronni, do you hear me, come when he honks the horn." All I could say again was, "Yes." "I'm hanging up now Ronni because I need to go back in the room with Momma and Marie. See you later." Cee Cee hung up on her end. For some reason, I couldn't do it on my end. It was as if I thought if I didn't hang up, then maybe somebody would come back and tell me something different. But I knew that wouldn't happen. All at once, my bravado was shattered. "Poppy!" I cried out, hurling the phone on the bed. I dropped to my knees, bending over and almost touching my head to the floor, calling my daddy's name several times through my tears. I stayed in that position for a while until I could start to compose myself enough to stand up, wiping my tear-stained face with my hands and then with tissues from the box on the nightstand. Part of me didn't want to go. But the other part of me knew I had to. I felt like a zombie, but I somehow found the willpower to gather my jacket, a purse, and a big handful of tissues from the box, placing them in my bag. From the window, I saw Barry pulling up and getting out of the car. I knew he wouldn't honk, rather come up to get me, but I didn't want to wait. I hurriedly locked the door and met him

A Love Deferred

at the entrance to the building. He put his arm around my shoulder and supported me on my walk to his car. He opened the passenger door and helped me in. I stared blankly out the passenger side window. Barry got in, put his hand on mine, put the key in the ignition and drove off. I never asked Barry how they got in touch with him. I never asked him anything on the drive to the hospital and he never spoke a word either. I was never more grateful for the silence

There was a small group of people already gathered in the family room down the hall from my dad's room. As I got closer, they came into focus – my sisters, two of my brothers and a few close friends. But I didn't see my mom. "Where's Mom?" I asked, as I hugged my sister Marie. "She's in there with daddy." "By herself? "At first yes," my sister answered. "But T.J. went in a little while later to be with her. T.J. was the oldest son, oldest of all of us, and although he and I were only separated by 5 years, I would always jokingly refer to him as my "Brother/Father." All the siblings did. It was a role he assumed, maybe a bit too enthusiastically, dating back to our childhood years, when our parents put him in charge when they went out. Even though we all now ranged in age from twenty something to thirty something, T.J. still took that role on, sometimes much to our annoyance. But deep down, he knew we loved him and we knew he could always be counted on. We were all glad he was with Momma now. "What happened?" I asked Marie. Still a little shaken, she had regained some of her composure, and began recounting the details as best she could remember. I could tell that she had told this story more than once already, maybe more than she wanted to, but the look on my face let her know I needed to hear it.

When Marie and Doris (my mom's daughter through a previous marriage) arrived at the hospital after work, they found my father awake, but not speaking. He acknowledged their presence by widening his eyes and following their movements in the room. They brushed his hair, put lotion on his hands, and wiped his face with a warm washcloth. They then proceeded to tell him about their day, making sure to add in a few humorous details. My father loved to laugh and so we always imagined him laughing with us when we told the silly stuff. The nurse came through to check on him and Marie pulled her to the side. "Is he in pain?" she asked. "He looks different today." The nurse responded by saying that daddy was resting comfortably and that, at this stage, that was what was best for him. She made notations on his chart and left the room. About 30 minutes later, Marie said daddy appeared to be falling asleep, so she and Doris took that opportunity to go to the snack bar to get a quick bite and come back to the room. It took them less than 20 minutes, but in the time that they made their trek and returned, there was a medical team congregating outside daddy's room. Marie ran over to find out what had happened. "Miss Bradley, I'm afraid your father has passed. His heart just stopped. If it's

A Love Deferred

any comfort to you, he was in no pain," said the doctor on call.

Immediately, Marie leaned against the wall and Doris rushed over to grab her before she sank to the floor. They began to cry on each other's shoulders. They waited outside for a minute while the nurse, with whom Marie had spoken with only minutes ago, unhooked daddy from the machines. "I'm truly sorry Marie," she said. "If it helps any at all, he went peacefully." Marie said she couldn't bear it at first because she felt that if she hadn't left the room, daddy might still be with us, or at least that he wouldn't have died alone. But she said when Cee Cee and Momma came with the boys, they let her know that God was always with daddy and in control and He knew it was his time. Marie found a bit of comfort when our mother went on to tell her that an all knowing God and a loving father knew that Marie could not have handled watching her father pass and spared her. That's what real love does — it tries to spare us from unnecessary pain. And that's what Jesus did for us through His sacrifice – spared us from unnecessary pain. I realized right then and there, that our father in Heaven and here on Earth, knew exactly what was happening that night. What love, I thought about that as I went in for one last time to stroke my father's soft, white hair, kiss him on the cheek, sing one last chorus from one of his favorite songs.

The week following Poppy's passing was especially hard. Two days before his burial, we went through the motions of celebrating Thanksgiving but there was no real joy. Friends and other family members prepared a meal at my momma's house so we could at least eat if we wanted to, but no one really wanted to. It was still all too fresh and impossible to celebrate anything. Even coming together proved taxing for me. All I wanted to do was revert back to my old childhood days, find a quiet corner and be still. Somehow, we all made it through Thanksgiving, but it would never be the same, or so we thought then.

That Saturday, we woke up to very bright sunshine. Even more unusual was the abnormally warm temperature. It was balmy and nearly 75 degrees. It was as if God was smiling down on us, knowing that we needed all the help we could get to make it through. As we entered the sanctuary, my brother, who was one year younger, and I walked in together. When he took hold of my hand, (something totally out of character for him) as we walked down the aisle to our seats, he gave me strength. I thought to myself and almost chuckled, "This is the brother who I always fought with over simple things now helping me to stand. I know daddy is smiling." Throughout the service, people who knew and loved Poppy, remembered him fondly. Many more offered words of encouragement to our family. We were all attentive to my mom, who had a peace about her. I know she knew her husband was in better hands. And then, Cee Cee stood and did what she had done numerous times in front of our father – she sang in tribute to him. I remember telling my sister before she sang that

A Love Deferred

she'd better hit every note right or daddy would rise up out of the casket. That was our inside joke and we both smiled. She sang a beautiful solo just before our cousin read part of the obituary – a line from each of his children. Mine simply read: *Till we meet again Music Man. Love, Harmonica.* Pastor Thomas delivered the eulogy. Pastor Thomas warmed our hearts when he said that, as can happen with some eulogies, he did not have to make up anything about Thomas Bradley. He knew my dad was head of his household. He knew my dad had the love of his wife and children. He knew my dad had a love for the Lord and, as pastor interjected on a personal note, for him as well. He recalled that on numerous occasions when he visited my dad and he ended his visit by praying for my father, he would take that same opportunity to say, "Now let me pray for you pastor." Years later, my mom would tell me that the day my father died, Pastor Thomas came to see her before sunrise. He had come directly from visiting my dad at the hospital and said he saw something different in my father's appearance and especially in his face, that particular morning. He said, "Sister Bradley, I believe God is ready to call him home today." He prayed and comforted my mom that morning and I believe that helped her have the calm she did when we arrived at the hospital that evening and even now in the service.

How I loved Pastor Thomas and thanked God for giving us a servant with so much compassion. Pastor Thomas charged those in the congregation to not worry about where

Brother Bradley would rest now, because he knew during his lifetime that my father's faithfulness dwelled with the Lord. Pastor Thomas sought any and every opportunity to win souls for Christ and he implored everyone "from the pulpit to the door, from the ceiling to the floor, to search their hearts and if they hadn't yet made the decision to follow Jesus, as Brother Bradley had, now was the time." It was a stirring message and even through the tears that were shed, provided a release and a relief to me. I followed Pastor Thomas with words to a song that I thought spoke to where we all went from this point on. The song was titled "I Know Who Holds Tomorrow," and, as I stood, tears running down my face, I found hope and strength in the words that echoed my personal testimony, "Many things about tomorrow, I don't seem to understand, but I know who holds tomorrow, and I know who holds my hand." Someone asked me later how I was able to do it. I simply answered, "I couldn't imagine not doing it."

At the cemetery, Poppy was buried with full military honors, which included removing and folding the flag draped atop his coffin and handing it to my mom. It ended with the twenty-one gun salute and *Taps*. The last memory I have of the service was so typical of a Bradley function. Even in the midst of our sorrow, we found laughter. When the first shots were fired, my then 7 year old nephew, scurried under one of the chairs for safety. Watching him in that one moment, helped lift some of our heaviness and remembering it helped get us through the rest of the day. We knew daddy must have been laughing too.

Days later I lay in bed, curled up in the fetal position, thinking that loving someone so deeply hurt too much, and deciding I could take the less painful way out by declaring that I wouldn't allow anyone to touch my heart that deeply again. But that would be easier said than done. For weeks after the funeral Barry was extremely attentive to my needs. Unfortunately for him, he was already in harm's way. He became my first casualty.

CHAPTER FOURTEEN

1984 –THROUGH THE NIGHT

Some book starts with the line "It was the best of times; it was the worst of times." I wish I paid more attention in English Lit but that's what 1984 was for me. I divorced my college sweetheart after six years in early 1983 and although I was emotionally drained, I still knew I had to go on. I left her with our suburban town-house and most of the belongings we collected over the years. I also left her with no hard feelings because I knew that deep down inside we were both good people, we just were not good for each other. When we left the courthouse, I didn't feel free. I felt like a failure. This was another relationship that didn't work. To fail at a relationship in college was one thing, but after investing six years with someone, failure takes on a whole new meaning. I found that friends took sides and most of our friends took her side. I found that food tasted different when I cooked it for me only, music sounded different when I played it for me only and getting dressed up for me only, well what's the use.

I moved into a studio apartment on the north side of Chicago. I could honestly tell visitors that I had a view of Lake Michigan. The problem was you had to put yourself tight against the window pane in the bathroom and look between two buildings to see it. After a few months that I called cleansing, i.e., no phone calls, no movies, no friends, just studying for my Masters Degree and going home at night I met someone quite unexpectedly. She was in my class and she and I were the sum total of African Americans in the class of about 60 people. She had a medium brown complexion with long black hair and was medium size. She had a very pretty face and a great figure. She looked to be about my age but it didn't matter. I made up my mind that I was going to talk to her the first chance I got. That chance came during the break of the next week's class. She was looking at something on a bulletin board when I sidled up to her and said "Hi. My name is Eric Lewis." I held out my hand to shake hers and she answered "Pleased to meet you. My name is Prentice Williams." I said "I guess you've noticed we are truly the minority in this class." She answered "Yes, I had noticed that but all of my classes have been like that. Sometimes I'm the only one." I told her this was my first class since changing my major and I was surprised by the low number of African Americans. She said "You shouldn't be. There are very few of us in this profession and fewer still seeking or holding advanced degrees." When the professor came to herd us back into the class room I quickly asked, "Do you want to study together sometime?" She looked at me, laughed and walked away. For the rest of the class I stewed over her reaction. Back in college, undergrad, that was a perfectly legitimate request for a meeting. I guess I had been out of it for a while. When class ended I caught up to her and said "You know I am a serious student. I am not trying to come on to you and I thought we could work on the mid-term together." She looked at me and answered, "The last guy that asked me to study just wanted to get into my panties and I don't really have any interest in that. So if you really want to study…" I raised my hand and said "Scout's honor." She handed me a slip of paper with her work number on it and said, "call me." "Maybe we can get together this weekend." I agreed, and we made our way to the parking lot and went our separate directions.

Needless to say, we got along very well. After our first study session we scheduled more sessions and found ourselves talking about things other than class. She invited me to her apartment on the south side of Chicago which put my little studio to shame. It was neat with expensive furniture and art pieces throughout. My apartment had reproduced prints and a fold-out bed. When we talked about going to my apartment to study, I always recommended that we meet at the library. We went on meeting even after our class ended and we found ourselves falling in love. I was surprised by that after being divorced only a few months earlier, but who questions God's wisdom. We kissed and got close several times but hadn't made love at that point. I like the fact that we waited until we were sure that this is what we wanted. We scheduled a trip to Lake Geneva, Wisconsin one weekend to one of the old lakeside hotels. We checked in planning to go to dinner, but all the pent up passion came out as soon as we entered the room and we found ourselves kissing passionately and our clothes lay in puddles around our feet. We made love that evening, later that night, the next day.. you get the picture. We couldn't get enough of each other.

When we got back to Chicago we were officially a couple. Our only decision was whose place we would stay at for the night. And it wasn't that we made love every night, we just wanted to be together every night. After a couple of months though we started experiencing friction about everything. She'd say, "You're too sloppy." I'd come back with, "You're too neat." She'd say, "You have too many activities." I'd complain, "You're a homebody." Then out of nowhere, she'd say, "You flirt too much!" Taken by surprise, I'd respond, "I flirt too much?!" Soon the phone calls trickled then stopped. Home visits ended and I figured it was time to move on. I started going out with a woman from church named Sedra and was putting Prentice in the past when a couple of months later she showed up at my apartment unannounced. I rang her up and was happy I had no guests. (A new policy I instituted after Prentice). She came to my door and I invited her in. After refusing drinks I had offered I asked her, "What brings you here?" She said simply, "I'm pregnant." At first I thought I heard her incorrectly and it must have been reflected in my expression because she said, "You heard me right, Eric, I'm pregnant, and I am going to keep this baby." I didn't ask whether the baby was mine because I knew Prentice, and she would never play those kinds of games. I also knew that the chances of her becoming pregnant were miniscule because of the damage that previous surgeries had done to her ovaries. She said, "Well aren't you going to say anything?" I sat down hard and said "I don't know what to say or what to think. You really came out of the blue and body slammed me with this." She started to cry and I did what came natural to me. I held her and cried too.

 To be honest, I was happy, but scared. We both had good jobs but I was just making it. It was going to be rough for a while but we could do this together. The real problem was that we were not a couple anymore. Fate or chance had thrown us back together and I wasn't so sure that was such a great thing. I asked her, "when is the baby due?" "The doctor says June of next year" she answered. "Man. That's not a lot of time" I said. "Well what do we have to do to get ready?" After an hour we had a list that included taking childbirth classes, finding a place to live that allows babies, picking a name, and the last item on her list, getting married. That item caught me by surprise. I mean people have committed relationships out of wedlock everyday. They last for years with children and are functioning family units. She logically explained that rising executives, especially female and Black are frowned upon and passed over for promotions if they are young single parents. I knew what she was saying is true. I had seen it where I work but was powerless to change it, except now. I said, "Okay, let's get married." She looked at me and said, "That's it?! That's how you are going to propose marriage to me?"

Her anger grew quickly and she grabbed her coat and left my apartment. I tried to get her to stay and be reasonable but no use, she was gone. I did not talk to her for a week after that even though I left messages for her at home and work. So I pulled one of her tricks, I showed up unannounced at her house. I waited for two hours for her to get home from work on a cold November night. As she got out of her car, I walked up to her and said, "Hi." She looked at me and said "What do you want?" I answered, "I want to take you to dinner so we can finish talking about our baby." She still seemed reluctant but gave in by saying "Just let me drop my things inside and then I have to pee." We both laughed and I said I'll get the car warmed up. When she came downstairs, I opened the door for her and helped her sit down. We had a pleasant conversation, that revolved around work and school, while we drove to the restaurant. I started to see the old Prentice, the Prentice I fell in love with during that drive and knew that what I planned was the right thing to do. We had dinner at a well known hotel restaurant in downtown Chicago. I really enjoyed being with her now and she was glowing that special way that people say that pregnant women do. As the waiter went away with our dessert orders I said, "Prentice, I have a serious question to ask you." I looked into her eyes as I took her hands in mine. I stepped out of my seat and took one knee next to her. This caused a stir amongst the other patrons in the restaurant. Prentice looked around embarrassed and said quietly "Get up, get up. You are making a spectacle." I said "What I have to ask you won't take too long. Prentice Williams, will you do me the honor of being my wife for the rest of our lives?" With tears in her eyes, she joined me on her knees and said "Yes for the rest of our lives." We kissed and held each other, crying for a long time.

We moved to a new apartment and married in February 1984. From February to June when our baby was born, we painted and cleaned and bought toys and got everything ready for what we now knew was our boy child, Christian. In May, I received an urgent call from my brother saying that our father had died suddenly and to hurry home. I was left numb. My father and I were never close, but he was my father. I quickly pulled up images of a good looking man who loved to cook and sing but just did know how to be around when the going got tough. He left us when I was 11 and started living with a woman some 10 miles from where we lived. I would stop to visit him from time to time and he would give me a ride home, but it wasn't the same as having you dad at home every night, or at your football games, or tying your prom tie. But I still found enough to cry about. The $20.00 he slipped in an envelope to me at college every so often, the Christmas gifts from years ago when he had to buy for 9 kids, and the singing and cooking.

Prentice came up behind me and hugged me, big belly and all, trying to stop my tears. All that did was make the dam burst and I let it all out and had a good cry. Later that week, my dad was buried with full military honors in a veteran's cemetery in Washington, D.C. The day of the funeral was unseasonably cold and rainy but when we arrived at the cemetery there was a tarpaulin set-up with a number of chairs facing the grave and the flag covered casket. Standing in the rain at full attention were seven soldiers in full dress uniform holding rifles. Under the tarp were two other soldiers and a Bugler. The ceremony of the flag folding, playing taps and the 21 gun salute was touching and the end brought tears to my eyes once again. I came to the funeral alone from Chicago because of the lateness of Prentice's term, but I felt her presence. I didn't stay long after the funeral. I quickly said hello to relatives and friends and hurried back to Chicago to be with my Prentice.

We were doing so well. We were happy, excited and full of wonder about being parents. We went to Lamaze classes and learned breathing techniques, had our bag packed and sitting by the door and were ready to go. That moment came on June 13. Prentice's mother was in town awaiting the big moment when her contractions got to the point where it was now time to get to the hospital. I got the car while Prentice took her shower and was dressed by her mother. I took Prentice and her bags to the car, put them both inside, and drove quickly but safely to the hospital 5 miles away. The doctor was there awaiting our arrival as they wheeled her in a room in the natal unit. The doctor and nurse put her on a bed and took a look at her under some sheets and said not time yet. The right time didn't come until 1:30 p.m. the next day. Christian was born naturally, a perfectly healthy baby boy. I held him as he cried his announcement "Hey world I am here." I handed him to Prentice who induced him to breastfeed right away. At that moment, I had never seen anything more beautiful in my life and I knew I would love and cherish this moment forever.

The weeks following Christian's birth were the happiest days of my life. Family and friends came from all over the country to see our son. "He's so beautiful, he looks just like you Prentice, but he's got his father's nose. Look at all that hair." Everyone adored him. I used to sit up at night and watch him sleep because I still had a hard time believing how precious and beautiful he was. Prentice relished her role as mother as much as I basked in the glow of being a proud father. She dressed, fed, washed, burped, and cleaned after Trey, all the while talking to him even when he put up a fuss. As I said before, my job was to take care of the laundry, and I took pride in washing and folding his clothes because they were my son's. I dreamed of what he would be when he grew up. Teacher, policeman, athlete, preacher, president, all were possibilities. Until one sunny day in August when all of my/our dreams were taken away from us.

On this day everything started out normally. I got up first, then woke Prentice and while she washed, I got Christian washed, dressed and ready to eat. Prentice would prepare his food and pack a bag to go to the babysitter's. Prentice looked at Christian and said, "That's the new outfit his aunt bought him. I'm going to take a picture and send it to her." I looked at Christian who at first was lying on the sofa and then lifted his head and tried to pull himself up. I yelled, "Hurry, you've got to see this." Prentice hurried back in time to see our son happily sitting and holding his head up on his own. Prentice smiled while she snapped pictures of Christian with her 35mm Nikon. With pictures taken it was time to go to the babysitter's and work. I kissed Prentice and grabbed Christian from her smothering kisses, which he seemed to love, and took off. The drive to drop Christian off was typical, traffic moved well because everyone was heading into the city while I was heading out. I dropped Christian off with Mrs. Kennedy who took Christian from my arms and started cooing and talking to him immediately. I told her I would see her at 5:00 she nodded and waived and they disappeared inside.

The day at work was typical. There were meetings, and grievance hearings. There were conversations with laid off workers and state unemployment offices in short typical until about 2:30 p.m. I stepped outside to get change from my car to buy a soda when my assistant Roberta, came to the door and screamed my name sobbing all the while. I ran to her quickly and asked what's wrong and tearfully she replied "On the phone, it's Mrs. Kennedy." With those words she broke down completely. Fear running through me I ran to my office and picked up the phone and breathlessly said, "Mrs. Kennedy what's wrong?" On the other end I could hear the sounds of people rushing around, telling children to stay calm, crying and other noise. Mrs. Kennedy spoke frantically saying "Eric, it's Christian. He stopped breathing and they took him to the hospital. Eric, I'm so sorry." I know she said other things, mouth to mouth, doctor across the street, here in minutes, but my head was spinning. I had to get there now. I needed to be there now. But I couldn't get my body to move. I fell into my chair and the tears came uninvited. One of my friends came in and said "Eric do you need me to do anything?" I think I answered no and unsteadily got to my feet. I went to the door and headed for my car thinking all the while, how am I going to tell Prentice what I knew in my heart was true. Our baby has died.

I somehow drove to Mrs. Kennedy's house whispering prayers and crying all the while. When I got to her house there were police cars on both sides of the street and parents consoling their children. Mrs. Kennedy was beside herself with grief. I ran directly to her and she grabbed me into her arms. At that moment I knew that what my heart had told me was true. She told me that she had laid Christian down for a nap and when she checked on him not 20 minutes later he was blue and not breathing. She added that she immediately began mouth to mouth with no response and had one of her staff call 911. Another staff member ran to the neighbor's house who happened to be doctor and who was home. She told me he rushed over and began treating Christian right away. Within minutes she said the ambulance arrived and the doctors and paramedic bundled Christian inside and rushed him to the nearby Trauma Center. With that I told her thank you for everything, got back in my car and rushed to the Trauma Center. There, I ran to the Emergency Room admissions desk and asked about my son. I must have appeared in bad shape because they attended to me immediately even though the Emergency Room was full.

A nurse quietly asked me my name and was I his father. I answered yes and that my name is Eric Lewis. She ushered me to a room and asked me to take a seat where she told me calmly and with great empathy that Christian had died a little more than 30 minutes ago. I heard a sound that broke my heart. I had never heard a person cry like that before and, unfortunately, it was coming from me and I knew I would hear that cry again in a few minutes when I called Prentice. After composing myself enough to go back into the waiting area to use the public phone, I dialed Prentice's work number. It rang twice and she answered cheerfully, "Prentice Lewis, may I help you?" All I could say was "Prentice." She must have heard something in my voice because her immediate question was "Eric, what's wrong with my baby." I answered by saying, "Prentice, Christian..." I never finished the statement when she screamed and dropped the phone. I heard people bustling into her office to help her and I could imagine her on her knees crying uncontrollably and no one being able to console her. I questioned myself as to whether I should have tried to get to her and tell her in person but it would have taken at least an hour to get to her office and more time to get back. The next voice I heard on the phone was that of one of her co-workers. She said "Eric is it true?" I said "Yes Marianne. He died a short while ago." In the background I could still hear Prentice's sobbing and Marianne continued by asking "Where are you now?" I told her the name of the Trauma unit and she promised to bring Prentice directly there. With our conversation over I hung up and joined the other people in the waiting room. I hung my head and cried.

Almost two hours later, Prentice and Marianne rushed into the hospital. Prentice ran past me and directly to the emergency room desk demanding to see her baby. The nurse was very accommodating and asked the two of us to take seats. While we waited more family and friends arrived. Each in turn came forward to ask questions and console but nothing really mattered now. Nothing could get past the numbness I/we felt at the loss of our child. Making matters worse, a police officer and a nurse came to ask questions about whether we suspected foul play in our son's death. We of course said no and went about recounting the details as we knew them. The officer closed his notebook, apologized and walked away. The nurse who asked us to wait returned and ushered us to a small room where Christian laid, wrapped in a blue blanket peacefully, as though he was just napping. Prentice picked him up and held him gently to her chest weeping the whole while. I stood numb looking at them thinking, the day he was born was the happiest day of my life and this by far was the saddest.

The next few days went by quickly. Relatives and friends had to be notified, funeral arrangements made, a cemetery had to be picked out, headstone, announcement, obituary, minister...all details that had to be tended to. When the day of his funeral arrived, there was a line of limousines outside our door to accommodate immediate family and still more cars were needed. We made our way slowly through the streets of Chicago from our North side home to our Southside Church where the service would be performed. Once there, Prentice and I sat quietly as hundreds of people, family, co-workers, friends, doctors, nurses, all filed by to look at our son for the last time and wish their condolences to us. There was mournful singing by the choir, and a stirring message from our pastor about getting right with God because "ye know neither the day nor the hour that it will be your time too."

At the end of the service, at the time to close Christian's casket, Prentice stepped forward, kissed his forehead, and

A Love Deferred

placed a flower next to him. I stepped forward to carry his casket to a waiting hearse. When I picked it up, he felt light inside there as though the casket had no weight at all. But as I walked closer to the doors leading outside to the hearse, I started to falter and cry as the casket became heavier and heavier. From that point until the time I actually placed the casket with my son inside the hearse, all I could remember is the feeling of the hands of men on my shoulders and words of encouragement that gave me the strength to go on.

Christian was buried between two sapling pines on a hot day in August 1984. He is missed and loved even to this day Those ten short weeks of his life taught me about unconditional love, sacrifice, pride and sorrow. I learned to cry then. It's a lesson I have used too often since.

CHAPTER FIFTEEN

JOY IN THE MORNING

It took a long time for Prentice and me to be able to accept the loss of our son. Everything in our home reminded us of him and we wanted it that way. We wanted to keep his memory fresh always. We dealt with our grief differently. Her tears came early and frequently. Mine came early but stayed locked inside later until some obscure event sent them tumbling over. We both sought professional counseling but I needed to get back to work and keep myself busy. In hindsight, I needed to stay with Prentice to make sure she was alright. After several months we were able to work with other couples to help them through their grief. Sometimes fathers who had experienced such a loss would be asked to talk to other men who had lost their child. Sometimes they would ask for couples. Through it all Prentice and I worked well together and it helped us handle our grief. After awhile we found that we could find comfort in the intimacy we shared before our son's passing. A little while after that we started dating each other again like we were starting all over. We started to feel some level of normalcy when one day in February, I came home from work to find all the lights out except the dimmed lights in the dining room. I called out "Prentice is the power out?" As I came into our apartment, I flicked the switch and found the lights to be in good order. Prentice called back, "The lights are fine. I made dinner and thought we would have it by candle light."

As I hung my coat in the hall closet, I could smell the delicious aroma of baked chicken, potatoes, greens and corn bread, all favorites of mine. As I stepped into the dining room, Prentice was placing piping hot bowls on the table and I could see a bottle of what looked like champagne chilling in an ice bucket by the side. I looked at Prentice and saw that she was dressed in a black silk night gown, the one she knew drove me crazy. She came over and kissed me deeply and said, "Why don't you sit down and relax. Can you open that bottle for me? By the way, it's only sparkling grape juice." I asked "What's the occasion?" I quickly ran through my mind and checked birthdays, anniversaries, holidays and came back blank. She responded, "Can't a woman make a special dinner for her man every once in a while?" "I'm not complaining." I answered while sitting at the table. "Anything I can do to help?" "No," she answered. "Everything is ready now. We were just waiting for you." "We?" I asked. "Are we having some guests?" That's when she came and sat in my lap. Without looking at me she took my right hand and placed it on her stomach. She looked into my eyes and said, "When I said, we, I meant me and our baby." With those words said, she laid her head on my shoulder as I held her close and we laughed and cried as we celebrated the coming of our second child, Trey Vernon Lewis. God had granted us a second miracle.

****

Trey, named after my grandfather, would be born in October the doctor told us, so once again we set about preparing for a new baby in our home. We went about it with the same fervor but simultaneously with more than a little reservation. I think it would have broken both of our hearts beyond repair if we were to lose another child. But we agreed that this child would receive all of our love and attention for as long as God granted us to have him. Once again we painted rooms and picked out clothes and toys, that would be his alone. (Christian's were now packed in a special place that we still opened from time to time just to be near him). We went about the child birthing classes like old pros and I went on midnight runs for chocolate milkshakes with tuna sandwiches. There was a second baby shower mixed in with classes and work and all was right with the world.

****

One night in September, as I entered my graduate studies class, the professor met me at the door and asked in a matter of fact way, "What are you doing here Mr. Lewis?" Thinking it was some kind of test I responded "I'm here for class. Is there a problem?" He said smiling "I don't know if there is a problem but your wife is at the hospital having a baby. I think you'd better get there." I turned on my heels and took off past the other student entering the class rooms and building. I got to my car and roared on to northbound Lake Shore Drive and into the parking lot of the hospital less than half an hour later. Sprinting into the Emergency Room and out of breath, I found the admitting station and asked if Prentice had been taken to the natal unit. But in my mind I was calculating the time and it was 3 weeks too soon. I started to worry but the nurse told me to relax and informed me that Prentice was doing fine. She was resting comfortably in the room next door. I walked into the room amazed to see her sitting in her street clothes. She said "Hi honey. False alarm but the doctor feels it could happen at any minute. Let's go home."

By the time we got home dinner was already prepared for us and sitting on the table. My mother in-law who was staying with us through the birth of her grandson was a wonderful cook and began cooking the moment she heard we were on our way home. She was as excited as Prentice and me about our son's impending birth and while we worked during the day, she busied herself putting final touches on the baby's room and puttering around our apartment. Whatever she did

A Love Deferred

she always managed to create a new bag of garbage for me to take out everyday. I'm not complaining but... Anyway, it's needless to say that the dinner was delicious and we sat around talking for some time afterwards. Around 9 p.m. Prentice said she felt tired and went to shower and go to bed. I stayed up and studied a little longer while my mother in-law watched the Cosby Show. After an hour of reading the same line over and over, I went to bed too.

Around 2:00 a.m., Prentice woke me from a deep sleep and cheerily said "Let's go shopping. We can go to the 24 grocery and pick up some things so my mom won't have to" Although what I wanted was more sleep, I said "Alright," through a yawn and went about the tasks of getting dressed and headed off shopping.

After locking our apartment door, we walked down the front steps and headed arm in arm to the grocery one block away. Strolling through the almost empty store, we stocked up on fruits, vegetables, fresh chicken and juices. On an impulse we bought a shopping basket with rollers to transport large amounts of groceries easier. After checking out, I turned left outside the store which would have been the most direct route home but Prentice pulled me to the right and said "I feel like walking for awhile." So we walked two blocks out of our way and if you could have drawn a straight line from our apartment to the middle point of the block south of our place, that's where you would have found us when the new contraction hit Prentice.

A Love Deferred

I could tell from her voice and the way she squeezed my arm that this was it. "Honey," She said, "It's time to go." I didn't panic but I was sort of lost. Should we hurry, should I go get the car, should we take a cab and just get to the hospital? It was Prentice who was thinking clearly when she said "Let's take our time and get home. Then we'll call the doctor and head to the hospital." "Good plan," I said starting to sweat a little. Prentice stopped along the way holding her side and taking short breaths. We would walk a little further and take breaks until we reached our front door. I hurried in, grabbed our bag and woke my mother in-law to let her know what was going on. Prentice made her way in and calmly went to the bathroom and began running a shower. I couldn't believe it. While my mother in-law and I paced outside the bathroom, Prentice calmly took a shower. Twenty minutes later she came out clean, dressed and ready to go. After giving her mother a kiss and a hug, we walked outside to my car and drove quickly to the hospital emergency entrance holding hands.

I got out of the car at the hospital and asked an attendant to help me with my wife. I explained the situation and he jumped into action, bringing a wheelchair along with him. While he got Prentice inside, I parked the car and sprinted back to her side with her bag. By the time I arrived, insurance information had been given and she was on her way to the natal unit. By the look on her face and the small beads of sweat starting to appear, we arrived not a minute too soon.

A Love Deferred

A sharp stab of pain caused her to arch her back and let out a hiss. She instinctively started her breathing techniques and I began my coaching. When we arrived on the floor of the natal unit, we were both happy to see that her doctor was there awaiting her arrival. Once there they whisked Prentice in one direction and me in another. They got us both gowned up and after a brief examination, settled into a private room. The doctor told us, "It won't be long now so let's get you prepped." Prentice just nodded and continued her breathing techniques. I continued holding her hand, wiping her face with a cool cloth and giving her ice chips for the next hour and a half. As if on cue, her doctor and several assistants entered the room announcing "It's show time." With that a flurry of activity followed. I was sort of jostled out of the way while tubes were attached and people moved into position to perform this surgical ballet. I remember instructions being given by the doctor to the nurses and from nurses to Prentice. I continued with my coaching, "Breathe Prentice" and the doctor saying "Alright give it one more push." A few minutes later I heard "I've got him" from the doctor. Then him handing Trey to a nurse who cleaned his nose and wiped his face. Soon after there was a cry of outrage in the tiniest of voices followed by the doctor handing Trey to me saying "*Heeeere's* Trey." Sounding a little like Ed McMahon. I held our little treasure wrapped in a blue blanket only briefly before placing him in Prentice's outstretched arms. Then the most amazing thing happened. As soon as she held him, kissed him and whispered how much she loved him, he stopped crying. Soon after he began breast feeding and opened his little eyes briefly catching sight of his mom.

Trey and Prentice bonded quickly and permanently. He was not perfect, what child is, but he grew up to be a fine young man. Unfortunately, while he grew up, Prentice and I grew apart. Our changing feelings had nothing to do with money, infidelity, or dislike of one another. The changes had more to do with the fact that without Trey we had nothing else in common and no basis to build a long term relationship on. Around his twelfth birthday, we decided to call it quits. We couldn't pretend anymore and it hurt too much to stay together in a loveless relationship. We talked to Trey together and separately and made sure he understood that he was number one in our lives and that nothing could change that. He is an amazing kid. He took both our hands and told us how much he loved us as a family, but we would all be alright just different. It was simple in his world and he was right. We would be alright.

I moved into my own place in Chicago and, a year later, to California when my job promoted me and transferred me to be branch manager of our Oakland location. Trey shuttled between us as often as he could. I tried not to miss the important events in his life and with few exceptions I didn't. We talked often and I came to town as frequently as I could. I saw his little league games and attended PTA meetings. I went on weekend camping trips with his Boy Scout Troop and helped sell tickets at his High School Basketball games. I went with him and Prentice on campus visits, we talked often about girls and sex, drugs and smoking. We talked about standing up for what's right and speaking out about what's wrong. Of course I was there to see him off to the Prom and at graduation. Somehow, through it all, Prentice and I remained friends. Trey was accepted at USC and Prentice planned to move her studio to LA so we were all going to be in California for a while.

After our separation and later our divorce, I spent most of my energy on raising my son. Sure, I dated a few women but, as one woman put it as our relationship came apart, as they all ultimately did, "You have a lot of unresolved things in your life. I truly enjoy being with you and when you are with me, I mean really with me, things are fine then. But sometimes we can be in the same room but you are emotionally somewhere else and that's not fair to me Eric. So when you are ready for a meaningful relationship, call me." That's what I heard time after time. So I stopped dating and concentrated on my career. The more successful I became in one, the more distant I became in the other.

I made my trips back east but they became more infrequent. I stayed in contact with my family, Eddie, Corrine and the twins. I sent gifts and attended gatherings when I could but I stayed out of Ronni's sphere. Of course I heard about her. I heard about her father's passing and sent flowers because I did not know what else to say or do. I heard about how successful she was in her career and her singing. I heard about her family and her dates but not in as much detail. I kept myself sequestered pretty much in my fortress of solitude. I found comfort in my martial arts and serenity in meditation. Somewhere along the way, I found myself again and started to feel good and confident.

****

CHAPTER 16

A NEW LEAF

My focus now was on family and my future. Anything outside of that became a distant third. For years following my father's passing, my siblings and I were careful to help my mom transition into life without dad around. My mom was remarkable. We knew she missed her bow-legged, quiet man. He always knew how to pull us all together with a quick phone call. Mom became our *Miss Ellie*, the glue that continued to make sure that this house, the *South Fork* that she and dad worked so hard for to get us out of the projects, remained the home, the refuge, the gathering place, for family functions and no-special-reason get-togethers. We continued the pot luck meals, cutthroat board game marathons and the football viewing frenzy.

It always amazed me and gave me pride to let people know not only had my mom, this Georgia belle, taught my dad everything there was to know about football, but would be the loudest voice holding a one-way conversation with

A Love Deferred

the television set, yelling at the coaches and players making what she considered wrong calls and costly mistakes on the field. I used to laugh when I thought what she wouldn't have given to spend just a minute with her favorite teams in the locker room to whip them into shape during halftime. And then, there was my family's notorious competitive spirit, fueled by both my parents, as we grew up. If you sat down at the game table with any Bradley, you had to be thick skinned. Whether it was a favorite board or card game, when we faced off against each other we, as I coined the phrase, "recognized no one as family or friends." Everyone was fair game. We were never mean-spirited in any competition, but we could tease you to no end if you were on the losing side. This exercise gave us some of the funniest and most memorable moments following some of the dark days, months, and for some, a bit longer, after Poppy died. There was always a method to my parents' madness. Word games like Scrabble, Upwords, and Boggle helped make us good spellers. Other games like Concentration and Connect Four sharpened our focus. And Monopoly helped us better understand the power of the dollar and the art of wheeling and dealing. These lessons weren't reserved exclusively for me and my siblings. As grandchildren became old enough to participate, my mom would engage them as well. One of my mom's funniest stories involved playing Connect Four with one of her 7 year old grandsons, who, once he saw she had the upper hand for the third straight time, pleaded, "Please don't win." My mom said her heart melted and she somehow lost the next five.

For years after Poppy's death, we came together for birthdays and most holidays during the spring and summer months. But without question, the turning of the leaves and the cool breezes of the Fall, only reminded us that November was nearing. This brought about a hollowness in all of us as we counted down the days, dreading the effort it would take to celebrate Thanksgiving. We began to find reasons, any excuse, to go a different way during that time, mostly because being in each other's presence left us all emotionally drained and mentally and physically exhausted. But little did we know that would soon change.

I continued my work at the health agency. It was a respite I needed following my father's passing. My colleagues and friends became the extended family I needed then. But even with the professional accomplishments I was making, I felt I needed other challenges, but couldn't quite put my finger on it until I received a call one spring day in 1989, from Patti Stevens, my mentor and dear friend. I met Patti when I was a senior in college. I interviewed her for a project and from the moment we met, we bonded. She was sophisticated, intelligent, approachable and generous. Following the interview, I stayed in touch with her, working on various projects under her direction. When I graduated from college, Patti offered me a position as her assistant, in a new public relations position she assumed with one of the then largest

African American owned radio networks. I learned a lot from Patti and she respected my input and ideas. We were a great team and her tutelage provided me a great foundation for building my professional career. We were more like sisters than employer and employee.

Even as I moved on to other positions, I always sought her valuable counsel. In 1989, Patti told me about a position in Long Island, New York that, she believed, had my name written all over it. It was a great opportunity, she said, for me to take a health campaign and put my signature on it – breathe life into it –mold it as I saw fit. The catch was I would have to move to Long Island. I took a big gulp when Patti told me that. Other than my two month internship in California during my senior year in college, I'd never been away from home, or the D.C. area, longer than a couple of weeks. This wasn't like any of those times. This required a real grown up Ronni Bradley to pull up stakes from familiar land, for at least a year, maybe longer, and establish a new home in unfamiliar territory. Patti must have heard the trepidation in my voice, but, like the true encourager that she was, urged me to step out of my comfort zone and, at the very least, interview for the position. I was single, with no dependents, and she convinced me that this was the perfect time to explore other options for my life. I arranged to drive up to Long Island with two friends on a Thursday and interviewed on Friday. I was instantly impressed and slightly intimidated by the spacious university campus, on which the job was

A Love Deferred

located. But most of those feelings dissipated when I met Dr. John Reiner, the head of the Transplant Department, a very soft spoken gentle man, with whom I connected immediately. He was Jewish, but his demeanor, and even some of his facial expressions, reminded me of my beloved Poppy. By the end of the interview, we could tell our conversation went beyond just knowing that our personalities complemented each other, but more importantly, a meeting of the minds for the mission at hand — to educate Long Islanders about organ donation and transplant. Within a week, I was offered and accepted the job.

The move entailed a lot of firsts for me. In my brand new car, I transported a thirteen inch television set, several of my favorite books and photos, and two suitcases of outfits and other necessities. I rented a room in the Long Island home of Rosa Cutler, the mom of a friend of mine from church, Philip Cutler. The house was a comfortable, split-level with four bedrooms, two baths, an eat-in kitchen, and combined living and dining room areas. There was a huge back yard. On one end surrounded by a tall fence, was a very colorful flower garden that attested to Mrs. Cutler's apparent green thumb. When you looked on the other end of the yard, you knew why the picturesque flower garden needed protecting. Two huge Great Danes pretty much ruled the remainder of the open space. While Mrs. Cutler said they were like big babies, I never journeyed into the back yard unaccompanied by either she or her teenage daughter, Leah, who still lived with her.

Philip told me that because Leah was so young when their father passed, he had assumed a surrogate father role. Even though I was much older when my father passed, I could understand how much of a help mate that must have been to his mom, and the void it must have left when he moved to the D.C. area with his wife a few years ago. But I also understood how the added layer of responsibility he assumed might have prevented Philip from taking full advantage of some of the good-humored life experiences that generally came during teen and young adult years. Philip could be very serious, maybe too, too serious, and could come off as the man with all the answers, which is why folks in church would generally appoint him as the "take charge" person when planning events. This could sometimes backfire when those same folks started complaining that their ideas and suggestions were not being heard. This was often Leah's main complaint about her big brother/father. Having a brother/father of my own, I understood her angst. As she grew into adolescence, she challenged everything Philip threw her way. But, true to her teen hood, one wouldn't expect anything different. I became the sometimes big sister to Leah while I stayed with the Cutlers.

The work at the Transplant Center presented me with a whole new challenge. I was responsible for developing a campaign that would enable us to demystify the purpose of organ donation and the process of transplantation. We wanted to let Long Islanders know how important it was to discuss this potentially life-saving issue with loved ones. I worked extremely close with Dr. Reiner and the other medical and administrative staff to build the campaign, detail by detail. One aspect addressed informing the medical community. We used, to our advantage, the scenic beauty and culinary talent that Long Island was famous for, planning a series of luncheon and dinner presentations for healthcare providers. Dr. Reiner and his medical team informed these doctors about the benefits of organ transplant. He also went the step further to train them on the sensitivities involved in approaching a prospective donor's family. While there was some resistance from the medical field, many were very receptive and wanted to know more. We conducted focus groups of Long Island residents to find out what they thought was good and bad about donating body parts. Here is where we received some of the most honest and insightful information, which we used to shape the campaign. One of the targeted groups I had to reach out to was African-Americans. Of all of the prospective donor groups on the Island, this particular segment of the population tended to need transplantation more, most likely because of the prevalence of diabetes and related problems – kidney failure and dialysis; but donated least. I called on my transplant contacts back in D.C. to help me develop a video that would reach out to African-Americans.

I was given the name of a family in the Midwest, whose loved one's fatal injury, confronted them with an organ donation decision. With video crew in tow, I flew to Chicago to interview the family of four that remained — mom, dad, and two adult sisters, who graciously allowed me into their lives, and home, to share their story. Although it had been nearly a year, retelling the events had them relive it almost as fresh as when it happened. It was a mother's worst fear – getting word that her son had been shot and then arriving at the hospital, only to be told that he was listed as "brain dead." This was a new concept to the mother, as well as her husband and daughters. Here they saw this young man lying in bed. They heard the heart monitors beeping, the hissing sounds from the breathing machine, but were also being told that he wasn't doing it on his own, rather, was only able survive because he was being assisted, one hundred percent by machines. While trying to process all of that, the family was confronted by a staffer who, without much introduction or explanation, asked if they would be interested in donating their son's and brother's organs. What followed next was outrage by the family at the impertinence of the staffer to ask that they share body parts to give to someone else to help them live, when they hadn't fully processed that this young man who laid before them was never coming back. What also followed were many intense and exhausting discussions among the family members, praying for a miracle, but also finally having to come to grips with the reality. After answers to endless questions regarding the process were provided by a more sensitive hospital staffer trained in counseling families regarding the ramifications of such a decision, and also after the family reached spiritual consensus, the decision to donate was made. It was a heart-wrenching account of love, life, death, denial, acceptance, and sharing that filled a full day of videotaping to capture their story. It was now up to me to tell it.

The crew and I returned to our downtown hotel late in the evening. I could tell from their faces that they were physically and emotionally drained. I know I was. I welcomed the thought of kicking off my shoes, ordering room service, and totally shutting down for the remainder of the evening. We had an early return flight to D.C. the next day to begin the pre-editing tasks. I had a self-imposed five-day turnaround on the finished product before returning to Long Island. There would be no rest for the weary.

We moved the equipment slowly through the hotel lobby. As we walked, the magnificent aromas from each of the three lobby-level restaurants seemed to follow us. We all looked at each other as if to say we were more than looking forward to dining in tonight. When an empty elevator became available, I hurried over to hold it while the others brought the heavy equipment on board. As I stood to the side and looked out, I could have sworn I saw a man, who was the spitting image of Eric Lewis coming out of the Italian restaurant. I remembered how much he loved Italian food. He was with two women – one about his age, and the other a little more matronly. I assumed it was Eric's wife and mother-in-law. Jessie told me of the loss of his father and son, the same year that I lost my dad. I thought it inappropriate to call during that time and sent a card instead. And prayers, my prayers were always with him. It was difficult to make out, through the crew's movements and from the distance, how warm this threesome was. It looked as if this Eric look alike, was hugging the younger woman, but I wasn't sure. They did all seem comfortable with each other. At one point as they continued to walk towards the hotel entrance, the look-alike started pointing around the lobby, as if he were commenting on the very distinctive architectural design, I thought he inadvertently pointed my way and wondered if he saw me. I don't think he did, and even if he did, so what? As they loaded the last piece of equipment on the elevator, we let the doors closed and pushed our floors. Maybe it was Eric, maybe it wasn't. I was too tired to process any kind of emotion I may have felt or anything else for that matter. Still emotionally spent from the day's events, I knew I was too tired to concern myself with it now.

I met my deadline, finishing the project and used it widely throughout Long Island. It had a poignant message and I like to think that it helped to inform and influence the way organ donation was viewed, not only on Long Island, but in other communities as well. We submitted the video to a national media competition and it took first place in community and health affairs. In eleven months I worked almost endlessly, feeling that what we did made a difference. My contract, and the funding for the project was ending in another month.

Even with the progress the program had made, the university's budget came seriously under attack and new programs were the first to go. Dr. Reiner attempted, unsuccessfully, to get the university to extend the project and the monies needed to retain my services for another year. I knew it was time to return home. I was to be there for a season, and that season had ended. I felt good about what I, what we, had been able to accomplish and promised to keep in touch with Dr. Reiner and the others when I returned home. Home. That sounded good. I had to admit that I missed it more than I had imagined I would. My new car was proof of that. In the year that I owned the car and lived on Long Island, I had taken a road trip to D.C. at least once, and sometimes, twice a month, logging more than 25,000 miles on Blessing, as I called the car, in less than 10 months. In the days before I left Long Island, Dr. Reiner, Mrs. Cutler, and the others I befriended while there, gave me a warm and touching sendoff. I would miss them all. I knew that I had grown from this experience was been able to attain a level of maturity, independence and confidence, over the past twelve months, that might have taken a bit longer, had I stayed in the comfort and safety of D.C. It was now time to go home and spread my new wings even wider.

With my newly acquired expertise, I took on the job as a consultant to a local transplant center in D.C., promoting and planning as I did in Long Island. It seemed a natural fit for me. It also provided me an occasional opportunity to stay in touch and work with some of my former colleagues in New York. Not long after, I landed a health communications position with a new federal agency, professionally doing what I liked to do best. I also jump started some of the activity I missed out on while in Long Island, including singing and working in my church. In the months I lived on Long Island, I only had the pleasure of playing host and tour guide to a few of my family and closest friends on a couple of occasions, so it was definitely a nice fit to be one-in-the-number on a more consistent basis now. It was especially nice to get back together with one of my main girls, Revae Wallace. We shared so many interests. Our passion included working with young people – infusing spiritual, educational, and moral lessons into creative ministry outlets such as plays, skits, and real down-to-earth rap sessions. We were both passionate about music – especially gospel music. We had both been part of a couple of short-lived gospel music groups and had talked about starting our own trio, with another one of our good friends, Victoria Harper, one of the *baddest* sopranos on this side of heaven. Revae and I were excited about adding the harmonic blend of alto and tenor, respectively.

We chose a name, **RVR**, that included the initials of our first names, Ronni, Victoria, and Revae. We agreed that, as a gospel trio, the group name would be better if it reflected the true meaning of our exalting. It didn't take long for us to agree that **RVR** should be the short title for **ReV'Rence**. We became a musical fixture with Pastor Thomas and our home

A Love Deferred

church, and a few other local fellowships and programs in the Metropolitan area. There was great freedom and release that took place in our ministering and we sought not to pigeonhole ourselves into any one particular vocal styling. We were amazed that, within a year after we began, there were talks of our recording, and not just a fly-by-night opportunity, but something solid and momentous. We decided not to rush this, but take the time to put all of if in place. Yes, this was our ministry, but recording and ultimately promoting the recording, would present us with an outreach opportunity that required spiritual savvy laced with a bit of business acumen that included good judgment, shrewdness, and insight. It seemed as if folks were knocking down our door to work with us. We chose to work with two dynamic sisters who Revae and I knew from our congregation, Laura and Grace Howard. They were not only highly motivated, and steadfast, but they also had some connection in the professional realm we sought.

Over the next several months, we met frequently and talked about perseverance and performance and product and packaging and positioning; but we always made sure we always included prayer. There was a lot of new stuff to learn and we wanted to take it one step at a time. Things appeared to be going quite well in the planning stage, until one fateful day. It started out as a regular coming together, meeting in one of the church's smaller classrooms. Revae, Victoria, and I were updating Laura and Grace on the status of the music project. After going through more than a few musicians, we had been blessed to find and work with an extremely gifted and talented keyboardist, with whom we connected almost immediately. This was a big hurdle we had successfully overcome. Generally, this would have been enough to get Laura and Grace excited. We came prepared to talk to the Howard sisters about a lot of other important things today. There were legal issues, of course, such as copyright and performance contracts down the road. And then there was a life-changing issue we needed to bring up too. But before we could do that, the three of us noticed there was something different in Laura and Grace's demeanor. They were strangely melancholy – an unusually quiet duo – something that made each of us take notice. Revae broke their silence. "Laura, Grace, is all ok? We thought you'd be overjoyed to hear how we've progressed. What gives?" Laura and Grace sat silent for another second, looking at each other, almost as if to signal who would be the spokesperson. It was Laura.

"Revae, Victoria, Ronni, I know we've been through a lot together these past several months working with you all. Certainly Grace and I have learned a lot about all the ins and outs and the myriad things that can go right and wrong in the recording industry. We know that there's no guarantee that people you work with, even in the gospel arena, won't try to do you wrong. We are grateful for how far we've been able to help bring RVR along. But,"...Laura looked at Grace first and then at the three of us as she said these next words, "We can't take you any farther." Laura and Grace sat motionless, with no more expression than they had previous to the announcement. Revae, Victoria, and I were stunned. Revae blurted out, "What are you talking about Laura?! When did all this come about and why now?!" Victoria jumped up, looked at me, then Revae, and shook her head in disbelief walking away from the table. I never stirred, but sat quietly, fixing my eyes on the sisters' eyes *[the eyes are the windows to the soul after all]*. Laura and Grace gave what might have been a somewhat plausible rationale for jumping ship with a different crew besides the three of us. By our standards, they were lame excuses — about a door opening for them on another idea they were working on before they came on board with us. It seems that it now called on them needing to spend more time developing that business plan.

"Liar!" Victoria shouted. "You could at least have the decency or the courage of your convictions to tell us the real deal. You owe us that much!" But in the next instant, Victoria said, "Forget it, I'm out of here," and stormed out of the room. "Vicky, wait!" Revae called after her, knowing she wouldn't. "Come on Ronni," she gestured, pointing towards the door. "It's over. Let's go get Vicky," she said as she too, departed hastily. Surprisingly, Laura and Grace never once moved or got up from their chairs. It was as if they anticipated our reaction – or at the least, most of it – and thought it better to remain as ambiguous as possible. I calmly and quietly got up from my chair, gathered my personal belongings, and the materials we shared with Laura and Grace and began to leave. But before I did, I turned and said, "Ok, the others are gone and I'll speak my peace. This isn't about new deals, but old sins." I looked at both of them. "You know, don't you?" They remained silent. "News sure travels fast within these so-called sacred walls," I said a bit sarcastically. "I only found out for sure a week ago. The real tragedy here is that from your non-response, I can tell that you two already see my being pregnant as some sordid end. True, I may not have gone about it the way that God intended it to happen, but I'm taking responsibility for my behavior. What I carry inside me doesn't translate to a death sentence—it's life.

Grace spoke. "Ronni, look. I'm sorry. We just thought it best not to get too involved and..." I cut her off. "And that's the sad part Grace, because now would actually be the best time to get involved. At least that's what my Bible teaches. I looked at Laura. "Yours read differently?" I paused. "God has already offered His grace and a fresh start, but not an easy one. He isn't kicking me to the curb." Turning to Grace, I said, "Maybe you should try to live up to your name a little better, huh?" I grabbed the door knob and turned to them again. "You know, you could have come to me before dropping the bomb on my friends the way you did, and even given us all a chance to talk about how we would handle it. Even if you decided to walk after that, I'd have more respect for you than I do now. Tell you what. I'll close the door behind me. Out of sight, out of mind." As I walked out of the church I saw Revae and Victoria at the car. We needed the long group hug that followed. Tears flowing, we affirmed that our number three was powerful and promised not to let this test ruin what was already ours to get – with or without the Howard duo.

For several months following after, we continued to sing in the area. Eventually, the traveling to and from rehearsals and programs, on top of my work schedule, and other commitments, became a physical and health challenge for me. Now in my 30's, I was considered a high risk pregnancy, and I didn't want to chance losing this blessing, and I didn't want to stand in the way of Revae and Victoria pursuing their dreams. *ReV'Rence* decided to disband. Something like this is never easy to work through. But there were those with whom I would now find out were truly in my corner. There would be my family, friends like my singing sisters, and, of course, Jeffrey.

Jeffrey Boyd was at least ten years my junior, but to look at both of us, you couldn't tell. It was my youthful appearance and vitality that was always a draw for younger men. Usually I would gently reject their advances, but with Jeffrey it was different. We met while working on a creative project that Revae and I were co-directing for an area theater group. Jeffrey could be serious one minute, and have me in stitches the next. He was a talker and I found his conversation and his observations fascinating. I liked the way his mind worked and his body moved. It was evident he worked out. Jeffrey had a maturity and a wild side about him that brought it out of me as well. Like the time I surprised him late at night at his place. Without going into detail, I will say lambskin leather, plush velour, and three-inch heels were involved. He had great moves – was smooth, and I'm sure he could challenge, and beat, anyone who tried to out-dance him. But aside from all of that, I liked his inner strength. He didn't appear to be fake. He reflected a real desire to find something more meaningful in his life, and he chose me to be part of it.

Ours was a whirlwind romance. We dated heavily. We talked nonstop. We taught each other new and different things. There were times when the age difference and our stubbornness became a sore spot, but never enough to split us up. We still seemed to bring out the best in each other. Almost a year into our relationship, I became pregnant. Funny thing is, I think we both knew date, time, and place when it happened. I was extremely troubled at first; wondering how I would tell my mom, my pastor, my friends, my coworkers; wondering what the advent of a baby on the way meant for Jeffrey and me; wondering how it would look to others. Nothing was set in stone. Nothing that is, except the fact that in about seven months, I would give birth to a new life. The months leading up to Mark's birth had its ups and downs. Physically, I was healthy as a horse. Emotionally and spiritually, I had my moments. I thanked God for the awesome blessing of being able to nurture a life inside of me. But after awhile, I found myself questioning God, seeking answers to why those who so openly professed their love and service *to* Him, were now working so hard behind my back to oust me from service *for* Him. It is amazing how miserably most people fail the litmus test for friendship when faced with things that make them uncomfortable. And my pregnancy did just that. Before I got pregnant, some were singing my praises to a fever pitch. After word of my pregnancy was out, the tide changed dramatically. While I didn't expect it to be smooth sailing, I had to admit that there were a few curve balls thrown my way that caught me totally off guard. When I finally opened my eyes and heart, I discovered that there were people, waiting in the wings, who I knew would be there, unconditionally.

Jeffrey was remarkable during these months. We spoke with Pastor Thomas openly about the baby, our responsibilities, and plans for our future. Jeffrey and I loved each other and there was talk of our marrying, but we wanted to make that decision when it was right for us, not just because concerned, well-meaning folks around us thought it best. Our seven pound, twelve ounce arrival came early one Friday morning in late November. It was a boy. He was perfection personified in our eyes. We named him Mark. Born five years to the day that Poppy passed, we gave him my dad's middle name, Alan. I saw the gleam in his eyes as I held him in my arms and knew that some part of my dear dad was definitely still with me. Jeffrey and I took pride in everything that Mark did, anxious to share photos and stories of his development, over the first five years, with all our loved ones. Jeffrey was a natural with Mark. He wasn't afraid to squeeze, hold, feed, change, and bounce him around. As Mark got a little older, he took extra care to teach, toughen, and discipline him. Jeffrey was man enough to show his soft side when he broke into tears on special occasions, such as watching him perform in a play, or practice with the other children at the martial arts school his godparents ran.

It was one Christmas Day when Jeffrey proposed marriage, and I accepted. It appeared to be the right time and the right decision, but within months, ours became a troubled relationship, unraveling right before our eyes. Whatever foundation we were building on prior to, and since Mark's birth, seemed to be riddled with cracks and faulty framework. We loved Mark, loved each other, but something was so wrong with the latter relationship. Maybe we should have cried out to each other instead of raising our voices in anger and frustration. We both dealt with personal and professional challenges. What came so natural with Mark didn't spill over between the two of us. Our ineffectiveness to make it work began to affect how we related to Mark. Eventually, it began to make Interactions involving our son really ugly at times. The counseling we started before Mark was born had long since ended. I suggested we start up again, but we never did. At some point, it became clear that even counseling didn't appear to be an option that held any hope for us.

A Love Deferred

We called off the engagement. For a time, we retreated to the respective corners of each of our worlds, for much needed healing and regrouping – me, to the solace of my two-bedroom apartment and Mark; Jeffrey to his place in D.C., and eventually a move back to his hometown in South Carolina. The good news was that eventually we came to a meeting of the minds, or maybe more accurately, the hearts, where our anger, our disagreements, our negative dealings, converted to healthier experiences, when we both realized that our love for and commitment to Mark was our primary focus in working together. It hasn't always been an easy task and it is a lifelong process, but thank God for where we are now.

CHAPTER SEVENTEEN

SWEET REUNION?

I laid down to rest for a few moments in my hotel room knowing that nothing was planned for this evening so a brief rest before heading to visit family members would be okay. Now I needed to rest my eyes and body it only for awhile. I woke up at about 8:00 p.m., washed up, shaved and got dressed. I got my car from the hotel parking lot and headed to my sister's house, gifts in hand. Since she lived in the Northwest part of the city, it only took me about 20 minutes to drive the 12 miles to her house at that time of night. I rang the doorbell and Puddles, her adopted Heinz 57 variety dog, began barking like crazy all the while backing away from the door. Next I heard my 11 year old niece, Gwen, ask through an intercom, "Who is it?" I answered, "It's your coolest, most hippest, most favoritest uncle in the whole wide world." I heard her, without benefit of the intercom scream "It's Uncle Eric, It's Uncle Eric!" The next thing I knew my pretty young niece flew out of the door and into my arms. "Hi Uncle Eric. Mom says you brought me some more money for my collection. Can I see, can I see?" she said in one breath. I answered, "By the way it's good to see you too cutie pie." "Uncle Eric, I'm Sweetie Pie. Shauna is Cutie Pie," She corrected. Shauna my niece, Gwen's older sister. was on a field trip with her school in Europe and one should never be confused for the other. "Oops, I'm sorry. You see when you get to be my age..." My sentence was cut short when my brother in-law grabbed me and picked me up off the ground in his customary hug. He was a big bear of a man but would never hurt even a fly unless provoked. "Hey man" I laughed "Put me down what would the neighbors think." We both laughed as he said "Come on in man. I just put some steaks on the grill." "Now that's what I am talkin' about." I put my arm around my niece's shoulders and walked inside their house.

Like a lot of the houses in D.C. proper, it was of older construction on the outside. But once inside you could see the extensive reconstruction that went into this house. More importantly you could feel the welcoming spirit of family once you stepped inside. That is if you don't count Puddles who just growled at me. "Jenny's on her way home now. Come on out to the patio and keep me company" my brother-in law Gary said. "Man you would have thought the president of the United States was coming to town with all the fixing up that has been goin' on around here. You want a beer?" "No thanks" I answered. "That's right you don't drink. Sorry

Man." Gary apologized. "No need, brother. I will take a cola if you got one." My niece happily dipped her hand into the ice bucket and pulled out two colas when my brother-in law cleared his throat and asked "And who is that second cola for?" Gwen shrugged her shoulders and said "Oh dad." "Oh dad nothin' girl. Put that soda back. I am not going to see all that pretty skin ruined by pimples." After handing me my soda and putting hers back she huffed back inside the house. "And no candy either" my brother-in law yelled after her. "She's getting to be a handful" he said almost apologetically. "Yes well she gets it legitimately from her mother" I said. "You got that right" Gary said and we both laughed. "What are you two laughing about and why is Gwen pouting in the TV Room?" my sister Jenny asked while coming over to give me a hug and her husband a kiss. "You know how it is Babe. I had to put my foot down" Gary answered. "Uh-huh" she said. "More likely you got your foot stomped on" Jenny retorted. "Ouch baby sister, why you got to be so cold." Gary said "Forget it man. I am a minority in my own household. Anyway dinner is ready." We went inside and got plates and glasses ready to do a buffet at the dining room table.

After washing our hands and saying a short prayer we got seated around the table and dug in. We got caught up on family business and Gwen told us all about how school was going. I asked her about boys and instead of the "Eeww" response I got the last time I asked that question she said there were some nice boys in her class. Jenny said "She means

Gregory. Eric that boy is like a puppy dog that follows her home, carries her books, wants to go to the movies, anything to be near her." "I see" I said. He sounds a lot like me with Cathy Bennett. Remember her?" "Oh Lord, I had forgotten all about her," Jenny laughed. "What ever happened to her?" I asked. "The last time I saw her she was living in Maryland, married with a couple of kids. She did ask about you though." We talked until past midnight when Gary said, "Listen I would love to stay and chat some more with you guys but I am about to crash so, I'm going to take Gwen upstairs and go to bed. Jenny, don't keep your brother up talking all night either." Gary picked Gwen up and carried her upstairs just like I had seen him do so many times in the past. "So now that it's just the two of us, how are things going?" Jenny asked. I told her I was doing fine. I gave her a quick update on how my company was doing and how Trey was enjoying school. "Child, I remember when that boy was a baby. Now look at him. He's all grown up. Now how is Prentice doing?" She asked. I answered by saying "We talk frequently and we visit Trey together on campus. I think she's dating someone but I'm not asking anyone to find out. If she is that's good. She deserves to be happy." I added. "And you don't?" Jenny asked. "Now I don't mean to pry but it's going on five years since you two divorced."

I started to interrupt but Jenny went on "Hold on a minute just let me say my piece." I relented and shrugged my shoulders as she went on. "Since your divorce, you've gone out with some nice people but you really have shown no interest in dating. Are you still holding a flame for her?" "Now can I speak?" I asked. "You may" she answered in a lawyerly voice. "Prentice will always be special to me and I know exactly what I lost when we divorced. I am not looking to replace her. I will know it when I see the right person." "So what about Ronni?" my sister asked looking directly into my eyes. I looked at my watch and said "Man, I didn't know it was this late. I have to go. You know they lock up hotels at night and..." "Uh huh. You have just answered my question," Jenny said. "You can run but you sure can't hide Eric Lewis." I got to my feet and Jenny walked me to the door. "Will we see you any more this weekend?" "I will see you on Sunday for church" I answered. I went on by saying, "Listen Jenny, I really don't know what's going on with me. I'm not trying to be evasive about your questions, I just don't know. And Ronni, well she is a big question mark. Maybe some questions will get answered this weekend. I'm going to see her tomorrow; that is if she is still coming to the celebration." Jenny smiled and gave me a hug. I hope she does. You two have a whole lot of 'splaining to do." We laughed and I headed back to the hotel. Only I didn't go directly there. I drove to my high school football stadium and parked in the lot. From there I had a clear view of the mall with the Washington Monument on my right and the United States Capitol closer on my left. I got out, stretched on the hood of my rental and let my mind go free. What am I doing here?

A Love Deferred

How had so many things happened to complicate my life so? Where do I go from here? And what about Ronni? Since 1975 I had only seen Ronni a few times but each time was memorable. The first time was shortly after my divorce was final from my first wife. The last time was several years after my divorce from my second wife. I had planned to call her but as it turned out she called me. I was at work when I received the call from Ronni who was coming through Chicago on business. I remember it as if it were yesterday.

****

I was working late in my Chicago office when the phone rang. I wasn't expecting any calls but sometimes our West Coast Office or Asian clients called after hours. "Good evening this is Eric Lewis can I help you?"

****

"That depends." Upon recognizing my voice Eric answered "Ma'am if this is a prank phone call I'll have to direct you to security." "Well, if you need security to help you deal with me, this was a wasted dime, Mr. Lewis," I said laughing. "Oh, since you went there Ms. Bradley, I'd better handle you as one of my special clients," Eric said laughing. "Hi Ronni. What a pleasant surprise," he continued. "I didn't really know if I would reach you Eric. I took a chance on catching you there. I actually expected to get your voicemail. "I'm almost embarrassed to tell you that I've been in town for the past 24 hours and about to move on to my next stop in Wisconsin. "

****

"Well, you should be embarrassed," I said, trying to sound offended, but not believable. "I'm glad you caught me now. I'm putting the final touches on a presentation I'm giving tomorrow. I was just about to leave, but glad now that I didn't. Since this sounds like a drive-by call, what's up? Of course if you had called 12 hours earlier, we could have had dinner last night. We could have..."

"You see that's what I was afraid of," I said. "It's all those could haves that lead to shouldn't haves when we get too comfortable, and you know where that generally leads don't you Mr. Lewis?" As if he was totally unawares, Eric asked, "Where?" "Yeah, right Eric. In one word, Nowhere!" Look Eric I really didn't call to talk about that right now. Truth is, I thought I might hitch a ride with you to the airport. Can you help a sister out?" "Sho' Miss Ronni. Eric be driving you to the airport quick as you please. Yowsuh." I could hear Ronni bursting out laughing. It was good to hear her laugh because it was always infectious. When she regained some of her composure, she gave me the address to her hotel and said she would be waiting for me outside. I went to the garage, retrieved my car and drove to the hotel. Fifteen minutes later I was sitting outside the Hyatt Regency Chicago waiting for Ronni Bradley. I knew, from past experience that when she said she would be waiting for me outside actually meant she would be in the general vicinity of outside. While waiting for Ronni, I checked myself out in the rear view mirror. I scraped my comb through my salt and pepper, mostly salt, hair and a couple of times through my mustache. I reached into my glove compartment and put two dots of Fahrenheit cologne on each cheek and checked my shirt collar. When I finished checking myself and turning the interior light off, I looked out of the front windshield just in time to see Ronni stepping out of the hotel. I noticed some guy talking to her and the two of them laughing about a joke they shared but all I could think was there she is. Tall and fine as ever in a tailored pants suit. She wore conservative and probably comfortable low heeled shoes and had her hair in a short perm cut that accented her brown skin and eyes. I got out of my car and leaned against the hood looking at her. She spotted me and we walked to meet each other. Instead of a handshake, hug, kiss or any combination thereof, I stretched out my hand and said "Here, let me take your bags." I quickly added "You look great. Who was that dude?"

****

A Love Deferred

"Thanks. You look good too. And that *dude* was Dr. James Whitney one of the key presenters at my meeting today." I squeezed Eric's arm, "Hmmm….looks like you've been taking care of yourself I see." He told me that he was working out regularly and cutting back on bad food, which meant a lot of comfort food. "Cuz you know," he added, "when you get to be my age…." I cut him stating emphatically, "Mr. Lewis, I will never get to be your age, you're 2 months older, remember. But that's a subject for another day. We both laughed. "If we're going to sit down and relax a bit, we should leave for the airport now, don't you think? My flight leaves in about two hours and I thought it would be nice to catch up, if only for a little bit. You game?"

****

"Aren't I always where you're concerned?" I said slyly. Ronni playfully jabbed me in my side with her elbow. I feigned injury. "Watch me work my driving magic and show you why they call this the windy city. Besides, I know the perfect place at the airport where we can sit down in relative quiet and be served quickly and the food ain't half bad either. "How do you rank?" Ronni probed. I pulled out a gold travel card. "Just one of the rewards when you're a frequent business traveler, which I am," I said. "Cool. Let's rock and roll," stepping up her stride to the passenger side. We arrived at O'Hare, parked and got to the airport restaurant in record time. After catching our breath, we talked. She told me that her job with the government health agency was rewarding and just by the way she talked about what she was doing, I could feel the passion she had for her work. I told her about my divorce and what I had been doing to stay close to my son.

****

Before Eric could say another word, I reached into my purse, pulled out my wallet and propped a wallet-sized photo of a smiling little boy in front of him and said, "That's my heart. A spirited, kindergartner named Mark." Confused, Eric asked, "How? When? Who?" I couldn't resist an open line like that and responded, laughing and saying, "Surely, Mr. Lewis, I would think you, of all people, would know how. Didn't you pass biology?" He was a bit flustered and said "I didn't mean…Ronni, you know what I mean." "Do I?" I asked smiling. I gave him the abbreviated version of Mark's father, Jeffrey, and my relationship.

****

I told Ronni that I had spoken to our mutual friend, Jessie, on her birthday a few months earlier and that my oldest brother was turning 55 this year. I was still jolted by the fact that Ronni had a son and in all the times over the past two years I had spoken with Eddie he never once mentioned it. I guess one of those head doctors would probably say I was more focused on the fact that I wasn't the father, more than anything else. Who knows? I wanted to talk to Ronni more, ask more questions but we both noticed that time was slipping away and we needed to get to her gate. As we walked through the terminal we talked more about how she and her family were doing since the death of her father. The crack in her voice as she told the story let me know that, even now, this was still an emotional topic for her to discuss. By the time we got to her gate, they were announcing that her flight would be boarding shortly. "You see" she said. "It's like the song says a taste of honey is worse than none at all. Just when the conversation was getting good." "I know what you mean," I agreed. "Well we'll just have to pick up from here when I get to D.C. next month." "Next month, really?" she asked. "That suddenly seems like a long way off," she said while she gathered her bags. "Come on. I'll walk you to your gate." I took her rolling bag. When we arrived, people were already boarding the commuter flight to Wisconsin and they were calling for all rows to board.

****

"I guess that means me." As I looked at Eric, he took me in his arms and we gave each other a huge hug. The next thing I know, our lips found each other. I think we both realized at the same time, how much of a release this was for us and as passionately as he was kissing me, I was kissing him back. This type of thing is so common in airports, that we must have been oblivious to those walking pass us and even the ticket taker. It really didn't matter to me or to him. At least twice during our goodbye, I felt my legs go totally limp and Eric holding me tighter. I never once lost my balance in his arms and knew I was secure, at least for now.

****

When we parted, I stood there shaking my head, saying "So you're just gonna leave a brother like this?" (With the unsaid wanting more, again). She said, "Well, you know, this plane has at least one more shuttle going to my destination tonight?" I told her that as much as I wanted to, I couldn't make it happen then. "Maybe next month we can finish what we started," I said. "Next month, or even tomorrow is not promised, Brother Lewis," she added. "Oh well, as the old song says See You in September," she said as she turned to hand the gate agent her ticket. She adjusted her carry on bags in her hand and started to walk down the walkway. Before she was totally out of sight, she took one last look over her shoulder, blew a kiss and with a wave she was gone. I stood in the gate area for a few moments, blood still racing to my head, wishing I could meet her in Wisconsin, but knew I still had a lot of work to do and nobody volunteering to do it for me. I watched her plane taxi away and then I left the airport. Next month could not come soon enough.

****

The next several weeks went by quickly. Eric and I spoke occasionally, but shared a lot more in the emails we exchanged, once or twice a week. As I shared more about my son and our exploits, such as trips to kiddie theme parks, museums, and book readings for children (he loved books), Eric said he felt as if he had already befriended Mark. It may have been moreso because of the fact that I told him that Mark was born five years to the day Poppy passed, and shared my belief that somehow, someway, a part of daddy definitely still lived on in him. Eric said he could tell that fact was reassuring to me, and then went on to tell me that just between me and him, it was just a little unnerving for him. I found that so funny. I told him that I had sacrificed much for Mark and would do it all again without a moment's hesitation. As we wrote, we both learned about our walks with God and how He stood by both of us during our trying times.

****

I knew that Ronni was more in-touch with her spirituality than me, regularly attended church services, enjoyed being active in her church choir and also just hanging out and talking to other members, who, like her, were crazy, fun-loving, and transparent too. I told her that my life pretty much revolved around work, and a lot of that was traveling, which was the reason I pushed back our reunion for another three weeks. I also told her that I was almost a little envious of the everyday contact she had with Mark, living under the same roof. I was crazy about my son. Generally, when I wasn't traveling, I wanted to be close to him as much as I could. He was now fifteen, and living with my ex-wife on the north side of Chicago. He was a rock for her. In many ways he did the things I should have done for her when we were married. He sensed when she needed to be hugged, he called to tell her he was alright when he was with me, he took out the garbage, cleaned his room, did his homework, and all with no questions asked. Most of all, he made her number one in his life and showed it everywhere, anytime to anyone. I wish I could have been more like him, but I live with the hope that it's not too late. I had also returned to my study of martial arts several years ago and like work, it kept me very busy. There was constant practice and tournaments to show what I learned. I had gotten quite good and was making a name for myself in the circuit. It was a part of me that I did not share with anyone, but it was a part of me.

****

I told Eric that I had been part of a trio called *ReV'Rence* for a while, did a bit of solo singing around the Washington area, and had recently declined an offer to join a well-known local recording artist, as a backup singer, because the travel schedule up and down the East Coast would take me away from Mark for longer periods than I was ready to commit to. We talked about past relationships and what we learned from them, we also talked about sex and sensuality and how conflicting it became for young, single, Christians. We delved into what the Bible said about it and how most people justified having sexual relations out of wedlock by invoking the words love and commitment and the all too misunderstood line, "God knows my heart," to absolve them of their behavior.

****

All of that rang hollow somehow when I looked at my past relationships, almost too many to count. Ronni, on the other hand, had been more selective in her life, but still dealt with the challenges we were discussing. We wrote about loneliness and longing. We also wrote about despair and prosperity. We talked about how we felt about each other and although the word love was never spoken, I felt it was very near and knew that fear was what kept us from saying it aloud.

****

About a week before Eric's visit, he called me. Nothing in our conversation was out of the ordinary. We shared a few funny stories; he asked about the long-term forecast; and we talked about our sons, of course. Just as I could tell the conversation was wrapping up, Eric got real silent – for only a moment, but it just seemed longer. "You okay Mr. Lewis?" I asked. No response. "Eric, why so quiet? What's up?" Finally, his silence lifted. "Ronni, I love you." I couldn't speak. Those words opened the floodgates and I began to cry. "Ronni, did I say something wrong? Why are you crying?" he asked concerned. "Eric," I said sobbing, "You don't know how long I wanted to tell you that I love you too." "Good night Sweetie Bradley. See you soon." "Good night, Eric." As I fell back on my sofa, I played those three words in my heard over and over again.

****

As my visit to D.C. came nearer, I got a call from Ronni one night. "Hello Eric," she said, sounding a bit weary on the other end of the phone. "Hi Ronni. What are you doing up this late? I quickly asked is anything wrong?" I couldn't quite pinpoint her frame of mind when she said, "Nothing is wrong, well maybe there is." Her voice changed and she said, "I think it's cold feet." She continued, "Eric we've started and stopped our relationship so many times that I can't help feeling a little reserved about your coming here. I want us to be honest with each other now about expectations." I heard something in her voice that I hadn't heard before – a fear, an anxiousness, whatever it was, I could tell this was her time to get it out. "Ronni, I'm listening. Talk to me, please?"

****

"Maybe I've internalized this fantasy about our relationship that perhaps made it more that what you may have believed it to be, Eric. Maybe that's why I seem to be on the short end of the stick with our starts and stops." Frustrated I said, "Look, maybe this call was a mistake. I guess I am just a bit leery to get too close to you again because if our history is any indication, I will end up getting hurt again."

****

While Ronni was talking I kept thinking about the old expression about flying that says, "It's not the flying part you have to worry about. It's the take offs and crash landings that should keep you up at night." As Ronni spoke I could see the truth of that old axiom in our relationship. Things worked smoothly when we were talking about easy stuff like family, friends, books, movies and music. It also helped when you are hundreds of miles apart and talking by phone or email.

But when it got to the tough stuff, like emotions, relationships and the future, I always started to fade away. It all reminded me of my father. The one who didn't know how to be around when things got tough. When I found my voice I said, "Ronni, all I expect of this weekend is a start. Because if we don't get a fresh start, we will never know what the end's going to be. The only thing that will sustain us to the end is building a foundation based first on friendship and trust, then love. I expect this weekend to be a time of discovery. First we have to find out if we can tolerate being in each others presence for three days and nights," I said lightheartedly. I could hear her laugh a bit on the other end of the line and hoped that her nerves were eased somewhat. "Most of all we have to see if the fantasy you talked about is just that or is it real this time. Does this sound like something we can work on this weekend Sweetie?" Ronni said yes. I said "Good then we will have something to do besides kissing and hugging and…" "Now see Eric," Ronni reacted. "I was just kidding," I said. "But I do want us to have fun this weekend as well. Deal." "Deal," Ronni responded. Yawning, I said, "Now go get some sleep and I will talk to you tomorrow. You got me up way past my bed-time."

****

I couldn't fight back the yawns either. "That's right, Eric, you do need your sleep. After all, you are much older than I."

"Yeah, very funny,"he said. "Two months does not equate to much, Ms. Bradley." "Maybe not in your book, but in mine, brother," I added. "But hey, I'm just having a little late night fun, sir." I said, not able to contain my laughter. I mellowed out and said, "Good night Eric. I want you to know when you show up next week, I'll turn the porch light on for you." Eric said he was a bit puzzled because he knew I didn't live in a house and the light on the patio was nowhere near my front door. I went on to tell him how, growing up, my father would always turn the porch light on for me and my brothers and sisters when it was time to come in. It was such a regular practice that almost everyone who lived in the neighborhood came to know that signal and would pass the word along if we didn't see it, to let us know our dad wanted us home. I told him how it embarrassed my older siblings at first, but after awhile, it was just something we were used to seeing. I told him that bright light shining was as good as a welcome mat any day. "Thanks for sharing that Sweetie," he said. "I'll certainly look out for it." "Good night, Eric."

****

I didn't go to sleep for another hour after we hung up. I had to look deep inside myself and ask the questions that needed to be answered this weekend. What was really keeping the two of us apart? Is it something about me that makes relationships fail? Will I disappoint Ronni again?

Should I not go and save us both the misery? All questions I needed to think about. Somewhere between asking the questions and finding answers, sleep clubbed me and dragged me away like a caveman. The next morning I woke up sitting in the chair I started thinking in last night. The really bad part was, I was no closer to the answers than I was before I fell asleep. The caveman didn't help. Not one little bit.

****

Friday arrived and wouldn't you know it, thunderstorms rumbled across Chicago and delayed all flights. My plan was to get to D.C., get my rental car, check into the hotel and surprise Ronni at her job. We could go have some dinner and I could take her home where we could continue our conversations. But the weather wasn't cooperating. After a two hour delay, our flight taxied onto the tarmac where the pilot announced we were number 30 in line. Luckily, I had my New York Times Crossword puzzle book. Unfortunately, I had plenty of time to work on them.

****

I arrived in D.C. at about 4:30 p.m. Too late to pick up Ronni and right in the middle of rush hour. After getting my bag and finding my rental car, I drove to my hotel in Georgetown, checked in and relaxed for awhile. According to plans we made I was to go to Ronni's, always assuming I could find her apartment in suburban Maryland, and pick her up for dinner. We also planned some sightseeing on Saturday and maybe a picnic in the afternoon and dinner in the evening. All of this was under the radar of my family. If they got any idea that I was in-town without visiting, I was a dead man. So this was our weekend. Ronni and Eric. Finally.

****

It was Friday, the start of Labor Day Weekend, the last official hurrah for the summer. Eric would be arriving in a few hours, and I was poised to greet him - hair freshly coiffed, manicure and pedicure in tact, new outfit (because nothing old in my closet would do), and wearing Caroline Herrera, a fragrance that would take us both back, but not too far. All was in place, but as I took stock of myself, even with all the attention to detail I had so carefully done, there was one thing clashing —I was sporting a crutch.

Forty-eight hours ago, I received what I thought was a mosquito bite on my left foot. I experienced slight swelling, but this was generally my body's response to things like this, whether I did anything to aggravate it or not. Generally, my father's old home remedy of a palm full of table salt, rubbed vigorously on the spot, would decrease the itching and gradually, any other allergic reaction, such as swelling, within a few hours after application. But twenty four hours later, while the itch was gone, my foot resembled that of a Sumo wrestler, and in addition to the throbbing, writhing pain when I applied any weight to it, I now had "foot fever." A visit to one of the area hospital's emergency room deduced that I had a severe allergic reaction to a bee sting. So, here I was looking like Miss Ebony Fashion Fair from my head to the top of my foot, and looking like the Hulk from my ankle to the tip of my toes. But, I thought, maybe if I dazzled Eric, he wouldn't notice it. All I could think of was a line from my dad's favorite sport, "game called on account of rain." Maybe I should have called him yesterday to let him know what was up. Sure, it would have been less than 24 hours notice to change his reservations, if he so chose, but I didn't even give him that option. Truth is, I wanted to see him, no matter what my physical condition. I laughed to myself as I thought that, the only position I would probably assume this weekend was my foot propped up somewhere.

It was now Friday evening. I had only worked half a day to give myself plenty of time to prepare. Eric would be arriving at my home in less than an hour, having already checked in to his hotel. When he called en route from his hotel to my apartment, I felt my pulse rushing a bit. It had been some time since our paths purposefully crossed, and, after all, we'd been through a lot, both individually and collectively. Since the death of our beloved family members, Eric's divorce, and my breakup with my fiancée, we kept in touch off and on. Over the years, we were always challenged to define our connection - sometimes soul mates, or two people who could easily finish each other's sentences and thoughts, often determining that for some things, we appeared to be cut from a mold that was familiar and complementary. Whatever it was, we did not stray from each other's lives for too, too long. And now, Eric was arriving soon, and as I picked up the phone and heard his voice, I realized soon was sooner than even I expected.

****

After eating a quick snack, I washed up, brushed my teeth and combed my hair. At 7:30, I got in my car and headed to Maryland. I got directions from a gas station attendant once I crossed the state line and ended up in the parking lot of her apartment complex. The buildings were neat colonial style buildings, none over three stories tall. Judging by her apartment number Ronni's was either on the first floor or Garden level. I found her building and as I got to the door a couple was leaving, so I just walked in. I found Ronni's apartment on the garden level and knocked on the door. After knocking twice, I worried that maybe I read the number wrong or maybe I was in the wrong building. I was about to walk away when I heard, "Who is it?" from the other side of the door. Heart racing I answered "Hi Ronni, it's me. Eric." I heard locks being opened and the door being left slightly ajar. I stepped into the cozy, tastefully decorated

A Love Deferred

living room to take in the sight of Ronni standing there in a nice sun-dress with a short jacket. I closed the door behind me and said, "You look wonderful and your place is great." "Ronni looked at me appraisingly and said "You look pretty good yourself." Awkwardly I said, "Thanks. Is it alright if I just give you a hug?" "I don't see why not. I won't bite you know," she said smiling. "Actually, that might not be a bad thing," I responded quickly. Ronni hit me playfully on my arm as I gave her a hug and a kiss.

We pulled apart knowing that any longer and our body chemistry would kick in and we'd never get to that dinner or anything resembling conversation. Ronni let out a little hiss of pain. I asked "What's wrong." Her response was not what I expected. She said "I got stung by a bee and..." She pointed to her left foot and I said, "Wow! Are you okay?" She told me she was better, but the swelling had caused occasional throbbing in her leg. "That's why it took me so long to get to the door when you knocked." I then realized that I was so focused on her face when I came in, that I never noticed her foot. "Maybe you should just sit down and relax and we can order in," I offered. "I will rest in a minute but would you like something to drink first?" I said no, but offered to get something for her instead. Seems neither one of us was very thirsty, so we prepared to leave. Ronni, determined to show that she was still mobile, insisted on getting the crutch from her bedroom herself. "You can keep talking while I get my crutch. I can hear you." As she limped off to her

A Love Deferred

bedroom I asked "Where is your son?" "He's with his grandmother this weekend," she replied. "My sister picked him up earlier today." "I'm sorry I'll miss him this trip but I have something in the car I think he'll like," I said. "What's that?" Ronni asked. "I'll tell you as long as you promise to keep it a secret," I answered. She hobbled back into the living room and said "I promise," motioning as if she were zipping her mouth. "It's a Chicago Bulls, Michael Jordan jersey" I said proudly. "It's one of those collector's edition jerseys." "I'm sure he'll like it" Ronni said. "He likes anything that has to do with MJ." "Well it looks like you'll have to give the jersey to him for me." I added as Ronni put on a light jacket. As we headed out the door Ronni said, "I think it will mean more to him if you gave it to him personally." "I know what you mean," I responded as we headed down the steps toward my rental car. "But for all practical purposes, it might be weeks before I could get back here and..." "Weeks? Really?" Ronni asked bleakly. "I'm afraid so" I said starting the car's engine and pulling out of my space. Noting Ronni's response and trying to put a positive spin on my comment I added, "It's not easy for me to get away but I will get here much more often, just to see you." In the darkness of the night and the car's interior, it was hard to make out Ronni's expression. We drove toward D.C. in silence for awhile until it dawned on me that I didn't know where the restaurant Ronni mentioned was located so I did the next best thing. I took her to one of our old favorite restaurants. It was a little out of the way but well worth the effort for pasta.

After 30 minutes of driving, with sparse conversation, we found ourselves on Wisconsin Avenue in Georgetown. The restaurant was near the University. I saw Ronni give a little smile when she realized where we were going and felt her loosen up a little once we were seated in a booth by the window. The atmosphere was one that made you feel that there was no one else in the restaurant but you and your date, the candles, soft music, the smell of garlic cooking, and light conversation to complete the ambience. After getting comfortable Ronni said "This place sure brings back memories and it hasn't changed a bit." I agreed. "I've often wondered whether this place had survived all of the trendy new places erected downtown but I guess this answers my questions. After ordering some calamari and anti-pasta, we talked about how the city had changed since my last visit. Knowing Ronni's love of her Redskins, I decided to give her a few good-natured jabs about how far the mighty had fallen. She returned, quite nimbly, with a kettle-calling-the-pot-black retort about the Bears. We talked about why I didn't pursue my law degree and how she pursued her singing career, only in a very limited geographical area, which she felt necessary after she had Mark. When dinner arrived, Angel Hair Pasta with Scallops for her and Chicken Vesuvio for me, we finally talked about us.

****

I said, "You know as much as I wanted this weekend to come to pass, I'm still feeling that I need to protect myself. Long distance relationships are always draining, and your remark earlier about uncertainty regarding seeing each other again only adds to my concern about getting too involved with you Eric. You sounded like a salesman or a sailor with a girl in every port of call and I won't be that Eric, no matter how lonely I may get." Eric finished chewing his forkful of food and took a sip of water before responding. He looked at me through the candle light and said, "I came here this weekend with few expectations, and fewer promises. It seems that's what always gets us into trouble. I thought we would try and see if this is what we truly want or is it what everyone else wants for us?" I stated, a bit bothered, "I really am not interested in *everyone's* position Eric, just *yours and mine* — the two that really count. We are the only ones that can answer that and this is as good a time and place as any to start."

From that point to the end of dinner we asked and answered questions that only people who have known each other for a long time and whose deep interest in each other's lives could ask. Some of the questions were embarrassing, "How many women have you been with?" "Well how many men have you been with?" "When you had the baby, why didn't you and Mark's dad stay together?" "Well, I need to ask that same question regarding you and your former wife. And what about the other women you slept with? Are you sure none of them ever became pregnant?" "How is it that such a gorgeous, sensitive woman like yourself hasn't been swept off her feet by some other guy?" "Well, it's not like I've been placing myself as bait on the end of a fishing pole and throwing myself out in the dating pool. Once I'm interested in someone, my heart is pretty much spoken for, unless someone or something proves otherwise." Some of the questions were hurtful. They weren't meant to be but the honest responses opened up old wounds that only the truth could heal. It was one of the most insightful and absorbing conversations we'd had in a long, long time. After our "Truth Session," after we got all our emotion out in the open, we talked about how, since our meeting at the airport, all we could think about was each other. We both needed to determine whether the relationship that had been stirring for sometime now had, as its foundation, solid rock or sand. Love or lust? If we both wanted to be with each other, was the only thing stopping us – us? At that moment we decided to get out of our way and see where this new unearthing took us.

****

After paying for dinner, I told Ronni to wait in the entrance of the restaurant while I got the car. I could tell that

A Love Deferred

her leg was bothering her and I could save her a little pain by trotting off to the car and picking her up at the door. Besides the brisk walk give me the chance to walk off some of the pasta I just put away. Five minutes later I was back. I helped her into the car, turned on some music and took the long way back to her apartment. It was a beautiful, clear night for cruising and star gazing. We held hands and talked as I drove slowly to Ronni's. When we reached Ronni's door it dawned on me that this was it. This is the moment that we have waited over twenty years to reach. There were no interruptions, no inconveniences, no voices from above and no excuses. When we stepped into the quiet of her apartment, away from prying eyes there would be no road-blocks. In short, nothing to stop us from seeing where we would go from our conversation earlier in the evening and 20 years of longing and questions that needed to be answered.

****

After parking, Eric hurried around to the passenger side to help me out of the car. I was actually getting by pretty independently on the crutch, but decided to take full advantage of this extra offering of chivalry and followed his lead. I barely used the crutch to take the few steps to my place, deciding instead to rely on Mr. Lewis' strong arms, now providing a firm, but comforting brace.

****

I took Ronni in my arms and held her close for a moment before picking her up. She traced the line of the bicep on my right arm as if to check whether there was strength enough to hold her. After reassuring her that I could and there was, she rested her head on my shoulder while I took the few steps to her sofa and laid her gently down. Knowing the pain she must be feeling in her ankle I propped it up on a couple of pillows and then I propped her head up with a third.

****

Knees bent on the floor in front of me, Eric leaned to within an inch of my face and asked "Comfortable?" "Very," I answered. He slowly, almost as if to tease me, leaned in further until his lips made a bulls-eye connection with my waiting mouth.

****

I swear, I only meant to sit with her a while longer but I had to kiss her and the more we kissed, the more urgent our needs became. I felt that old heat and passion rising as if we were in her basement and it was 1975 again. The difference though is then we were a couple of kids, but now, a man and a woman. No voices from above and no other stop signs.

****

The precision that accompanied Eric's next movements while we were still interlocked were very smooth. He lifted himself from the floor to a space on the sofa directly in front of me. In one fell swoop, he lifted my head from the pillows, replacing them with his lap, and continued to set off internal spark plugs of passion through our kisses.

****

I approached the buttons on Ronni's blouse, as if I were painstakingly unwrapping a gift, knowing what was inside, but nevertheless, not wanting to spoil the pleasure it brought to her and me, to reveal its contents slowly. Our mouths enjoyed exploring each other so much that I can't remember when we came up for air. I kissed her chin and continued my vertical descent to her neck.

****

When I looked into Eric's eyes, I could tell he had no intention of ending his exploration there. I believe my eyes must have given him the unspoken approval he sought to go on. His right hand stationed behind my head, I felt the warmth of Eric's left hand as his fingers began to move in a circular motion, stroking, as if he were an artist, creating his own unique design. My eyes then closed and I could feel him using another artist-like technique that only increased my response – a tingling all over me. In contrast to the dry, brush strokes of his fingers earlier, I now experienced the warmth of even softer strokes engulfing other parts of my body.

****

I could hear her short gasps each time I kissed her. She seemed to have entered that area of anticipation before love making begins and foreplay ends. But I remained patient. This moment was a long time coming and I did not want to rush it. I wanted it to be perfect for both of us.

****

My body came to attention. It drove me wild and Eric knew it. But true artist that he was, it only inspired him to do even more, with more intensity. I was completely his at that point, or would have been, until the loud ring from the telephone brought me out of the trance I had so willingly and enjoyably succumbed to.

****

It was at that point, a point we had never reached before that the phone rang. I thought to myself, "This can't

A Love Deferred

be happening." I tried to get Ronni not to answer but she insisted. However, I still had hope because she didn't try to re-dress herself...immediately.

****

I didn't usually get calls this late, so I had to make sure it wasn't an emergency. I had to check the number at least." I'm glad I did because it was my mom's number.

****

After picking up the phone and hearing her son's voice, Ronni's mood changed pretty quickly. She started buttoning up her blouse and straightening her skirt as she sat up to talk to her son. It was almost as if Ronni's dad was even now speaking through his grandson, just by having him call at this precise moment. I thought I could hear those words that used to scare the heck out of me "It's awfully quiet down there." I knew then, there would be no love making, in this apartment tonight. With a few words after the conversation with her son, that sentiment was confirmed.

****

Mark liked spending some weekends with his grandma, his TuTu or G'Ma as he lovingly called her. He was never

A Love Deferred

comfortable with the fact that she stayed by herself on the weekends, when my sister, her housemate, hung out with her friends. I loved that he was so caring of her. I picked up the phone before it reached the fourth ring, which would have put it in voicemail. "Hello, Ma, Mark, is everything alright?" "Hi Ma," Mark replied. "I was calling to tell you that one of our favorite movies, "The Terminator," is on." Mark and I loved to imitate Arnold S. in these movies. We had the video cassette and watched it endlessly, never tiring of the action or dialogue. Any other time, I would have loved to know so I could to be entertained by the celluloid master of action movies, but this clearly wasn't the right time. But I knew I couldn't let on to Mark that that was how I felt. "It is?" I said, trying to sound interested. "Is TuTu watching it with you?" "No, she fell asleep about an hour ago and I'm glad too because she looked real tired mom. I think she's trying to do too much. Can you talk to her" he asked sounding very concerned. "I will Mark, I will, soon." As I answered I looked at Eric's expression and it was one of defeat. As he saw me engage in more of the conversation with Mark, he knew that any plans he may have had for full body contact were now defunct.

   I stroked his face with my hand, over his forehead, eyes, nose, and lips. He took my hand, kissed it, and then placed it over his heart, giving me a hurt puppy frown. I had to smile. Deep down inside, I was actually relieved. I did not want our first night to be too intense and I knew that as long as I was

A Love Deferred

in as close proximity as we were before the phone call, there was no way I could have refused him, or refused myself for wanting him. It was very late and I needed to rest my foot, my body, my mind. Tomorrow was another day. I said goodnight to Mark, hung up the phone and then got up to stretch my leg and move my foot a bit. "Baby, it's getting real late. Maybe we should call it a night for now, don't you think?

****

I thought, Foreplay – Touchdown! Love Making – Fumble! However, the consolation was the promise that tomorrow held. I would have to set up a situation where no interruptions were guaranteed. When I left Ronni's apartment, a few deep kisses later, almost but not quite reigniting the fire, I could accept holding on to the wish that twenty-four hours from now, outcomes would be different.

Eric had been gone for a little while and I found myself wide awake. After tending to some things in the kitchen, I did my last minute check of the front and patio doors, before gingerly walking to my bathroom. I undressed and stood in the tub, letting the warm water from the shower hit me, first softly, then more forcefully. It felt good. I closed my eyes and relived some of tonight's moments in my mind. After several minutes, I got out of the shower, wrapped myself in the oversized bath towel and hobbled to my bedroom. The clock on my nightstand read Eleven-thirty. I changed into my nightie and sat on the bed, rested, but still not quite sleepy. Even in the peace and quiet of the room, my mind was busy with thoughts and questions that I couldn't answer, and I knew I needed to talk to someone now, but who? And who would pick up the phone at 11:30 and not have choice words for me if I just happened to disturb their sleep. Only one name came right to mind, my former roommate, Sandra. I met Sandra at church. She was a bit on the quiet, conservative side, or so I thought at first, but found out later that wasn't totally true. She would generally give me the "straight up" word if I asked her take on things, and that's what I needed right now. I dialed her number and just as I thought I would get her voicemail, she picked up. "Hello," she said a bit groggy. "Hey girl, did I wake you?" I asked. "Not really. I was actually watching a movie, "The Terminator," but I think the last thirty minutes it may have been watching me more," she laughed. "What's up?" I don't get many midnight calls from you."

"I know," I said, but, I need to bend your ear for a little bit." "Oh, oh, what's his name?" she asked. "You think you know me like that don't you?" I said. "Ok," Sandra said, acting as if she was clueless. "I'll bite. But people don't generally call this late unless it's about a man or somebody hurt or sick. So, what's up?" "Well, it's about a friend of mine – Eric," I said. Sandra laughed and said, "I rest my case." "Ok, Sandra, you got me on this one," I said laughing too. "But seriously girl, I need to talk to you. You remember I told you about Eric."

"How could I forget?" she asked. "Seems he's popped in and out of your life enough over the years." I wanted to tell her what was on my mind and decided to try to do it all at once before any more of her comments. "Look Sandra, you know how this thing with me and Eric is. It's one of those things that takes me there, lifts me up, and then either lets me down gently, or drops me with a thud. He and I are spending some time together this weekend, and right now, I think my fate is somewhere in between." Sandra asked the question that I knew she would. "And knowing this, you called me to tell you what?" "I'm not sure. Maybe to tell me nothing more than follow my heart or watch out for falling comets or get out now before the tide overflows." Sandra could hear the anxiety in my voice and kept her advice to a minimum. "Look, Ronni. True, you and Eric go way back. And what you feel for each other may be more unresolved feelings than anything else, but only you two can figure that out. From where I sit, and that's on the outside looking in, but always trying to look out for you, it appears you've made your share of sacrifices and then some waiting on this brother. You may be a bit crazy to put yourself on the line unless you can figure out for sure where he sees the two of you going and, most importantly, if you want to continue to take that journey with him. You gotta find out sista, or the thumps you think you might feel this time could get harder and harder to heal." There was a brief silence. "Ok, sista," Sandra said yawning, "my backup energy generator has blown a fuse, so I have to get me some sleep now." "I know it's really late, and I can appreciate what you said Sandra. I'm just going to have to figure it out for myself, huh?" I asked. "That's the bottom line, girlfriend. Look, hit me back tomorrow or whenever if you need me, because you know I got your back, right?" she said comfortingly. "Right, Sandra. Good night girl." We both hung up. Now, I really had stuff on my mind. But it was late, and I couldn't try to think rationally now. It was too late and I was too tired. I put the phone back on the night stand, turned off the light, and plopped down on the pillow. I needed sleep and hoped that would help me think more clearly tomorrow. As I drifted off to sleep, it never occurred to me that tomorrow had already come.

****

I woke up Saturday morning to a forecast of warm temperatures and overcast skies in the morning but thunderstorms by afternoon. At 7:00 a.m. though, it was hazy outside and perfect for me to work Karate techniques and Katas in my hotel room. After thirty minutes of practice, I went about the business of getting ready for the rest of the day. I knew I was going to meet Ronni at 9:00 for breakfast. We then planned to do some sightseeing in and around the Mall. We also planned to have a picnic lunch near the Tidal basin followed by more sightseeing. I tried to change her mind on the sightseeing because it would require a lot of

A Love Deferred

walking, but true to Ronni's spirit, she wanted to keep the plans as is. We would end the day with dinner and whatever the night leads us to. After showering, shaving and dressing, I went to the concierge's desk and asked her to order a picnic basket from a nearby restaurant. With that done, I left the hotel to drive to Ronni's.

I listened to a mindless talk show on the radio while driving and only slightly noticed the scenery along the way. I sometimes zoned out so I snapped myself back to paying attention to the road ahead and not to Ms. Bradley. Last night was like a dream now. We came so close but God, fate, or her father stepped in and said "Uh uh, not time yet." Undaunted, I felt there are only so many road blocks that can be thrown up and haven't we been patient long enough? Before I knew it I was passing through Southeast D.C. and the sign that read "Welcome to Maryland." Ronni's apartment was no more than five miles from here and I arrived 15 minutes early so when I got there, I sat in her parking lot, in my car and waited until 9:00 before ringing her doorbell. To my surprise Ronni answered immediately saying she would be right out and she was. She stepped outside with a medium sized garment bag in hand which I took from her so she could free her hands to use the cane which she now sported instead of her crutch. She said her foot had improved more than she expected overnight and she didn't need the full support of the crutch. I admit I was delighted when I saw the bag, thinking that she had already made up her mind that she was all mine tonight.

A Love Deferred

I guess she saw my look of glee and said, "Uh, don't get the wrong idea, Mr. Lewis. This is actually a change of clothes for our evening activity. Because I'm still moving a little slower than usual, I thought it might save time for me to bring this with me now and change in your hotel room instead of driving all the way back here." I put the bag in the trunk and we gave each other a quick kiss, nothing like the fire starting kisses from last night, and exchanged our morning salutations. "Looks like it's going to be a very warm day and we may get some rain," I added. "Yes, I saw that on the news this morning" Ronni said as she walked gingerly to my car. She was indeed, relying less on her cane today than the crutch last night. Seeing that I asked, "Are you sure you're up to all this sightseeing? I mean, it's not like we haven't seen it all before." "I'm fine," Ronni replied. "Besides, I think limited walking will do me some good." Before Ronni sat down, I noticed her comfortable jeans and blouse but more important her soft soled walking shoes. "We could be twins you know," I said pointing at my jeans and walking shoes." While I put the key in the ignition and started the car, "I don't think any twins would have done what we did last night and still claim to be brother and sister." "Point taken," I said and we both laughed, In fact everything we talked about most of the day seemed to be funny or easy going. After a light breakfast we began our day in earnest. There was nothing forced between us as we talked and walked through the first museum. It was only natural that her hand found its way into mine.

****

I pretty much held my own, but when the walking proved a bit much for me, Eric and I decided to stop. When we reached the Tidal Basin, we found a spot under a nice Cherry Tree and spread a blanket to sit on and have our lunch. Although we noticed the sky gradually darkening all morning and the temperature dropping, it wasn't until we stopped completely that we noticed how fast the black clouds were gathering. Having been in Chicago long enough to know that the rain would be coming sooner than predicted, Eric suggested that we make our way back to the car. I agreed and we quickly packed up the remains of our lunch and tried to make our way back the few blocks. We were fine for the first two blocks but before we could make that last one, the rain came, first in light drops, then in fat, heavy droplets pelting all who hadn't made it to shelter. Then it came in sheets pushed sideways by the wind. The grass that looked parched by the summer heat probably welcomed the rain but the hard dry earth gave the water no purchase. So it ran in torrents down the streets sending people scurrying in all directions. We were caught in a no man's land midway between a museum, offering potential shelter, or the car, which seemed like a long block away. It didn't matter. Unspoken, we opted for the car. I think we figured, we were already soaked so what difference would a shelter make now. Plus, I wasn't going to be running anywhere so we took our time and let the storm rage around as we stroked our way to the car.

We made it to the car, soaked to the bone, as my grandmother used to say, and surprisingly cold. I had the key in hand ready to open the passenger side door. Suddenly I lost my footing on the wet grass and went down hard on my rear end. Ronni let out a slight scream but after seeing that I was okay, started to laugh. As my attempts to gain my footing continue to fail she laughed harder and after awhile I had to laugh as well. Once inside the car we sat shivering. I then suggested to Ronni that we go to my hotel and change into dry clothes. Ronni said "All I have in my bag are the clothes I planned to wear to dinner tonight. We should probably go back to my place so I can get more things and something for my hair. I again suggested that we go to my hotel since it was closer, to let me change clothes and then we could go to her apartment. We could also get some towels and she could at least dry off in the meantime. Ronni agreed with my plan and we headed off to Georgetown and the Hotel Presidential.

Driving through the pouring rain in the warm dry cocoon the rental car provided for us, we arrived at the hotel a short time later and pulled into the valet parking lane. I turned over my keys and went to help a now damp Ronni from the car. As we started to walk away Ronni said "Maybe you should get my bag from the car just in case." Seeing the valet about to pull away, I ran forward and tapped the passenger window startling the young driver. I pulled open the door, apologized for frightening him and grabbed Ronni's bag from the trunk. Bag in one hand and Ronni supported on my free arm, we entered the hotel and took the elevator to the 17th floor. When I opened the door, Ronni stepped in and appraised the well appointed room. She said "Nice," as she walked to the window and opened the curtains to get a better view of the city. While she did that, I grabbed a couple of towels from the bathroom and started drying my hair with one and handing the other to Ronni. "I like that view, "I told her. "I sleep with the curtains open to let the city lights fill the room. This room is too high to let anyone see in so it's safe to stand there at night and look out, even undressed." Moving on I added, "It will only take a couple of minutes for me to change. But I'm worried about you. I'm not trying to flirt, although I wouldn't put it past me, but why don't you get out of those wet clothes? You know the old folks would say you'll catch your death of cold if you don't. The hotel room came supplied with really plush terry cloth bath robes and there's a hair dryer in the bathroom. If you'd like to take a warm shower and then dry off, I promise I'll be on my best behavior," I said as convincingly as I could. "I'll also order up some hot tea if you'd like."

Ronni made me promise Scout's Honor and said she liked both suggestions. "After the rain stops, we can decide what we want to do next," she added. "That sounds good to me," I replied. "A little down time after all that activity today will do both of us some good. I tell you what, I'll go in there now and get these wet things off and put on a robe. Then, you can go in and take care of what you need to do. That sound okay to you?" I asked caringly. "If you want to hand me your clothes after you get in the bathroom, I can lay them out here." "Sure," Ronni answered. "Besides, it will probably take me longer." I hurried into the bathroom, peeled off my wet clothes, dried off as much as I could with a couple of towels and put on my bathrobe. I decided I could take my shower after Ronni finished and was out of there in less than 5 minutes. Ronni hobbled a little going in and said, "If you just hand me a robe and my bag, I'll get started." I handed her both items and she closed the door....... A few moments later I could hear the shower going and Ronni humming in the background. I stood by the window watching the city under the darkening clouds and the lights starting to come on even though it was still only 2:00 in the afternoon. As I mused about the rain, I heard Ronni' call out my name. I wasn't sure if it was the first time she called or not but I was snapped back into the moment and shouted, "Coming!" I stood at the bathroom door and said. "Ronni, did you call me? Are you okay?" She said, "I'm fine, but I do need your help." I could hear the water running and figured she was still in the shower. "What do you need?" I asked. "I'm almost too embarrassed to ask, but when I was reaching for another washcloth, I dropped the soap on the bathroom floor and with my ankle the way it is, I need your help to pick it up for me. It's alright; you have my *permission* to enter," she

A Love Deferred

said jokingly. When I entered the bathroom I could smell the fragrance of her bath soaps and oils mixed in with the vapors from the hot shower. Ronni stood behind the clouded glass of the shower stall but I could still make out her figure as she stood to the side of the stream of water, a towel covering her front. I picked up the soap and opened the shower door to hand it to her. I couldn't take my eyes off this marvelous being standing before me and said, "You're beautiful. With the towel soaked like that, it drives a brother's imagination wild." She seemed to blush at that, and even more when I opened my robe, let it drop to the floor and stepped into the shower with her. "At least let me wash your back for you."

After looking into my eyes for a moment, Ronni silently turned around, still holding the soaked towel to her front. I took a wash cloth from the rack, soaped it generously and slowly began washing her upper back. I let the warm water rinse the soap from her and then I moved on lower, to her back, those long, lovely legs, being extra careful with her ankles and feet. After letting her rinse, I slowly turned her to face me.

****

When Eric's eyes met mine, he instinctively pulled me in close to him. The kiss we shared was deeper than any we'd experienced before that moment. Now, with us both standing here, we slowly explored bodies that were so familiar but still unknown to each other. The washing became an exercise in sensuality.

****

It was while I washed Ronni that she softly called my name. I kept listening for a phone to ring or a voice from above but there was nothing to stop us. Not this time. We held each other tightly, letting each other know that what was happening was alright. And finally, in that defining moment, we were together as we'd never, ever been before.

****

Breathless and still locked in our embrace Eric lowered me, and we slowly slumped against the wall, warm water still cascading over us. He reached up and turned the water off while we both caught our breath.

****

"Sweetie, I — I didn't know anyone could make me feel like that."

****

Dripping, we made our way to the bedroom. Sunset and an imposing street light invaded the privacy that the darkness had previously provided, and painted silhouettes of perfect body proportions on the walls and the ceiling. The sheets continued to consume the water from the shower and the perspiration pouring from every muscle movement, from the top of our heads to the tips of our toes. "Eric, if we never share this again, let tonight be our forever." At the height of passion, our syncopated rhythms gave way to multiple eruptions of volcanic proportion. Our *forever* was recreated again and again

We never made it outside the walls of the room that night. Actually, outside of the bathrobes we wore earlier and when we ordered room service, we never made it into much of any other clothing that night either. Needless to say, I didn't need that evening outfit that hung in my garment bag in the closet. I was out $200. But wasn't what we shared tonight priceless? Who was I kidding? Something like this always comes with a price, and a hefty one at that.

At one point during the wee hours of the early morning and one of our silent moments, as I lay next to Eric, I studied him. His eyes were closed, but he wasn't asleep. His breathing was calm. The moonlight streaming through the window, provided a silhouette of his left side, and I took stock of his stately features. I couldn't resist running my index finger through his salt and pepper, wavy hair, as soft as a baby's, I thought. I traveled farther along his distinguished forehead and nose, then across the salt and pepper moustache that accented the full lips that I had grown so accustomed to, always affording me the most pleasurable experiences. I took my hand away, propped up a couple of pillows against the headboard and stared aimlessly at the ceiling above. Eric turned towards me.

****

Are you alright, Sweetie?" I asked, wanting to make sure Ronni wasn't in pain. She nodded yes and said she wasn't quite sleepy yet and just wanted to know if I was up to talking for a bit, what I refer to as the *bearing of souls* session. I don't know, but it just seems like this is an inherent practice for the female psyche following lovemaking. Maybe women think that a man's defenses and barriers are weakened during this period and we're more likely to open up with our true feelings and definitely be more sensitive to theirs as well. I became a believer this night. I found myself sharing things that at least in my case, had never been shared with anyone else. I told her about how empty I felt after my failed marriages and how I had lost some of my confidence. I knew that it was affecting my work but I also knew that I had to work through it. We both talked about how the loss of our fathers, and also for me, my son, still affected us deeply. Unexpectedly the tears came. I don't know why, but they are closer to the surface for me lately.

****

I told Eric that I was wrestling inside, being here, now, with him. Yes, he and Prentice had been separated for almost a year, but that was only semantics – their marital situation was unresolved. *Separation limbo*, I called it. Maybe if I could turn off inside, what I know always kicks me on the outside after we're together, it would be alright. Or maybe, like one of my confidantes told me after I spoke with her yesterday, I must be crazy setting myself up like this. I told Eric this is that thing that happens to me when the choices I make compromise my relationship with God. The more I spoke, the weirder it seemed saying it now, in this room, especially after what took place between us earlier.

****

I don't think my response was all that reassuring when all I could say was, "I know Ronni, I know." Leading the conversation away from just being caught up in the moment to the implications it may have on our eternal souls, made us both feel guilty about the moments of pleasure we shared. For a long time we were quiet, she on her side of the bed, me on mine. It sort of reminded me of Adam and Eve, discovering their nakedness after taking a bite from the fruit of the forbidden tree.

****

Eric and I both felt the need to cover ourselves and eventually, exhaustion got the best of us. I started to sniffle and tried to keep as quiet as I could, but Eric heard me and put his hand on my back to comfort me. "I'm okay Eric," I whispered. "Why don't we both get some sleep." At that point, I think he knew I just needed to go through this without him. Once Eric fell asleep, I slipped quietly out of bed and into the bathroom. I stood for several minutes blankly staring at the reflection in the mirror. Who was she, and aside from the obvious, what was she really doing here? I felt first an emptiness and then a sharp pain in the pit of my stomach. I doubled over and found myself on my knees leaning against the commode. Every time I tried to take a full breath the pain seemed almost unbearable. I found myself praying, but surprisingly, not for relief from the relentless pain, but for guidance. I called on the name of Jesus, the only one I knew who could give it to me. But here in this place, and now, I wasn't sure if I should expect Him to hear me. In this very humbling stance, I softly spoke, openly and honestly sharing how this night felt to me; how the energy, athletics, and emotion that I just shared with Eric gave me immense pleasure, and yet, now had weighted me down to where it pained me to move even a muscle. Part of me knew this was more than any physical ailment for which I sought help; it went much, much deeper. I laid there quietly for a while. Later, as I stood to my feet, I began to feel as if I were no longer a victim of the pain that had overtaken me so before. It had subsided. I rose thinking that this was perhaps a sign that the guidance and sleep I sought might come a little easier to me now.

****

Ronni and I had breakfast at the hotel's buffet the next morning, but ended up wasting food and money because neither one of us was really hungry. We shared polite conversation, but we knew a lot of issues were left unresolved. Inside, I struggled, and sitting here now with Ronni made me feel like it was our *last supper*. How long had we wanted to be together and the time was wrong, the place was wrong, the situation was wrong? Now, when we believed we had finally found the opportunity to be together, something inside of us individually and collectively, based on this morning's interaction, let us know that what we thought was so right, was so wrong. Physically, coming together was incredible, but ultimately, spiritually it was wrong. Neither of us could put into a coherent sentence, or face where this was, or wasn't leading us to at this point. I know Ronni was struggling with it spiritually. Sitting here facing each other, we felt emotionally drained and maybe more than a little empty. I left for Chicago early that afternoon with still more questions than I had answers to give. The cloud that hovered over me left

A Love Deferred

me with an uneasy feeling. I'm sure that if my home girl Oprah could put a spin on this for one of her theme shows, she would probably say what I offered Ronni now reeked of, what was it Ronni called it – a life of separation limbo. It was a relationship that could never sufficiently address the depths of her feelings and would not be fulfilling for either of us. As I saw it, I would more than likely come out to be the villain. I boarded the 727 knowing that without a more decisive commitment, Ronni and I may have just run our course.

****

CHAPTER EIGHTEEN

THE BLOOM COMES OFF THE ROSE

Years have passed since our last meeting and Ronni and I have had very little contact. We attended functions in D.C. related to the twins, since we were godmother and godfather to Chris and E.J., respectively. I think we may have been intentionally avoiding events judging by the last minute cancellations on both sides. Eddie and I talked regularly and took pleasure in the fact that we had long ago given up basketball and taken up the more civilized game of golf. Unfortunately, it gave him more time to give me Ronni updates. They typically went like this. "So are you dating anybody?" "I have friends I see off and on. Nothing serious," I would answer. "Seems like there's a lot of that going around." He would say. "Oh really. What do you mean?" I would ask. "Just that Ronni was at the house last week for dinner and when asked the same question, we got a similar response." We would chat some more about other things, the children, work, politics but the conversation would always get back to Ronni and me somehow. "You know she is really singing up a storm now. She has really found her calling." "That's great," I would say. "I remember that summer when all of you sang together. Has anybody ever thought of having a reunion?" He would ask. "Nobody has asked me and I probably couldn't do it anymore. I haven't really sung in awhile." I would reply. "It's like riding a bike, you never forget how." He would say. Then he would sneak in, "Why doesn't somebody give somebody else a call and work out the details – hint, hint. I'm sure Corrine, Terry, Joy and Jessie would be open to it." That's when I would call an end to the conversation saying "It's not going to happen. Or let's just play golf please." We would play on in silence until I eventually apologized, thanking him for being my friend and asking him to let the Ronni and Eric situation resolve itself. Invariably he would say that he would. And he meant it, until the next time we met and he gave me the latest Ronni update.

****

Maybe if I could have stayed out of Chicago, it would have been better. But it seemed that much of my professional life took me there. From 1999-2000, I, and a colleague from my organization, were part of a planning committee for a major international health conference being held in Chicago.

I traveled to the Windy City at least twice that year, to walk through the sites and put the finishing touches on a program that had commanded much of my attention. Both visits were one night stays. I was so totally focused on the tasks at hand that, even though I had fleeting thoughts about contacting Mr. Lewis, the round-the-clock planning sessions and dinner meetings, didn't allow much, if any, free time.

With everything in place and the conference about to kick off, the summer of 2000 meant that Chicago would, once again, be my temporary home, but for much longer. Unlike the previous visits, I felt a need to connect with someone other than my colleagues while there for the next week or so and informed Mr. Lewis of my travel and lodging plans. He had been living in Chicago for almost 20 years and was now living in an apartment on Chicago's scenic lakefront. The day of my arrival, Eric had planned to meet me at my hotel for dinner. It was one of Chicago's oldest hotels, an architectural masterpiece with high ceilings and huge chandeliers. Although they had modernized it somewhat, it still had the flavor of the early 1900s. With such impressive décor, it came as a total shock to me when the room they gave me was half the size of an efficiency. Surely, the front desk made a mistake and I planned to rectify it. Just to make sure I wasn't overreacting, I had Eric meet me upstairs. When he saw the matchbox space, he laughed in disbelief. A luck of the draw and it looks like you lost, he teased. We hugged and laughed about how difficult it was for me to move around in this space. Just shifting my luggage took some maneuvering and when I asked for his help with one of the larger pieces, we almost tumbled over. This was not the space for two people of height. Eric came bearing gifts — some Chicago Bulls paraphernalia for my son. He knew Mark was fascinated with anything Michael Jordan and was always thoughtful about sending him memorabilia of No. 23. I thanked him and we left for dinner, which was at a quaint restaurant a short driving distance from the hotel. It was good seeing my friend.

For the first time in a long time, we actually just sat and chatted and chewed without any overwhelming sexual tensions between us. Living alone was something he had been doing for some time and he admitted to still being a bit uncomfortable cooking for one, which usually meant eating out a lot. He welcomed my companionship at the dinner table. He shared with me some of what was happening between him and his ex-wife which turned out to be a lot of unresolved issues that caused a huge divide in the Lewis family, at least between the adults. Both were working to make sure their son, whom they loved dearly, would suffer least from their split. I let him know that a lot of my energy was focused on raising Mark, who was growing bigger and smarter everyday. He was definitely his mother's pride. His father and I continued to work on resolving some of the back-and-forth issues between us and it helped to make our

A Love Deferred

relating as parents and the support we gave our son, a much more pleasant and beneficial experience.

I suggested some diplomatic and spiritual approaches that Eric and his ex-wife might also consider in resolving issues. I let Eric know that prayer and talking to confidantes, even considering ministerial counsel, even though we weren't married, did help to change things for Jeffrey and me. We first sought individual counseling, then managed to work through laying it all out during a couple of joint sessions. Making the parenting thing work for Mark was that important to us. But it took time to get there. I emphasized that the important thing was not just to pray, but to be open to the spirit within him and move toward the action steps that were being revealed even if they didn't make complete sense to him. When he asked how to do that, I suggested he work on first being real with his inner feelings –anger, frustration, failure, whatever. Once he could confront those things then he could ask God to help him start the healing process and work through the challenges that, he admitted, at times, overtook him. Only then, I believed would he begin to get direction on where he should be in his relationship with his ex-wife and his son.

Needless to say, this was an unexpected paradigm shift from some of the lighter fare we generally shared, but when we left the restaurant, I felt we both had lifted at least some of the emotional weight that we had been carrying. When we pulled up in front of my hotel, I knew our good night wishes

A Love Deferred

would go no further than where we sat in the car. I turned to Eric, thanking him for the dinner and the conversation, gave him a kiss on the cheek, and got out. After waving good night, I disappeared into the hotel lobby. I was feeling good about the events of this night and was looking forward to a good night's sleep. It was too late and I was too tired to move a stitch of clothing or luggage from the matchbox. The next morning, I was moved to a much larger room, hassle-free.

Over the next several days, I was on a roller coaster ride attending round-the-clock professional sessions and playing troubleshooter during the long days, and attending official receptions, one after another at night. All of this meant very early mornings and extremely late evenings. When Eric called to meet with me again, I invited him to attend one of the high-level receptions with me. It gave him an opportunity to see me in my professional habitat, outside of our personal arena. He was witty and very comfortable schmoozing in this setting of global medical experts and international ministers of health, some of whom, through the planning process, had become my new colleagues. My coworker also enjoyed Eric's savvy. I was happy to have my childhood friend with me to see how I transitioned from high school student to real-world professional. Eric had to leave before the end of the reception, and we again gave each other respectable parting hugs and kisses. I felt we were relating on a whole new level and it felt good. It was the night before the close of the conference and it was going out with a bang!

A Love Deferred

I again invited Eric to accompany me to the last formal gathering, celebrating the success of the week's events. Eric had to work late that night, but said he would try to make it. He didn't.

Hours later, feet and body overworked, I welcomed the quiet of my hotel room, a reward, I thought to myself, for a job well done. I slipped out of my shoes and jacket and plopped down on my king-size bed. Then the phone rang. I groaned as I reached for it. "Hello," I said, trying to sound a little energetic. "Hi Ronni. Eric Lewis here. How are you?" I sat up on the bed. "Good, Eric. Sorry you missed the big bash. It was a lot of fun." "I'm sorry I couldn't make it too. There was just no way to break away from what I had to finish up here," he said. "Not a problem. I understand," I said, trying to remove some of the guilt in his voice. "Hey, I'm finished now and headed downtown. I know you're out of here in a day or so, and would like to see you at least one more time before you go. You up to it tonight? I'd really like to see you Ronni, so please say yes?" There was something different in Eric's request. Maybe he was feeling a bit homesick for Washington, D.C. and being with me here was as good as being there. Maybe he thought he only had one more chance with his old friend to rekindle the flames of passion we'd shared in the not too distant past. I wasn't quite sure, but something in his voice connected with something inside of me and I knew I couldn't refuse seeing him one more time before I left. "Yes," I answered. "I'm on my way. Be there in a few." With that he hung up.

I fell back on the bed. What was I thinking? What am I thinking? We'd enjoyed just "being" this past week and now part of me felt we were about to fall into one of those passion-plagued potholes that had become our trademark. Could I resist him this time? Would I fall victim once again to my *flesh back*? Could I refuse him this time? Oh, brother, why does this have to seem so good and bad at the same time? I stood up and looked at myself in the mirror in front of me. I was still wearing everything but the suit jacket. And then the questions came again. Do I keep this on and look appealingly conservative? Do I change into something more casual? More alluring? What message do I want to send? Ronni, why is this so hard? Help me somebody?!

Almost as quickly as I thought that, there was a knock on the door. I jumped at first, startled, thinking that there was no way Eric could have gotten here that fast. I went to the door and asked, "Who is it?" "It's Gail, Ronni," the voice on the other side of the door said. My colleague, Gail had been close by my side all week. Even though she was short in stature, I considered her my big sister and a mentor. I learned a lot about professional development and posturing from Gail. It was a little late and she generally hit the sack early, so I was surprised to be hearing from her now. I opened the door and saw nothing but her smile. I motioned for her to come in, but she kindly refused the offer. "Girl, you know it's way past this sister's bedtime. But before I clocked out for the night, I had one special errand to run," she said. "I have never been more proud of you than this week." I was speechless. She continued, "I wanted a little help in expressing it to you in words that described it best, so this is for you. With that, she handed me an envelope. I felt a little teary-eyed. "Good night little sister," she said as she reached up to hug me, and made her exit. "Good night Gail." I closed and latched the door and sat back down on the bed, envelope in hand. I opened the envelope to find a beautiful card, its front adorned with two Black, statuesque female figures, clothed in African dress. I opened the card and began to read the message: "I am so glad that we are sisters. Sisters in the spirit, sisters in love, sisters in harmony, sisters when we're hurting, sisters when we need a helping hand. God has placed us in each other's lives for a reason and I want you to know I am here for you." It was signed, Love, your sister, Gail. The tears started rolling down my cheek more steadily. But they weren't tears of sadness, rather, tears of joy, tears of love, tears of amazement, knowing that an omnipresent God heard my call for help and sent Gail, with a message that offered me, as the Bible says, the means to *a way to escape* what was potentially about to happen.

I placed the card on the dresser, thinking that this very visual source of strength would help me decide how best to receive the man with whom I had received so passionately, so many times before. But this was different. I thought. If we were ever to really determine if we could rebuild the foundation of our relationship on something that didn't have to end in intimacy, this was the time to do it. I changed into something more casual and comfortable, but not tantalizing and awaited Eric's arrival. I decided, that in order to avoid the temptation my hotel room, and more specifically, the king-size bed provided, we would talk out in the huge, but private, seating area directly adjacent to the elevator bank on my floor. When he knocked on the door a few minutes later, I sent a prayer up asking for help, as I unlatched the locks. As I grabbed the key card to the door, I opened the door to Eric's warm smile. "Hi, Sweetie Bradley," he said. He handed me a dozen roses, and I knew I had a hard road to trod. Still standing at the door, I thanked him for the roses, placed them on the night stand, and stepped outside the room.

I closed the door from the outside, much to his alarm and disappointment, took his hand and led him to one of the huge sofas in the enormous hallway. "Let's sit here Eric." I looked into his puzzled eyes. "I know I've caught you off guard with this, but something about you and me hit me hard tonight and I needed to share it with you," I said. "Ronni, what's wrong with you and me. I love you. You know that," Eric said, still not able to make heads or tails out of what was happening. "I know you do, and I love you too Eric. But right now, we may need more than love to help us make the right choices. And choice is what God is giving us; has given us all along. I know I'm sounding triple deep and catching you totally off guard, but I have got to tell you where I am right now. You see, you and I have planted such deep roots in each other that it makes our connection and our connecting extremely intense. And the wild thing about it is that it doesn't matter if we're next to each other, hundreds of miles away, talking on the phone, or even emailing, our synergy is potent and passionate, almost to a boiling point. The trappings of our relationship are breathtaking, but is that enough when what we have never been able to realize is a union that is reflective and representative of the lifelong love that we share — one that is pleasing to both of us — to God? I just don't think we can ignore or gloss over that fact anymore Eric, and I don't have the insides to act like it doesn't matter that much to me. So I've got to make some decisions for me that will help me, but I've got to be honest with you about what that means to me and for us, provided there is or will be an us, beyond tonight. Am I making sense to you?

****

There it is again. One of Ronni's famous silver bullet questions. I thought to myself "What was I thinking coming here like this?" Did I think that Ronni would just fall all over herself for me and say "Eric come in and make love to me?" Of course not. She is an amazing woman and has grown so strong in the word, I couldn't help but be proud of her. This is wrong and everything she is saying is true. She's said it so many times over the years and the last time I saw her she made it very clear where I stood in her spiritual life. And now this is the punctuation mark. "Ronni, I understand exactly what you are saying. I just wanted to see you before you left and to tell you how much I enjoyed spending just a little time with you over the past few days." I went on to say, "I guess we proved we can be friends without being lovers. That's important to know because lovers are everywhere but friends are like treasures. Our friendship has endured for a long time. We have been through and seen some things that would have ended a lot of relationships. And yet we are still here. Even though we have done some things that are not in pleasing God's eyes, our enduring friendship still counts for a lot."

****

I thought about Eric's comments and said, "Eric, when I told you about the decision I faced entering college late, you said I was being very mature. I'll respond like I did then when I said that sometimes you have to make mature decisions in your life, even when you don't want to. This is one of them. I love you and I know you love me. If we are meant to be together, it will happen. This has been cathartic and a long time coming for me, but I now know that I also have to submit to the belief that God won't hold *any* good thing from us. When I honestly take stock of how we've related over the years, I can't say that we've really given *Him* a chance to show us how to be *good together*."

****

It always comes back to God with her. Any answer I might have given without God or the Bible as my basis would have been shot down so I thought I may as well exit as gracefully as I could. "You're right. I know I haven't listened for what God may have said in our relationship, or others, to be quite honest. Too often I have let myself get chosen and got pulled along in any direction by the chooser. By my track record you can tell that being chosen hasn't worked out too well for me. I agree with you. For the longest time, I thought it would always be you and I. There is no reason it shouldn't have been so I have some inner reflection to do to figure out how to present myself, whole to you. In the meantime, I respect what you are saying and appreciate your "God" concern."

****

I repeated his last words in my head, *"my God concern?"* We both sat silent for a moment, looking at each other. All at once, as if we both understood where we needed to go and what needed to happen, we smiled. "Look, it's late and I've got a lot of packing to do before I'm out of here tomorrow afternoon," I said a bit tired. "I think we should call it a night. Thank you again for the lovely flowers. Eric stood up and took my hand, lifting me to my feet. We embraced each other tighter than we'd ever done before. I rested my head on his shoulder as we walked to the elevator. "One parting request Mr. Lewis." "What's that?" he asked. I gestured to Eric to come closer. We shared a very long, warm hug. As the elevator door opened, and he stepped in, I said, "I just want you to know that you shouldn't let pride stand in the way of coming to me, when and if you're ready to come to me." As the doors closed, I blew Eric an imaginary kiss. He grabbed it and placed it on his heart. As I walked towards my room, I thought about how I loved this man. But I knew this time, that whether we were or weren't to be, was not something that my hands or my heart could direct.

****

When the elevator door opened on the ground floor, I felt as though, no, I knew that my relationship with Ronni was now defined. I knew there were things that I had to do if we were ever going to be together. I knew her love for me was sincere but the test of time had shown signs of waning. It was time for me to step up and do some choosing of my own. I needed to choose which path to follow, and who I wanted to walk that path with me. I knew I wanted to be with Ronni but I still felt as though I was inadequate when I was with her, but never because of anything she said or did. When the valet pulled my car up, I was still thinking about how strong she was and that I needed to decide who I was and what I wanted to be if I was going to have any chance with Ronni. In short I felt as if my life had been imitating art, and similar to that old show "To Tell the Truth," it was now time for the real Eric Lewis to "stand up."

****

Weeks after making my declaration of self-determination to Eric, life took an interesting turn, unexplainable to me. Seems like most of the males I encountered professionally and socially, were in some stage of "marriage-dom," as they told it, either separated, in open relationships, and, oh yes, even so-called wedded bliss. I became weary of fighting off their subtle and sometimes not so subtle advances. This must surely have been a test of some kind. I shared my no-win-situation with my good friend Revae who came up with an unusual solution. She suggested I call my insurance company to find out if it would be considered elective surgery or a covered mental health benefit to remove, what surely must be, a sign imprinted on my forehead *(only visible to married men)* reading: "Available." It was the first really good laugh I'd had in a while. Although I knew she was being facetious, I couldn't help but think that if it were doable, I'd be under the laser now. Wherever they were all coming from, I wanted no part of it.

CHAPTER NINETEEN

BEEN FOUND

After leaving my high school's parking lot on Friday night, I found my way back to the hotel in Georgetown. I was too restless to go directly to sleep so I spent the rest of the night watching television. Late night television was different than daytime or even early evening. The public networks became a little bolder on what they were willing to show and the cable just got even looser on their standards. If I can't watch sports, then I prefer to watch a channel I can learn from. I especially liked watching the Discovery Channel because it sometimes gave me good ideas for places to go on vacation. The problem with deciding to go on vacations alone is that you get to see once in a lifetime events but you can't share them with somebody. "Remember that sunset in Venice? Oh that's right you weren't there. I went alone. My bad."

The discovery Channel also presented shows that opened your mind to a lot of strange and interesting things in the world. Tonight I was watching a show about people who changed their bodies to look like animals until, as my Grandmom used to say, "The television started watching me." I woke up Saturday morning with infomercials on, still propped up on the bed with pillows behind my back. I got up and looked out my window at the sunny, and undoubtedly hot day outside. As was my practice, I went to the bathroom, washed my face and brushed my teeth. I then walked back into the room and worked my short Katas. Katas are good mind and body exercises because they teach you to perfect the individual techniques that go into making up the total form. I started out slow making sure that my body was aligned properly and my strikes were aimed in the correct places. I then moved through the form at the proper speed. I worked my forms until I was hot, then I sat and meditated with a towel over my head and shoulders. While meditating, I assessed my life and where I was going with it. Overall, I have had a good life but there was an emptiness that kept eating away at me and if I didn't do something about it, I would be left as empty as a wheat field after the locust had had their fill. I also thought about how much stronger I had become since I concentrated on healing my body and spirit. I knew now that I could take whatever life could throw my way because I have been through the storm and I'm still here to tell about it.

After meditation, I showered, dressed and went downstairs for breakfast. Now I was ready to start the day. My plan was to visit relatives and rest up for tonight and the rest of the weekend. My first stop was my brother Ben's house. Unfortunately, as it turned out, I never made it to see any other relatives that day. Ben, with very little arm twisting talked me into filling the fourth spot in his golf group and there went the next six hours. After playing an extremely slow round of golf, in what had to be at least 100 degree heat, I was exhausted. With most of the day shot, I went back to my room to shower and rest until the barbeque at my cousin's house where I planned to see at least some of my relatives. I will make my apologies there.

Around 7:00 p.m., I got up put on a fresh pair of jeans and a polo shirt and went to my cousin Lena's house where I ate and partied like it was 1999. A lot of the family was there talking jive, playing cards, dominoes and basically cuttin' up. There was music and old school dance demonstrations mixed in with hip-hop and salsa. There were questions about Ronni from my aunt who always thought the world of her and from my uncle who thought about her very differently. There were still others who thought about her because wherever there was a competition, she was normally all up in the middle of it. But not tonight. Tonight she was all up in the middle of some Congressional report. That's alright I thought. She'd probably be beating me liked she used to do. About 11:00 p.m., my son Trey called to check in on me. "What's up dad," came his cheerful voice over my cell phone. "Ain't no thing but a chicken wing," was my old-school reply.

"Dad, you really have to get some new lines," Trey said. "But I haven't worn this one out yet," I replied. "Trust me dad, that line is long gone" he said laughing. I joined him in laughing and said "How are you doing Kid?" He answered "Fine, we just finished having some pizza and we are going to catch a late flick. You can tell summer session is winding down." "Good" I said. "Because I really want to see you." "I'm coming to see you soon dad, but first Mom and I are going on a little vacation to Cabo. Then I'll head up the coast to see you. Cool?" "Cool," I said adding "The party is just starting here. Your uncle Eddie and Aunt Corrine really laid it out this time." "I'm glad you are enjoying yourself. Listen dad, I don't want to rush you but we gotta run if we're going to catch this show. I'll check in with you next week. Love you." "I love you too. Have fun and stay safe." I said before hanging up. No matter how old he is, I still worry about him even though he has shown nothing but maturity and responsibility in everything he has done so far. I guess it's a father's right to worry.

After hanging up the phone, I really got an idea of how noisy the party had gotten and how late it was. I went around and said my goodbyes before heading out. I was still feeling good when I arrived at my hotel 30 minutes later. There's nothing like talking trash while playing cut throat dominoes with good friends and family one minute and talking with your son the next to let you know everything is going to be alright. Those were my last thought as I fell asleep.

Sunday Morning

As promised, I arrived at Tried Stone Missionary Baptist Church at 10:45, fifteen minutes before service was scheduled to begin. I saw my sister Jenny and her family sitting in the middle section of the packed Church and had an usher show me to her pew. I knew she saved a seat for me. In greeting she said "Boy, you don't know how many people I had to beat off to save this seat. I almost had to lose my 'ligion up in here." I kissed her and my niece before taking my seat. I shook my brother-in law's hand and sat back taking in the old church. It still had a lot of character, even though there were cracks in the plaster and patches in the walls and ceiling where it looked like water had seeped in. As I looked toward the front, there was still the mahogany colored pulpit and the lush red and purple velvet sashes hanging over the sides. On one side of the pulpit stood the American Flag with the stars and stripes. On the other side stood the Christian Flag with the blood red cross. On the wall behind the pulpit, above the choir stand there was a stained glass window that depicted Jesus, kneeling, hands folded in prayer with a dove holding an olive branch in his beak forever suspended above his head. The red, yellow, white, green and blue chips of glass, often streamed color combinations on many of the robed choir members when they were seated in their stand. I looked further and all around me I could see the colorful hats, suits, dresses, wraps and trappings that always distinguished our churches from anyone else's. I also saw a sea of fans throughout the sanctuary. Waving back and forth the fans were only successful in cooling the warm air immediately in front of your face but very little else.

A few minutes before eleven, the deacons started the praise and testimonial service. One older deacon stood up and started the church going like a warm up act in a concert. He started signing "There's A Leak in This Old Building." Before you knew it the whole church was up on its collective feet and we were off singing "And my soul has got to move." I marveled at how this old spiritual still roused the spirits of even the younger people. I always felt that songs like this that inspired our slavery bound ancestors, were inside all of us through manifest destiny. That's why we could feel it all through our bodies when the old deacons half sang and half moaned the song.

After the song, the Bible verse was read by a very nervous Junior Deacon. People were still being seated by the ushers while a stream of people started testifying about what the Lord had done for them, after the invitation was given by the Senior Deacons. Others asked for prayer in their time of need and still others just wanted to say thank you for how good God has been to them. After about fifteen minutes, the testimonial service was ended when the choir formed in the back of the Church and the Pastor and Associate Ministers took their seats on the Pulpit. The choir sang the invocation as the Pastor gestured for all of us to stand. Pastor Earl had

A Love Deferred

been our spiritual leader for almost forty years and he still had a commanding presence. He was washed in the blood and ordained by God at an early age to take up his calling. He often spoke about his life BJ, Before Jesus. He told the story of how he was imprisoned in Mississippi for three years for a crime he did not commit. In a different way of speaking about it, he talked about God finding him one night in his prison cell when he had no place to go and no one else to turn to. And just when he did that, his life was turned around. He spoke about being freed because a young attorney would not give up on him. He talked about walking out of jail a free man with a second chance at life and a commitment to lead as many people as he could to discover what he found in the Lord before they had to suffer what he did before God found him. Anyone who ever heard him speak heard some version of his personal testimony. And if you were lucky, you got to experience Pastor Earl's touch. I can't explain it but every time he physically touched me I got a jolt from him and it left you feeling lifted. I was thinking about his touch as the choir processed in on "Marching up to Zion." After the choir was seated, the service proceeded with the prayer of invocation, the reading of the Bible verse, more prayer, announcements and the welcoming of visitors. It was at this point in the service that I was a little uncomfortable because, even though I grew up in this church, I hadn't attended it regularly since the late '70s. So it was a surprise to me when after recognizing the visitors that Pastor Earl recognized me.

A Love Deferred

He stood at the pulpit after the offering was taken and said in his baritone voice, "I want to acknowledge another visitor today. He didn't stand up with the other visitors because in fact, he is part of our extended family. But since he doesn't get here very often I want to ask him to stand up, So Brother Eric Lewis would you please stand." I was surprised again when I got a warm round of applause and some "Amens" mixed in when I stood. I waved and said thank you as I sat down. Pastor Earl went on to say "It's always good to recognize family and Eric Lewis is part of this family. But that's not the only reason I had him stand today. You see God sent me a message for you today Brother Eric and I want the choir to help me sing it." That's when Pastor Earl did another extraordinary thing. He started singing a song and he touched me again, this time with his voice. I always knew the man could sing but this time... Well this time was special. He started out half singing and half moaning softly into the microphone, "Safe was the night, ninety nine in the fold." The pianist quickly picked up his key as Pastor sang a little louder, "And safe was the night, it was so chilly and so cold." Then Pastor grabbed up the microphone as he sang "But said the shepherd as he was counting them all." Pastor started counting heads in the audience just like the shepherd. "One of my sheep is missing, somewhere there's got to be one more." Now in full voice the Pastor and choir sang "The shepherd went out, to search for his sheep." Now the Pastor was walking down the stairs and up and down the aisles singing "And all through the night, on a cold mountain peak." Shading his eyes as if he was scouring the horizon for that lost sheep the Pastor sang, "He searched till he found it, he loved and he bound it and I was that one lost sheep." Pastor kept on singing as he looked at me but by that time the message was clear. I was the lost sheep but today, I could be found if I only let him. I could be a better person if I only believed and I could stand up for what I believe if I would only trust. As he sang I saw, heard and felt the open emotions he evoked with his voice. I know the message wasn't mine alone because it touched so many. But the power of his words made me feel as though I had been found. His words could do that because our Father in Heaven told him so, and gave him the power to change lives. And in him we could place our complete trust.

After the service, I felt lifted. There were so many things going through my head. I felt as though I had been awakened, renewed, and revived and now it was time to start living again. I stood in line to greet the Pastor as I had so many times in the past but as I got closer to him I started to feel unworthy of his touch and almost darted out of the line. It was his voice that stopped me. "Brother Lewis it's so good to see you." And instead of reaching out to shake my hand he pulled me into a brotherly embrace and added, "I miss seeing you here on Sundays. As much as I try to keep tabs on everybody, I can't seem to stay up with you. Tell me, how are things going for you in California?" I answered,

"Things are going fine out there but I hate being so far away from my family." "Yes, I know the feeling. With so much of my family down South its hard to stay in contact with all of them." "But," He added, "That will all be changing soon." "How so?" I inquired. "Why I thought your family would have told you. I'm retiring at the end of this year and I am moving back to Mississippi. Back to the same town I was jailed in more than 40 years ago." I told him, "I'm happy for you but I know it won't be the same here without you." He surprised me by saying, "I hope not. I hope this old church gets better and stronger." That's when I heard the Amens of the people behind me waiting to touch the Pastor. I again gave my congratulations and went outside to see my family. Jenny saw me first and waved me over to their car. She said, "We are going home to get dinner started. We are planning to eat around 4:30 and everybody's coming so what time should we expect you? I responded cheerfully, "As soon as I can go to the hotel and change. I can come right to the house and help to cook." My sister, brother in-law and niece all looked at me with that comic look of disbelief that you sometimes see in cartoons. "What. Did I say something wrong?" I asked. As a group they all burst out laughing. Jenny through her laughter said, "That would be a sight to see. Eric Lewis in the kitchen cooking. Gary bring out the video camera for this because we might be able to sell it for television. I had to admit, it was funny. I must have gotten caught up in the moment because, I have been known to ruin salads. So it was

A Love Deferred

with relief that my brother in-law said, "No Brother. You just show up. We'll handle the cooking, won't we ladies?" My sister and niece agreed and that left me off the hook. "Well, since my services are unwanted, I will see you at 4:00." Laughing still my sister said, "Don't pretend like you feeling are hurt. We just saved you from potential embarrassment and all of us from a potential stomach pumping." I agreed saying "You got that right. I don't know what I was thinking" and we all laughed until we were almost crying.

****

After dinner, some spirited games of Backgammon, Bid-Whist and Pictionary, I finally left for the hotel at around 12:30 a.m. When I got in my room, I was still thinking about how wonderful this day had been. More importantly, I thought about how much more excited I was about tomorrow. The Pastor's words on Sunday morning changed how I looked at the celebration at Ed and Corrine's. Of course, I always looked forward to seeing all of my old friends and family, but this weekend has always been about me seeing, and talking to Ronni. At first I thought about it as something to get over with. Now it was something I looked forward to. I now couldn't wait for tomorrow to see what, if anything, life held in store for me and Ronni.

CHAPTER TWENTY

<u>WHEN IT'S ALL SAID AND DONE</u>

Monday morning. Finally, Five-Fourth Day! I woke up to sunshine and knew that God had blessed us with another beautiful day. I have been up for a while now, still rummaging through portions of the Sunday paper. I was challenged to give it my full attention on yesterday, and thought the quiet of the holiday morning, sitting at my dining room table, orange juice in hand, presented the perfect opportunity, or so I thought. My solitude was interrupted by the phone ringing. The caller I.D. let me know instantly that it was the Rush household on the line, and I, of course, figured it was my girl, Corinne. "Good morning sista, sista," I said cheerfully. "My aren't we full of energy this morning," said Corinne. "Yes, I'm a bit surprised too," I agreed. "The report is coming along nicely and I got some really good rest last night. Beauty sleep I needed for today, huh?" Corinne laughed. "Yeah, you and me both!" "So, to what do I owe the pleasure of this call Ms. Pointer-Rush? You sound pretty calm for a woman who's about to have hordes of folks christen your new domain." "Girl, don't let this early morning calm fool you. I've still got a lot of loose ends to tie up, which is why I'm calling you now," she said. "Uh oh, should I prepare for the bomb to drop? Good thing I'm already sitting down. What's up?" I asked cautiously.

"No, silly, nothing that serious. It's just that I know that I promised you I'd come get you personally to bring you this way and it looks like I may need to stay here to make sure everything is in place. You know how obsessive I am about stuff being in place." "Hey, I've known that for most of our lives, but I love you anyway," I said jokingly. Corinne laughed, saying, "Well, baby girl, it takes one to know one, 'cuz didn't you just share with me a short time ago, a detailed itinerary for getting my godson off to college in another week? Watch out pot!" "True dat kettle!" I said trying to sound cool, but knowing I was sorely missing the mark. We both let out a loud laugh. Corinne continued, "I didn't want to leave you hanging, so thought I'd let you know that your handsome godson, E.J., graciously volunteered to come get his favorite aunt and will be there promptly at one o'clock to get you." "Are you sure?" I asked. "You know I don't want to be a bother to anyone. I would have driven myself but I let my brother, T.J., borrow my SUV to take his wife and son, on a much needed long weekend. Unfortunately, since I didn't drive a stick, his car is of little use for me." I then cleared my throat. "Of course, up until 72 hours ago I didn't think I needed transporting anywhere this weekend, until someone whose name I won't mention "twisted" my arm to come to this little bash."

My only company was to be the mega report I brought home with me on Friday. Now, as I looked at the dwindling stack of papers on the dining room table that I had yet to read, I marveled at the progress I had made. I knew how intense I got when I needed to get my work done, but, somewhere in the back of my mind, I had to confess to myself, if to no one else, that my added motivation did involve my curiosity, if nothing more, to get the 4-1-1- right from the horse's mouth, and that thoroughbred was none other than Eric Lewis. But I couldn't let Corinne know how bought in I was to her plan, so, staying in character, I still protested somewhat. "Yeah, yeah, yeah, Ms. Bradley," Corinne said, "heard it already and it still ain't workin'. You just be ready when your chauffeur comes a' callin' for you at 1:00 pm." As if she wanted to rush off before I got another word in, she said hurriedly, "Okay, see you soon, smooches, bye now," and hung up the phone. All I could do was shake my head and laugh, saying, "If I didn't love that chile so much." I still had to laugh out loud when I wondered whether Eric still had a little kick in him or whether he was ready to be put out to pasture. Focus, girl, focus.

I put the paper aside, finished my juice, cleaned up in the kitchen, and started for my bedroom and bathroom. Getting ready might mean a little extra touch, but not too much, and I didn't want to rush. I sat in a nice, warm bubble bath and played my favorite Donny Hathaway and Roberta Flack CD, repeating one or two of my favorite songs at least ten times before the bubbles started to dissolve. Bubble baths and the soothing comfort they provided, were my favorite luxuries and escapes, and when the last bubble disappeared, that was my cue to get up, get out, and move on. I continued to pamper myself, using a light lotion, lest the heat overtake me, and putting on light makeup and some of my favorite jewelry. I'd already treated myself to a manicure and pedicure a couple of days earlier. I chose a very simple sundress in my favorite color, orange, to wear, and accented the dress perfectly with the open-toed, two-inch sandals that I bought when I picked out the dress on one of my shopping trips. I couldn't believe it when I looked at the clock and realized an hour and forty-five minutes had already gone by. E.J. would be here in another 30 minutes, but not to worry, I was more than ready and most importantly, relaxed.

E.J. called me from his cell phone to let me know he was outside. I told him that was nice, but he hadn't "arrived" until he came up to my door to "fetch" me. This was something that I constantly told he and Mark was important. Always meet a lady at the door, always. It just showed the gentle man in a male. For the most part, the boys remembered, but every now and then, I've have to help them out. In took less than 30 seconds for my doorbell to ring. "Who is it?" I asked playfully. "Aunt Ronni, it's me, E.J." I opened the door and we greeted each other with a hug and kiss. I remember the early teen days when E.J. and Mark thought it social death to kiss and hug them around others in public. I guess now, in their latter teen years, they had matured enough to make it acceptable once again. I grabbed my purse, put the alarm on and we headed out to the car. On the drive to the house, E.J. and I talked about a lot of things, his preparing to go to college in another couple of weeks, his summer, and when I could get it out of him, a little more information about the young lady who he now referred to as his "special lady." My how they were growing up, or at least they thought so. If they only knew how much growing they had left to do. But the one thing I knew is that he, Mark and Chris had good heads on their shoulders, good hearts, and common sense – all pretty good starters for developing young minds and bodies. They would be alright.

 We pulled up in front of the house and at least 4 cars I knew didn't belong, were parked on the street along the front sidewalk. I could already smell the aroma of grilled something or other as I got out of the car. I knew it had to be the work of Grill Master, Eddie, Sr., on the job. I greeted some old friends whom I hadn't seen in a few years, met a couple of children new to the group, and then walked outside to greet the host and hostess, who were both knee deep in preparation. On one table, the Rush spread looked like a combination Thanksgiving meal and cookout. The spread already looked quite appetizing and a few of the folks were making themselves at home in the back yard and at the fabulous buffet. On one table Corrine laid out Eddie's famous barbequed ribs and chicken wings, grilled Teriyaki shrimp, garlic potatoes, candied yams, macaroni and cheese, and of course, collard greens. On a second table there were sweet potato salad, pecan pies, coconut and chocolate cakes, watermelons, grapes and strawberries, ice cream and sweets enough to give you ""The Sugar," "" just looking at them. Another table was loaded with enough refreshment to quench anyone's thirst including soda, juice, water, and a choice of light beer and wine coolers. There was beer, wine, water and sodas enough to keep everyone well lubricated and from the looks of things, some people were well on the way to getting oiled up.

    I pulled up in front of Eddie and Corinne's nearly an hour late, solo, except for the dozen roses I carried gingerly in my hands for Corinne. As Eddie and Corinne approached me, I said, "These are for the beautiful head of the household, and you know that ain't you, Brother Eddie," I joked. I planted a kiss on Corinne's cheek, handed her the flowers, and did that manly greeting that guys do, with Eddie. I continued to move around and greet others who were closest to me. And then I finally made my way to *her*. Ronni was a vision, and if, as the saying goes, she was a *sight for sore eyes*, then she healed mine completely.

Eric and I stood for a few seconds, just looking. He was very handsome in his beige slacks and short-sleeved, loose fitting white cotton shirt. It seems I'd seen him mostly in black or navy blue, so the color choice, while a change, befit him nicely. His hair was still as I remember it, precision clipped and salt and pepper. I was tempted to greet him rubbing my hand over it, but fought back the urge. We hugged. He smelled soooo good. He kissed me on the cheek, and I did the same in return.

The delicate scent of Ronni's perfume was intoxicating and I wanted to hold her longer, but not wanting to make her feel awkward or self-conscious, I gently let go. "Really good to see you, Ronni," I said. She acknowledged the same and added that she was doing great. When she asked about my family, I went on to tell her about my brief visit the day before and plans for the next day. "There is never enough time to see everyone," I added, "but I have to try because if I don't, I can never come home again," I said jokingly. "How's your son doing?"

A Love Deferred

Saying these words out loud really let me know that Mark had grown up. "Preparing to leave, Eric. Well, actually, he's already left me. He's spending some time with his dad in South Carolina and then heads off to Xavier in a couple of weeks," I said proudly. I let Eric know that I had plans to meet them in New Orleans for the first few days. Eric shared similar proud papa stories about Trey's progress. "I guess we both have a lot to be thankful for when it comes to our kids," I said. "Amen," he agreed. Phew! We passed the first hurdle – re-introduction. At least, for now, talking about our children wasn't a forced conversation.

I could tell Corinne and Eddie were up to something, but couldn't quite put my finger on it. Then Corinne spoke. "Eric, since you've haven't been to our new home before, you are due a grand tour. Eddie and I have our hands full playing host and hostess, and the kids are so involved with other things, they would give you the express tour." Just then, I could feel the bomb drop and I knew there was no place for me to take shelter. "But Ronni has been through here enough to really do it justice, Haven't you Ronni?" Corinne continued. "So do us a big favor dear sister and take Mr. Lewis on a personal tour while Ed and I go check on everything, pleeeeeze." Oh, if looks could kill, Corinne knew my eyes were giving her the last rites, and she wasn't Catholic. I had no choice. What could I have said that would have

A Love Deferred

sounded believable? Besides, I didn't want Eric to think I was totally trying to avoid him, but I certainly thought that any relating at this shindig would be with one or two others in the mix. But it was obvious, our closest friends thought otherwise.

As the others returned to the festivities outside, I led Eric farther into the house. "Look, Ronni," Eric said apologetically, "I know this was unfairly thrown at you, so if you don't feel like it, no problem, I......" "Hey, no problem for me Eric," I insisted, "after all it is a lovely home and Corinne and Eddie have filled it with love and character. As we made our way from upstairs to downstairs, one of the last steps on the tour was the Family Room. It was my favorite room in the house. A collage of family and friends photographic memories aligned two of the three spacious walls and artfully told the story of much of the Rush's lives. A full entertainment center, with plasma television, Bose surround sound, DVD and video games galore, made this the true "living" room.

As I walked around the room, I slowed my focus on the myriad of photographs chronicling Corinne and Eddie lives – prom, college graduations, their wedding, the birth of their twins, the kids' high school graduation, and special family gatherings and vacations. Scattered throughout the photos, were occasional images of Ronni and me, as best man and maid of honor, and much later at different functions with our significant others at the time of the event. It was very surreal, but in this setting, this surrounding – everything seemed in place, even, to some odd extent, Ronni and me right now. The picture told almost as much of our lives as theirs. As I looked over the photos again, almost stalling to keep us in the room, I said, "You know these memories should have been ours too Ronni."

"Please don't go there Eric," I said, "because this isn't the time or the place," I added, slightly annoyed, but not so much at him for saying what he was feeling, but moreso at myself for having fleeting thoughts about the same thing. I had determined right then and there, I wouldn't get sentimental. No way.

"When was, when is, when will there ever be the right time or place for us to come totally clean Ronni? "I'd be lying to you if I said I hadn't been slightly consumed with thoughts of how we'd react or what we'd say t to each other here today," I confessed. "Something similar must have been going through your mind as well."

As much as I wanted to fight responding, I couldn't, but only mustered up nodding yes. "Maybe it would be best if we joined the others Eric. It has been a while." When we stepped back outside, someone shouted, "There you two are. I thought maybe you had eloped or something." I turned to see Larry Johnson's wife jab him in his side to silence him. Realizing that there couldn't have been a more awkward moment for Eric and me, Corinne came over, took my hand and led me to the food table. Eddie gestured to Eric to join him as his Bid Whist partner. For the next couple of hours, we stole an occasional glance at each other. Three hours later, the big bash was still going strong. I knew I was at the end of my festive line, with so much on my mind, and decided it was time to leave. I told Corinne and she went to look for E.J. She returned shortly to say that sometime in the past hour, E.J. had taken his girlfriend for a spin around Hanes Point, so there was no telling what time he'd be back. She suggested I wait and continue to hang out. I told Corinne and Eddie I had no problem calling a taxi.

"I can take you home Ronni," an all too familiar voice from behind said. It was Eric. "That's alright, Eric, I don't want to take anyone else away from the fun. You stay. I'll be fine calling a cab." "Don't be silly Ronni," said Corinne. "Besides, you'll have to wait forever to get a cab on the holiday." Eric did all he could to assure me I wasn't ending his fun. He added that he needed to get some rest so he would have energy to visit with his family again at his sister's house the next day. So, whenever you're ready," he gestured, trying to relax us both, "your carriage awaits." All I could think was this was anything but a fairy tale. But knowing it was pointless to play verbal volleyball with both he and Corinne, I said, "Thanks Eric."

It took us nearly 30 minutes to say our goodbyes to the crew, and to gather our things, including take home food that Corinne and Eddie insisted we both pack up, since neither of us really ate much. About twenty hugs and kisses later, with promises to keep in touch with everyone, Eric and I were finally headed to my home. The night air was warm and humid, but we opted to leave the windows down instead of turning on the car's air conditioning. We had light conversation during the 40 minute ride, mostly about the weather, the city and anything that didn't pertain to us. We pulled into the driveway of my townhouse and Eric turned the car off. I thought that might have prompted him to realize that if there ever was a time to talk about something more meaningful, it was now. But after sitting silently for a minute, I realized I was wrong. I also realized now was time for me to *woman up,* gather my things, cut my losses, and go home. Eric broke the silence.

A Love Deferred

"Ronni I've been trying to form the right words to say to you. Seems like it's been a lifelong issue for me where you're concerned, and it's no easier now." Frustrated, I thrust my head back on the headrest and looked out the front window of the car.

I took stock of Eric's striking features as I'd done so many times over these thirty years. The wrinkle in his forehead let me know that he was struggling, but there was nothing I could do or say, that I hadn't done or said before, to help him. I was still resolved to follow my present course of action. His next words were almost a whisper.

"You know it seems to me that we are always driving away from each other and not toward one another." Caught off-guard, Ronni asked what I meant. I looked directly at her. "What I mean Ronni, is that after thirty years, we're still always leaving each other. Instead of drawing you closer *to* me, I'm always driving you away *from* me, and I don't know why that is. There are still so many unanswered questions that I don't know whether we really want to know the answers."

I could feel the aggravation rising in me when I said, "Eric, I never got the impression that you were really sure what you wanted when it came to me." I said. "Leaving you? In order to leave you, in the true sense of the word, I would have had to been with you, been part of you first. Somehow, we've had one of the longest runs avoiding that very important caveat to a working, meaningful relationship. I thought it was because you never seemed quite available enough, and then when it seemed as if you were, there was no follow-through. Sure, there was physical desire, but never quite the desire to be together emphatically, with no reservations. The thing is, I was willing to wait for you because I believed you were the one for me, but whatever I tried to do, I misdirected it every time. There came a point when I had to realize that I couldn't provide the answers I needed, and stopped leaning to my own understanding."

Ronni and I looked at each other for another silent minute. I took hold of her left hand, and then the finger that I should have placed a ring on decades ago. "Ronni, I know you are right. I let my selfishness in wanting to have you in my life, but not *being* my life, get in the way of our happiness. Do you know what I mean?" The blank expression on her face answered my question. "What I mean is," I continued, putting my other hand over my heart, "when you love someone as much as I've always loved you in here, the natural progression should be to make that person the most important focus in your life, after God. It was a painful admittance. "I never did that with you," I said now looking straight into her eyes. "I know now that somehow over these years, I idolized the image of the woman I saw named Ronni. Putting you up on that pedestal was totally unfair to you, because the times when I should have made you my only choice, I placed you too far out of reach and I'm sorry. Her expression when I said those two words let me know that I could, that I had to, finish what needed to be said. She continued to listen, silently. "I look at you and I see, all grown up, the beautiful young girl I took to the prom all those years ago. But my reflection in your beautiful brown eyes also shows me a man who should have had the courage to take you fully into his life years ago too."

"So what does it really mean that you didn't Eric," I asked, perhaps a bit uneasy, knowing his answer to some extent.

"At first, I blamed it on insecurity, then instability in my life, next uncertainty. Now I'm not so sure Ronni. Maybe it was insanity all along." I turned and looked at her again.

I cleared my throat. "Since this is true confessions Eric, I know I have to accept some of this too because I can now admit that I kept this image of what we could be safely tucked away in my subconscious mind. While most of my relationships ended friendly, when I dealt with a difficult and failed relationship, I unfairly or unrealistically put my faith in a false sense of satisfaction that I found in an image of you and I ultimately coming together. But we both know that faith without works is, is..."

"is dead Ronni, I added. "This may sound a bit selfish," I said, my eyes studying her and not quite sure if or how I should say these next words, "but I'm grateful for that part of you that held on to your love for me, although now I can only imagine, what you may have gone through. "

I turned away from him as I shook my head acknowledging the truth in his words. "You have no idea Eric."

He continued, "And you never said one damning word about me?" he asked.

I didn't speak a word, but, for a second I flashed back remembering, thinking maybe not damning Eric, but sometimes demeaning.

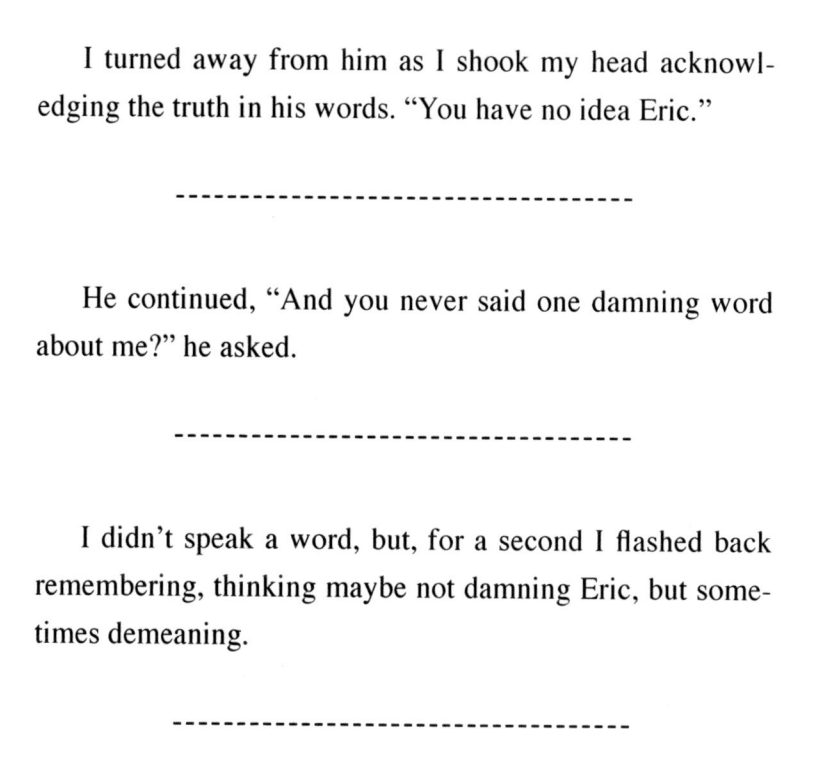

I went on. "Even my sister calls me a fool Ronni, for not coming back to you. Every relationship I have been in, on some level, made me feel that I was being unfaithful to you, and the ultimate result is that through many of them, even those that lasted for years, I found myself eventually just going through the motions moreso than experiencing real feelings." I know you're probably wondering why then, did I keep going down that same path? I think that's where the insanity part comes in. The truth of the matter is for the past few years I have just been letting life happen around me but I haven't really been living." As if that last line summed up everything, I let out a long sigh, while grabbing my head and shaking it. "Ronni, I don't know if you know what I am trying to say. Maybe I've just been rambling on and..."

I raised my hand to cut him off in mid-sentence. "No Eric", I said, somewhat baffled that this otherwise well-spoken, rational-thinking, sharp businessman would try to excuse his personal failings as acts of insanity. "You don't get off that easy. Hear me out now. You can't possibly know how hurt I was when you got married not once, but twice; or how many times I ached to hear your voice but knew it wasn't right because you were unavailable. And when you appeared to be available, I didn't know whether there was anything of me left inside of you. Things I'd wish you had done, had said, you didn't." Now, not caring that he saw the tears welling in my eyes, I said, "You can't know how I wished that we could have had a child together, as husband and wife – someone that Mark and Trey would embrace as the sibling tie that binds."

I gathered my purse and other belongings as best I could and opened the car door, dropping my bag on the ground in my haste. Picking it up almost as quickly, I said, "You know, life is funny. I can't tell you how many times I hoped we could have had this bearing of souls discussion. But, but now? It's probably too late for this cleansing, this "fessing

A Love Deferred

up." So why don't I make it easy for both of us and I just go on in. I got out and started to walk towards the front door. "Goodnight Eric." I paused and added, "Goodbye."

I stepped out of the driver's side, a bit bewildered by what I had just heard. "So this is how it ends Ronni? Nothing more than a goodbye?" Lights on, car door open, I hurried around the front of the car, almost double-timing towards Ronni.

I was resolute about getting inside. I fished around my purse for my keys, my vision slightly blurred by tears. Eric caught up to me as I reached the steps and triggered the motion-sensor light that illuminated the front porch. He touched me on my shoulder, turned me towards him, and took me in his arms, whispering, "Ronni." My heretofore steady composure took a hit. I fell victim to this *flesh back.* The long, passionate kiss we shared was different from any others we'd shared before. Eric embraced me tightly, almost in desperation; aware that once he let me go, he might never have that opportunity again. When we finally came up for air, I said, "This is probably the most romantic moment of our lives Eric." In one split second, he looked at me, as if wondering if he now had reason to smile. Then I added, "but romance was never our shortcoming." It was a sobering reality. Our embrace ended and for a brief moment time seemed to stand still as we just stood and looked at each other.

"Eric, after one of the last times we were together, I remember writing in my journal that *our follow through or lack thereof, had made what we thought we had, begin to lose its luster, and polluted the sweet fragrance that once was. Like any plant or flower, if it's not rooted solidly and if it doesn't get enough nourishment or attention – the basic necessities of life, it will perish.* Standing here looking into your eyes, this moment is magical Eric. But after this has worn off, what's left isn't enough to help *us* survive. We're too caught up in the emotions of this moment. This is textbook fairytale and you and I live in reality." Whatever we had was over and we both needed to acknowledge and face that fact, no matter how hard it was. Here, on the porch, this scene started to feel a bit like déjà vu to me. I put my bags on the porch rocker and turned to face Eric.

"This has been coming for a long time, but we just didn't want to, or couldn't, face it. We've lived much of our lives thinking that ours was *a love deferred*, and when we came together we believed it was *a love deserved*. But, in actuality, the signs that we have chosen to ignore and much of what we've been going through has been..."

"...the longest goodbye," Eric said reluctantly again finishing my sentence.

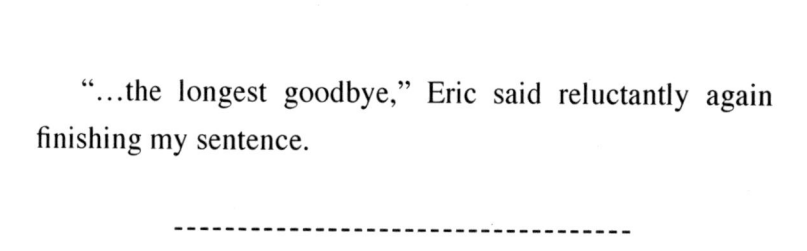

"Eric, maybe now we can both find what we really need in our lives. I've got to bring it back to God again. Seeking Him first will help. If we really want to add to our wholeness, both of us have got to be led right."

"Ronni, maybe it's not too late. It's never too late, if we love each other enough to work this through. And God knows our potential is great if we give it one last, and our best shot." Ronni looked at me, shaking her head in disagreement, acknowledging that this was the same conversation we'd had so many times before.

"That's just it, Eric," I said, "God *does* know, and He's shown us as clearly as He can, that this isn't it. If we don't act on it this time, we are destined to repeat this lesson over and over until we do get it. Well, I never thought I'd have the strength to say it, but, for me, thus endeth the lesson." Looking into my eyes, I guess he realized that his words were more desperate than true and defeat made him sink into himself. As if surrendering, Eric too shook his head and smiled his old half smile.

I stood erect, and with a tinge of sorrow in my voice said, "then I guess this is goodbye Sweetie, or should I say, Miss Bradley." "Miss Bradley" I said, with such a formality and a finality, recognizing that the Sweetie I once knew, was no longer. Through her past responses, Ronni had given me the right to call her that name, all those years ago.

I took Eric's hands in mine and said, "You may find this hard to believe now, and as clichéd as it sounds, today could be the first day of the *best* of our lives." I ran one of my hands through the mane I'd come to love so much, kissed him on the cheek, and he did the same. I freed his other hand. At that moment, it was clear that we had released each other from the emotional binds that tied us together for three decades. I picked up my purse and keys and opened the door. Once inside, I realized how calm I was. The tears had stopped and I knew then that, this was the right thing to do.

A Love Deferred

Ronni stood in her door and watched as I walked slowly back to my car. Somehow I knew she would still be looking and I turned towards the house, placed my left hand on the side of my heart and with my right hand, blew a kiss in her direction. I then sat in the car for several minutes, as though contemplating what to do next. Finally, key in ignition, I backed out of her driveway and slowly drove away.

I knew Eric would be alright. We both would be – maybe not today, or tomorrow – but, eventually. As I closed the door, my last words echoed the same finality Eric had spoken to me earlier. I said, "Take good care, Mr. Lewis."

It's never too late to step into your destiny, especially with the right *One* leading. God never once stopped being God in Eric's life or mine. We just needed to trust Him more — *(Proverbs 3:5-6)*. For the first time in a long time, I felt like I finally opened the door to have someone in my life who would recognize me, as I read somewhere once, as *the pearl of great price in his life*, and would do whatever he had to do in order to gain my hand. Maybe there was still enough about someone else I had yet to discover, and he about me, to build upon.

As I locked my door, I couldn't help but notice how the glow from the porch light made the path leading to my door so clear. I finally fully understood how something as simple as a porch light brought comfort to my dad. Turning it on meant that his loved ones would be home soon. Turning it on helped us find our way safely. And now, as I turned it off, I realized that *walking in the Light* would be the only way that Eric or I would ever be able to reach that place, called home, with someone else, deserving of our love, a love no longer deferred.

The End

EPILOGUE

Her Story *(Ronni)*

It is amazing to me how much you can discover about yourself when you start to take stock of your life. One thing is clear – it is never too late to learn! Through chronicling these years, I've had a chance to set out on understanding how the chapters of my life thus far have helped me to acknowledge that I had been acting out the longest *"Dear John"* letter ever, where it concerned Eric. It also helped bring me to a point where I began to see through the *glass darkly*. When I self-diagnosed my mystified myopia, the spiritual insight I discovered finally allowed me to see things, up close and personal, that I purposely avoided beforehand. It wasn't always pretty and didn't always put me on my best behavior. Although there are adjustments with this new *I* sight, my *new vision* chart has shown me that the most seeing, healing, and strengthening comes from not only having, but cultivating, an intimate relationship with Jesus, the *One* who, in *His* Word, proclaims, *"I am your first love."* Even as someone who had given her life to the Lord many years ago, I oftentimes found myself at a point where I was in Christ, but needed to show more of Christ in me. Once I understood and operated in that, I discovered that my experiences only sought to draw me closer to that first love. Those same experiences and the lessons learned also helped to raise my consciousness, and, more importantly, my spiritual awareness and maturity, for the woman I am becoming. To help keep me on track, I have come up with what I call the *Essential Eight Edicts* — things to know and live by:

- *Love deferred* from one person should *never* separate you from *love available* from others. *[Romans 8:35-39]*
- The love of a man or woman should not add or subtract from your wholeness, but the love of God increases it exponentially.
- The path that seems straightest can often be full of passion-perforated potholes and rocky-relationship roadblocks, and only divine guidance can get you around and through them.
- God's perfect timing doesn't run on a battery or a calendar and doesn't spring ahead or fall back because of our wants and desires.
- God doesn't need us to second guess His plan. When we do, our attempts ultimately meet with defeat.

- God can't speak to us or through us if we're always interrupting and giving Him our opinion.
- Love deferred challenges us to wait on the Lord's directing and then follow it without question.
- God wants us to discover our self-worth and purpose. Finding real love, and someone in this life to share that with along the way, is a bonus.

HIS STORY *(Eric)*

It is clear that we often make life far too complicated. The really sad part is that, nine times out of ten, we know what is right before we make the wrong life choices, but make them anyway hoping for the best. Some people say that it's the following of some of those wayward choices that makes us truly appreciate the end of the journey. They are the ones that say you can't appreciate the good times unless you've had some bad ones. I imagine myself as a survivor of a ship wreck, holding on to a piece of flotsam. I have been tossed around by waves and strong winds and just as I'm about to give up, I see help on the horizon. Sometimes that help is going my way, but not all the way to my destination. The help lets me off, in a life boat, better off than before, but still far from home. These life boats come along from time to time and I float through life, sometimes so close to my goal that I can almost grasp it and sometimes so far away that I forget where I was heading. I sit in my boat parched and hungry not knowing that salvation is within my reach. It is not until I open my heart and let in my true savior that I open my eyes and see that my answer was always there. Maybe I will be stronger because I did make it through the storm. Maybe I will be wiser for surviving the wind and the waves. Hopefully that will be the case for Ronni and me, and others like us. Our relationship was forged by trials that, if we survived this long, surely will help us endure the times of peace ahead. We now have an opportunity to pursue the love and happiness we have long sought, without the fetters and scars of 30 years of false labor pains of the love that was never born, but forever deferred.